CW01096081

One Man's Nightmare

JOSHUA FOX

One Man's Nightmare

by

JOSHUA FOX

Volume II

310 Kennington Road, London, SE11 4LD

Issued by Volume II*
Printed and bound by BWD Ltd. Northolt, Middx.
ISBN 1 85846 015 8

*An imprint of the Professional Authors' and Publishers' Associstion

I dedicate this book to all Expat's working worldwide.
We know the score. Good luck lads.

He lay on his back, the rain pounding on his face and body, at peace. There was no weariness, no pain, as if the mind was outside the body, looking down at the unreality of the whole thing, a nightmare developed from a torment of his own making, possibly he was dead.

The blood from the bullet wounds in his neck, back and thigh slowly seeped into the grass and was dissipated by the rain. Bullets can stop a body, but the mind is not matter. It is abstract and you cannot see to shoot at abstract thought.

There was the sound of the river as it rippled and flowed on its endless path, the rustle of the wind in the trees, the rain as it thrashed the vegetation and the occasional cry of the beast in the wilderness.

How had it all begun? Is there an inherent evil in all men, waiting for something to awaken it, be it greed, lust or power? Or is it bred into a child from an early age?

He remembers his own happy childhood days as the youngest of a large family in a working class neighbourhood. The boys were rough, but harmless. They perfected the way to enter the cinema without paying and the way to pick apples from the grocer's shop display. One group would fight in the fairground boxing booths for five bob a fight. Joe Tully was one of that group. They would fight for reward, but were never criminal.

What his tormented mind wanted to know was, what could induce an honest man to commit the ultimate crime? The small fortune offered? It was academic now, he was dead. But if the mind goes on forever, then that in itself will become the torment. One always pays a price. Was this the price his maker required?

"Hello sweetheart. How are you today?"

"Good news Joe, I have the results of my test. It was positive, I'm pregnant!"

"That's great news!" cried Joe, "tonight we celebrate!" He took Jane in his arms, saying "Come here the pair of you."

"Never mind the celebrating," said Jane, "we'll have to start saving. Life will be very expensive now, and with your overtime being stopped, we will have to be careful."

"No problem!" Joe replied cheerfully. "I have two fights lined up next week at twenty quid a fight. That's forty quid, it's not a lot but it's not to be sneezed at either. It will help."

"Oh Joe! That's a ridiculous way to earn money. Who wants to watch old men fighting?"

"Hey! thirty three isn't old.."

"It's old for boxing and you know it!"

"Wait a minute, this is not a professional bill for young contenders. Nobody gets hurt. Its just the floor show at a booze up." Joe kissed her, "I love you." he said.

"Joe Tully, you're crazy!"

About you, my petal, definitely."

"Come on!" she said. "Let me get dinner finished."

Joe kissed her again before he left her to prepare their meal. He went into the lounge, got his briefcase and opened it on the table. He took out his work and began reading. He was studying for his Higher National Diploma in Mechanical Engineering. Half an hour later his wife put her head round the door.

"Dinner's ready love." she called.

"Right m'love, I'm coming." He followed her back into the kitchen. After the meal, Joe went to the living room and switched on the television. The six o'clock news was beginning. "Look at this, war all over the world. The Middle East, Far East, Central America, and the bloody IRA in London. I tell you its depressing." Joe muttered in his wife's direction as he returned to his studying. When it

3

got to nine o'clock Jane entered the lounge.

"Are you here all night then?" she asked.

"No love, I'll only be a minute, I'm just finishing." Half an hour later he went into the living room again.

"That was a long minute!" said Jane.

Joe just cocked his head on one side and grinned.

"Are you really happy with the news Joe?" asked Jane. There was a note of slight anxiety in her voice.

"Come here!" said Joe, sitting her on his knee. As tenderly as he could, nuzzling her ear and gently stroking her fine dark auburn hair, he reassured her. "Sweetheart, it's the best news I've had since you said yes to my proposal. I love you Misses Tully." He kissed her. "Come on," he said, "Lets go to bed."

It was her beautiful auburn hair that had first attracted his attention more than six years earlier. He had not long been out of the army then. He had accompanied his brother, Eddie, to a 'knees up' at the local ex-services club. She was sitting with her father, her back to them, as the whole audience enjoyed the performance of the stand-up comedian. When she laughed, her long auburn hair had waved wildly. His attention had been attracted by that silky waving. He wanted to see her face but could not because of their relative positions. When the dancing started he had made sure he was first to reach her, to get a dance before any one of the many other young bucks could beat him to it. He had approached her with the intention of being bold and macho but, when she turned her face to him, he had melted into a stammering unconfident schoolboy.

"D-d'ya wanna dance?"

He had planned to take her arm firmly and say something clever, like, "fancy a trot with an old soldier," or perhaps more formally, "may I have the pleasure." But her beauty had literally stunned him and he had made a complete hash of it, leaving himself awkwardly fumbling, not knowing whether to take her arm or turn and run. She had looked at him curiously, amused at his discomfort, her hazel eyes smiling up at him. "Love to," she had said in those musical tones that further enthralled him, "Joe Tully, isn't it?" He was

4

amazed that she knew his name but, before he could ask, she went on, "my dad's the club secretary, all applications for membership pass through him." Then she had laughed as she saw she had made a double impression on a poor fool's consciousness. They had danced together for the rest of the evening. People had noticed the new light in both pairs of eyes. They were married four months later.

During the course of the next 5 years Joe qualified. By that time they had two children, Jonathan, now aged 4 and Elizabeth, aged 6 months. They were the apples of his eye. It was September and it was raining, as usual, in Manchester. "There is a letter for you Joe."

"OK love," he shouted from the bathroom as he finished shaving. "I'll read it later, I must rush." He hurried down the stairs, grabbed the letter from the hall table, kissed Jane and hurried out to his car and to work.

Over the evening meal Jane asked, "What was the letter you got this morning Joe?"

"Well," he said, "I sent my CV to a recruitment agent to see if he could find me something better."

"What do you mean, a job?"

"No, a new wife." She slapped air at him across the table but he had already carried on. "Yes love, a job."

"But why? You have a good job."

He deliberated for a second or two before answering. He knew she would be upset if he had to go away and he anticipated her reluctance to let that happen. But he was determined to improve all of their lives. "Yes love, I know, but I'm bored, so I thought I would broaden my outlook and find something better, with more money."

"But you're on good enough money now! We're managing all right." She came around and threw her arms around his neck, kissing him between syllables as she spoke. "You've done great since you qualified. I love you, I want nothing more."

"I want you to have more, everything there is." Joe responded passionately. "You and the children, I want you to have the best. The children will need the best education and everything in life that matters. That all costs money."

"But they have everything in life that really matters Joe, they have us, and we have them."

"I know, Jane. With the job I have now, this is it. This is our lot, but I want you to have more." He stressed the "I" and continued quickly, trying to end the debate. "Anyway, this agent replied to my CV. He has a contract in Ligeria worth twenty four thousand pounds a year. Think of it, two grand every pay day! It's only for one year and there's two weeks paid home leave every three months. With that kind of money we could get the bigger house we need. I think it is worth giving it some consideration." There, it was out. She knew now it meant his going away.

"You'd be away for a whole year." She said unhappily.

"Look Jane, if you don't want me to look into it, I won't." He allowed a note of irritation to creep into his voice.

"I didn't say that Joe. It's your decision. I know you are doing your best for us. If you think it's the right thing ...." Her voice trailed off. It was settled. She had capitulated. Joe finalised the details of his meeting in London with the agent the following day.

He travelled down by rail on the appointed day. He arrived ten minutes too early at the designated offices in London's West End. He introduced himself to the seated receptionist, an attractive blonde girl wearing a tight fitting black suit with a white blouse that formed an open vee almost to her navel which clearly displayed both sides of her ample charms. She had a small badge with the name "Claire" pinned to her lapel. "Please take a seat mister Tully," she said in a sing-song voice, "you're a bit early. Would you like a coffee, or something, while you're waiting?" She smiled pleasantly, leaning forward at the same time, but Joe declined the offer. "Mr Cross will be with you shortly, he has a client with him just now." She picked up the telephone and spoke quietly into it, observing Joe's lean but fit body frame all the while. Joe ignored her and idly picked up and leafed through a magazine that lay on the counter. A few minutes later the phone buzzed. Claire picked it up and listened. "He will see you now Sir." Her manner had changed to one of cold indifference. As they walked down the corridor they passed a tall white haired man who smiled at Claire, looking down at her assets. She returned the smile and looking at Joe raised her eyebrows. Joe acknowledged with a smile. He thought it better to be friendly, who knows, she might have influence. She knocked on a door about half way down the office corridor and entered. "Mister Tully Sir," said the receptionist introducing Joe, who stepped forward, smiling politely, to shake hands with the agent.

"Take a seat please, mister Tully. My name is Harry Cross." Cross smiled back at Joe, showing a single gold incisor as they shook hands. He was a big man with a large beer belly. "Our clients in Ligeria require a mechanical engineer to manage the installation and initial servicing of a large air-conditioning system in a new residential and office complex. I see from your CV that you have the qualifications and experience to handle this sort of job." He had a large folder in front of him that obviously contained more than just the one-page curriculum vitae Joe had sent. Probably the details of the site and specifications. "You would, of course, be responsible for commissioning and hand over. The entire project would be yours. What do you think Mr Tully?"

Joe thought he should ask to look at the folder to assess the scale of the project and the difficulties that might be involved, but he needed the job and was confident in his abilities, so he decided to be bold: "As long as the materials and equipment, and the skilled labour, are up to standard I would do a first class job." He was ready to elaborate, to push his qualifications and assert his competence, to explain that, despite never having had sole responsibility for an installation project of this size, or indeed any, size, he knew he was up to the task, but, as he took a deep breath and prepared himself, the agent just closed his folder, sat back, and beamed broadly at Joe. "We have no doubt of your ability to carry out this project. You had already been short listed from your CV." Then he added, "what we really want to know is a bit more about your background." He produced Joe's CV from below the folder. "For example, your military service. You left the army about six years ago?" He looked quizzically at Joe across the desk, waiting.

"Yes; I served for five years."

"In the Paratroop Regiment. A good outfit." The smile beamed again, encouragingly.

"Yes," said Joe slowly. He had not expected to being asked more about his service than his engineering experience, and could not see where this was leading.

Now the smiled slackened slightly. "I had a lot to do with recruiting training personnel for various African countries. Mostly British." He stressed the word "personnel". Joe suspected he was referring to the recruitment of mercenaries but he made no comment. He was beginning to feel uncomfortable about the interview. What did this fat man want him to say? As if reading his mind, the agent explained. "I have an admiration for the British army, and outfits like the paras and marines. I just wondered if you had done any," he paused momentarily, "special assignments?"

"Well" Joe answered, in as friendly a tone as he could muster, "I wouldn't be at liberty to talk about it if I had, Mister Cross. I'm sure you would know that."

Cross beamed again, "Just the answer I wanted to hear, Joe. You don't mind if I call you Joe, do you?" He continued, lowering his voice conspiratorially, "you see, this project is concerned with the building of a Presidential retreat outside Bakra, the capital. We have to be absolutely sure that anybody working on the project is one hundred per cent conscious of the security implications, you see." He was beaming again. Joe smiled, a bit relieved. "I understand, I signed the Official Secrets Act when I went into the army here and I have never betrayed any confidences to this date. You can be certain that I will maintain the same standard of secrecy if I am accepted for this position."

Cross nodded approvingly. "In that case, Joe, it is my pleasure to inform you that the position is yours. You will want to know about the method of payment. As we explained in our letter, you will be paid twenty four thousand pounds for the one year contract. That will be in sterling, or any other currency you require. It will paid monthly into your bank account here in the UK, or anywhere else for that matter, just give me the details and all will be arranged. Should you complete the job earlier you would be paid the balance of the twenty four thousand as a bonus. On the other hand, if the contract takes longer due to circumstances beyond your control, you will be paid two thousand per month until completion. In addition you will get two weeks paid home leave every three months, plus free board and accommodation. I think you will agree, Joe, those are very good terms. Any questions?" Cross smiled expansively again.

"Just one. When do I start?" Joe was elated that he had got the job but he did not want to appear too exuberant.

"The main construction is still not complete but we want you there to make sure the ducting is in order before the main contractor finishes. I will contact Akeja Construction by telex to see exactly when you should travel. Then I will send you two copies of the contract, one to sign and return to me, the other you keep for your own reference. How much notice do you need to give your present employer?"

"One month, but I could get away with two weeks if necessary."

"Good. I can have all necessary details ready within a week. Then we will give you a firm date with airline tickets and travelling instructions. That's about it then, Joe." Cross stood up, extending his hand. "All that remains is for me to wish you the best of luck."

Joe also stood, reaching forward to shake hands. As he extended his hand the bottom of his coat sleeve caught the lip of the folder and it opened allowing him for a second to see a buff coloured document bearing a crown. He recognised it instantly as the first page of a British Army service record.

The smiling agent shook his hand and lumbered to the door with him. "Goodbye Joe, perhaps we'll have more professional contacts when this job is done." He winked conspiratorially at Joe as the door closed.

Joe was perplexed. How could Cross have got hold of his service record? And why should he want it? Probably the Ligerian Government had wanted some extra security screening, and Cross had been able to use his old army contacts to get hold of it. Maybe the Foreign Office had even allowed it because of the nature of the project. Still, what matter? He had the job and the terms were great.

This would change his whole life. He almost danced down the corridor to make his exit and get back to tell Jane the good news.

He arrived back in Manchester late that evening. It was raining again by the time he got home. He related the good news to Jane but her reaction was predictable. She was not as concerned about the extra money as he was.

"But that means we won't see you for three months."

"No," Joe agreed, "but it's only for the one year, then I could always get a job back here. At least it's a good start. I don't really want to leave you, you know that, but I'm doing it for you. I love you. You deserve the best and now we can have it."

With that Jane threw her arms around him and hugged him. "I love you Joe and I'll miss you, but do it love, do what you think you ought to."

Less than one week later another letter from the agent arrived. It contained an open return ticket from Heathrow to Bakra. The letter confirmed Joe's appointment to the post of engineer in charge of the installation of the air-conditioning system in the new complex as well as his salary and terms of employment. It ended with an instruction to leave England on Thursday 22nd September by way of Flight LA404 for Bakra leaving Heathrow Airport at 2.30pm.. That gave him just over three weeks to resign from his present employment. The date of departure did, at least, allow him to prepare for the trip. Jane fussed a bit as the due date got nearer. She was reluctant to see him go but, at the same time, she constantly reassured him not to worry about her and the kids while he was away.

Joe had to make his own way to London for the flight to Africa and so, to allow as much time as possible with Jane and the kids, he decided to take the shuttle from Manchester Airport directly to Heathrow rather than endure the longer train journey. After a slightly tearful farewell, and many emotional embraces, with Jane and the kids waving furiously from the promenade lounge as he boarded the BAC 1-11, he departed for London and a new job in Africa.

When Joe arrived at London's main airport he transferred through into the departure lounge for international travel after checking in at the Ligerian Airlines desk. He bought a beer and sat down thinking about Jane and the children, Jonathan had not really understood the significance to the farewell but he had given his dad a big hug and a kiss anyway. He had held Elizabeth, who couldn't have understood, and he had held his Janie, who was trying unsuccessfully not to cry. Joe was still a bit choked up as he waited for his flight to be called. He would miss them. He loved that girl and the children and considered himself very lucky to have such a lovely family. What Joe couldn't have known was that his future was about to become an unbelievable nightmare.

The departure of flight LA404 to Bakra was announced. Joe finished his beer and went to the departure gate. He boarded the plane with the throng of other, mostly African, passengers. He managed to secure an aisle seat and settled back to wait for the take-off. When the seat belt sign went off Joe called the stewardess over and ordered a whisky with a beer chaser.

EXPAT IN THE THIRD WORLD

On arrival at Bakra, Joe cleared passport control easily enough, but customs officers went through his belongings with a fine tooth comb and made things very difficult by asking a lot of ridiculous questions. Yet he noticed that some people were going through without difficulty. He was new at this game, but he would learn. Having cleared all formalities, he went out to the entrance hall and into total chaos. People were milling about all over the place. Small boys and adult males were fighting to get his suitcase as he fought to hang on to it. He spotted his own name on a piece of card held aloft above the mass of heads and bodies crowding around the main hall. Then he saw it was held by a large powerful looking Ligerian wearing a shabby grey chauffeur's jacket. Joe fought his way over and introduced himself. The man grinned and shook hands. "My name is God Bless, Sir, I am your driver." He took Joe's suitcase and they went out to the car park. The weather was pleasantly warm and sunny, contrasting favourably with the cold and rainy Manchester he had just left. God Bless led him to a large black Chevrolet and they drove out of the airport and on to a fairly modern dual carriageway.

"You have been booked into the Airport Hotel tonight, Sir. Tomorrow you will be contacted by an Akeja Construction representative." God Bless told him, still displaying a wide friendly grin.

At the hotel God Bless parked the car and they went in and up to the reception desk. "This is Mr Tully. He has a reservation for tonight." The clerk checked the book, "Yes Sir, just one night." The large Ligerian looked at Joe, "If you go out it is best to stay on the main roads, there are plenty of bad people in Bakra, I will collect you tomorrow, Sir." He offered his hand. Joe acknowledged the advice with a nod and a grin at the smiling face as they shook hands. The big Ligerian turned and left as a young boy appeared and picked up Joe's suitcase. "Follow me Sir." They went up in a modern lift to the third floor and Room 323. The boy opened the door and stepped back. Joe walked in followed by the boy who put the suitcase on the bed." "Will there be anything else Sir?" "No thank you," replied Joe, handing him a British fifty pence piece. The boy was thrilled. Joe knew only too well that hard currency, even coinage, is valued much more than local money in countries like Ligeria. He also knew that the official exchange rate was unrealistic and that more could be obtained for his money on the black market but, as it was against the law to change money other than in banks or registered cash bureaux, it could also be dangerous. He had promised Jane not to put himself at any risk, and that covered breaking local currency exchange laws.

Joe's room overlooked the forecourt at the front of the hotel and from his window he could see the swimming pool and bar. He realised the clothes he was wearing were unsuitable for the tropics for, although he had arrived in the late afternoon, he was already perspiring freely. He showered and then dressed in a T-shirt, lightweight slacks and sandals. He decided to have a beer before dinner and went down to reception, "Could you change me some currency?" he asked the clerk. "Yes Sir, how much would you like?" "Fifty pounds please." The clerk made out the paperwork and Joe gave him a single fifty pound note in return for which he got two hundred and fifty six Ligerian guineas. Joe then went into the bar by the swimming pool. He sat down at one of the vacant tables and ordered a beer from one of the hovering waiters. There were only a few Ligerians, male and female, and a couple of European men in the bar. He was thinking of Jane when one of the young Ligerian girls left her companions and walked to Joe's table. She was a slim, large breasted girl. "Do you mind?" she asked, sitting in the chair beside him. "Not at all," Joe replied, although he had no intention of being one of her customers. His army days had taught him to recognise a whore when he saw one but he could tolerate her company until she became a nuisance. She started to make small talk and Joe responded politely. He saw no harm in getting to know the locals, even those on the seedier side of life. Then she asked him if there was anything she could do for him, sliding forward in her chair to reveal most of her upper legs. He politely refused the offer. She then put both her hands on his thigh and squeezed encouragingly. "Oh, you're teasing me," she said, "you must be missing you home comforts." She pouted her

13

crimson coloured lips and assumed a hurt expression, but started to stroke his thigh at the same time. He moved his leg away from her hands. "No," he responded firmly, "but I'll buy you a beer to show there's nothing personal about it. It's just that I'm a happily married man". He gave her a friendly smile and beckoned a passing waiter. Her face showed genuine disappointment and she stood up. "No," she said, loudly enough for everyone in the bar to hear. "I don't want to drink with you." She strolled haughtily back to her companions leaving Joe slightly embarrassed. He finished his beer quickly and left the bar. He went straight to the hotel restaurant and had a steak for dinner. After the meal he bought a newspaper from the reception clerk and retired to his room for safety. He knew he had been foolish to allow a prostitute to score a point over him and he resolved to be less friendly in future. The paper carried details of world news as well as local political and economic matters. The current govern-ment, under President Elido, had introduced fiscal cuts and reduc-tions in spending that were unpopular with most of the people. Joe thought it ironic that he was being employed in a major spending project that would benefit only the President. He noted that there was no mention of that project in the paper. Still, it was not his country and he felt no real concern at the way others ran their af-fairs. Later, he wrote a long letter to Jane, and then took it down to reception. "Would you have a stamp, please?" he asked the clerk. "Leave that with us Sir, we will attend to it." He handed the letter to the clerk and went back to his room and to bed. Next morning Joe was up, showered, shaved and eating breakfast by 7am. He bought a new edition of the same newspaper and seated himself in the lobby to wait for his contact. At 9am an Asian walked in and went up to reception. After speaking to the clerk, he turned and came across to Joe. "Mr Tully?" "Yes," said Joe, standing up. The man introduced himself as Asad Bashire, the chief administrator of Akeja Construction . They shook hands. "Would you come with me Sir?" They walked out to his car and drove to head office, where they sorted out Joe's resident visa, work permit and driving licence, then they went to the site. Bakra city proper was built on an island, linked to the mainland by a network of bridges. The site of the new Presidential offices was in Akeja, a large town on the North West side of the city. They went to a Portakabin on the site. It would be Joe's office for the next year. Joe was introduced to the foreman, Les, the clerk, Daniel, and again the driver, God Bless, the big guy who had met him at the airport. "OK," said Joe to Les "First I would like to see the architects drawing to make myself familiar with the lay out." Les took Joe to his own office and went over to the drawing table and laid out the drawing. Joe studied the way the office suite was laid out in the plan view. The block stood in its own land area, covering several acres. Across the front of the complex ran the main Akeja Road. Branching off east were two secondary roads, Pupil Road and Slay Road, linking up with the main Torridor Road about half a mile north of the site. The whole complex at this stage was surrounded by barbed wire with Akeja Construction's own security men in attendance. "OK," said Joe "Now I would like you to show me round the site before I brief the men, then we will check all packing crates against the shipping lists." Joe and the foreman had a busy morning. After lunch, which for Joe was a sandwich and a beer, they checked all equipment on site against the bill of quantities. It was now 6pm and Joe was weary after a busy day. He suddenly realised he didn't even know where he was to live. "I will drive you home, Sir," said his driver God Bless. The two of them set off in the Chevrolet. They drove about two miles West of the site to a quiet residential area. God Bless drove the car into the car port of a bungalow, and gave Joe the car and house keys. "What time shall I call for you tomorrow Sir?" "6.30 please," answered Joe. "Good night Sir." "Good night, God Bless." Joe smiled when he realised what he had just said. He let himself in and heard the sound of bare feet scurrying across the tiled kitchen floor, it was the house boy 'Good Luck', who came and greeted Joe warmly. He was a pleasant little fellow and inquired what master would like for dinner. "My name is Joe, not master." Joe replied, "You call me Joe, is that understood?" "Yes master." replied Good Luck, "There is steak or chicken. I can do salad with them or I can make chips, Sir, if you give me a menu each morning I can do whatever you wish." "Well," said Joe, "Chicken and salad will be fine for now thank you." Joe showered first and then ate with relish. Afterwards, he gave Good Luck some money and sent him out to buy a six-pack of imported European beer. While Good Luck was out Joe unpacked and got himself sorted out.

Joe enjoyed his first three months in Ligeria, finding his way around the job, and the country a little. He had become a member of the country club and spent his weekends playing darts or snooker and having a few beers. The club was expensive by Ligerian standards so only the more prosperous Ligerians would frequent the place. Most Westerners working in the Capital spent their spare time in the club. Joe had made a few friends with fellow Brits at the club who were working on the new Guinness brewery. One, Ray Taylor, with whom Joe would throw darts, had been in Bakra for a year or so and knew his way around. "Have you seen much of the place, Joe?" asked Ray. "No, it's been all bed and work," replied Joe, "and the club of course." "Do you fancy a run down town for a change?" asked Ray. "Good idea," said Joe. "Come on, we will use my driver, that way we don't get lost," said Ray. The brewery where Ray worked insisted that he always use their driver. He could go anywhere on social outings using his company car and the only stipulation was that he use their driver. Joe could use his driver or he could drive himself, the choice was his. He always used the driver for business but socially he drove himself. Ray's car was a Ford. They drove down to an area of the city known as Happy Valley, where most of the nightclubs and hotels were situated. There was a cinema showing the film 'True Grit' staring John Wayne. They stopped at a few bars for a beer or two, where they were pestered by women, which neither of them wanted. "One sure way to catch a dose," said Ray, "is to go with a Ligerian prostitute." The driver would always wait for them in the car. On their way back to collect Joe's car from the country club the driver suddenly stopped and reversed into a side road. "What are you doing?" asked Ray. "Turning round Sir," said the driver, "this is a very bad place, I must have missed my turn off." "What do you mean Timmy, a bad place?" "Yes Sir, a very bad place." "Then we must have a look. Carry on." But Timmy was adamant. "Come on Timmy, move it!" Ray shouted, but by now Timmy was beginning to get excited, stammering and waving his arms about. Ray elbowed Joe "Come on, we'll walk." They both got out of the car, leaving Timmy screaming his warnings. The road was macadam but was in a terrible state of repair, there was no pavement and the dwellings were made from old packing crates, corrugated iron and mud It was a terrible slum and the stench was fiendish. It got worse the further they went. The odd beggar would appear, clutching at their clothing with one hand and trying to put the other into their pockets. Joe was not happy. "I think we have come far enough." "I agree," said Ray. Just then a whole tribe of beggars appeared out of nowhere. There seemed to be hundreds of them. What was even more upsetting was the fact they were all Lepers. One man approaching Joe had one side of his face a pastel pink in colour, his nose, upper lip and ear were missing and his face, or what there was of it, was like a big running blister. Another had one leg a pastel pink colour, the foot of which had virtually rotted away, what was left was just a wet grizzly mess. They were all alike, grotesquely twisted, hideous creatures. Among them , there were the spider boys. Cripples whose legs were twisted up under their backsides and who move about with a block of wood in each hand. By putting them on the floor and swinging forward between their arms, they can move at tremendous speed when they want to. Joe and Ray found themselves surrounded by an army of deformed ragged creatures. "We have a problem Ray," said Joe, "Let's run for it!" "How?" Ray said with a note of panic in his voice. "We are surrounded." "Start punching and kicking," said Joe. Just then there was one hell of a din. A car horn was blaring and head lights flashing, Rays driver brought the car toward them at them at speed, the beggars were being scattered in all directions, Joe and Ray lost no time diving in through the already open doors. The car never stopped, but they made it. Timmy went on screaming and stuttering at them, they could not pacify him. If anything were to happen to Ray, and he surely would have been killed, neither man would ever have been seen again, and the driver would be held responsible, not just by the company but by the authorities. Timmy could have spent many years in prison. "I never thought such depravity could exist anywhere in the world," said Joe, "that was unbelievable." Timmy went on stammering and swearing. They drove on with Joe and Ray in silence. Both of them were shocked. After a while Ray spoke, clearly attempting to keep his voice at a normal pitch. "When do you leave, Joe?" "Wednesday," said Joe "and it can't come soon enough." They stopped the car in the country club car park, Joe walked round to the drivers open window and gave Timmy a five Guinea note Timmy took it, smiling. At twelve guineas a month, it was worth almost two weeks pay.

On December 21st Joe arrived back in England for what he hoped would be the best Christmas of his life. He couldn't wait to see his family and to hold Jane in his arms again. For him it was, therefore, truly magic just to hold Jane as she flew into his arms in the arrivals lounge at Manchester Airport. This was Joe's whole world here and, with Jane in his arms, it was pure ecstasy. When he finally pulled away from his darling wife he turned to his son. Jonathan just stood there watching, with a big grin on his face. Joe bent down and grabbed him. The little boy's arms circled his Dad's neck and he gave him a big kiss on the cheek. The baby was asleep in her pram and the sight of her caused an emotional feeling in Joe that he had not experienced since he was a child himself. He almost cried with happiness. They took a taxi home and he carried Jonathan through into the living room while Jane put the now awakened baby Elizabeth into her high chair with a rusk. Joe leaned over kissed his daughter and held his cheek next to hers getting rusk all over himself. He put Jonathan down and lifted Elizabeth out of her chair. This was real living thought Joe. After the greetings were over he opened is suitcase, and took out a radio controlled motor car for Jonathan and a doll for Elizabeth. The children were thrilled with their presents. For Jane he took out an 18ct gold locket and chain. "Joe, it is beautiful! You shouldn't go spending money on me!"

The two blissful weeks of his leave soon passed. They had a wonderful time, but all good things must come to an end. "Those two weeks were the best of my life." he said to Jane on the day before he was due to return to Ligeria. "Mine too." she said. The following day, with the taxi waiting outside, he hugged and kissed his baby daughter and put her back on the bottom step of the stairs near the front door. He picked up Jonathan, hugged him and said "Look after Mum for me, won't you son." "Yes Daddy." he said. Joe put him down and looked at Jane. Tears were in her eyes, then in his eyes, neither speaking as they were both too choked. They just held each other tightly. He released Jane, picked up his suitcase and walked out quickly and got into the taxi. He looked back through the window as the taxi was moving off. Jane stood on the doorstep with Elizabeth in her arms and Jonathan standing beside her as they all waved. On the drive to the airport, Joe was deep in thought. Was it worth it? Was all the money worth it? The answer was no. But he had signed a contract and, on principle, he would not break it. He had nine months to do, less in fact, because he knew he could finish well within the twelve month period. He could make it. But little did he know of the drama that was soon to unfold in his life as he arrived back at Bakra airport and cleared passport control. He went into the customs hall, put his suitcase on the table still closed and locked. The customs officer approached him and Joe leaned on his suitcase with both fists closed. In one hand he had a five pound note rolled up and sticking out. The customs man leaned over, slipped the fiver out of Joe's fist and chalked his suitcase, saying, "thank you Sir, please move along." God Bless was waiting for him. They shook hands, went to the car and drove off. They went to Joe's home and parked in the car port. God Bless gave him the keys, "I will pick you up at 6.30am Sir." "Yes, thank you," said Joe. He let himself in and Good Luck came out of the kitchen to greet him.

Next morning Les took Joe round the site to show the slight progress they had made. They had completed the programme he left with them. As they drove down into the industrial area to pick up some materials, travelling down the main Torridor Road, where the pavements were busy with the everyday bustle of a normal working day, people going about their business and traffic heavy. Suddenly Joe shouted "Stop!" but God Bless carried on. "Stop will you!" The car slowed, moved over and came to a halt. Joe then made to get out. Just as he released the door catch, Les took hold of his arm. "Leave it Sir! You can do nothing." "You saw it?" "Yes Sir." What they had seen was a child of about twelve months old lying in the gutter, like a dog that had been hit by a car and dragged there, which was probably the case. "The child is dead Sir," said Les. "How can you know that?" "The child was there last night Sir, by now the body will be infested with vermin of all kinds." "We can't just leave it there!" said Joe. "If you interfere you will become responsible for the body and it will prove very expensive. Doctors will become involved, not because they care but to collect their fat fees from you. Also the police and the fake relatives will take all your money, and more. Believe me Sir, you can do nothing." Joe then remembered the last time he had not taken the advice of Ray's driver on a Ligerian matter, with the beggar episode, so he snapped the door shut and they drove off. It was late afternoon when they passed the area where the child's body lay. Joe noticed that it had been covered over with a huge banana leaf. That was not to be Joe's only experience of corpses by the roadside. Two months later there was a terrible smell, getting worse each day, finally Joe said, "Anybody know where that terrible smell is coming from? It is getting worse each day." "It is crazy man Sir." Said God Bless. "What do you mean, crazy man?" "Crazy man die by road side Sir," said God Bless. "Are you serious?" asked Joe "Show me." "No Sir, please, you get yourself all concerned, then big problem." "No. I promise God Bless I will not get concerned. I will leave well alone." Joe was then reluctantly taken about 200 yards up Pupil Road at the back of the site and there, by the roadside just out from the bush, was a sun swollen male corpse, partly mutilated by wild dogs. Two days later the police came with three prisoners who dug a shallow hole, rolled the body in and covered it up, and that was that. "Life is cheap here." thought Joe. The following morning there was a visit to site by the chief admin guy, to inform Joe that the President was going to visit the site. Joe's staff always referred to the President as Chief Elido, he was the chief of the Mausa tribe, the largest tribe in Ligeria. "I thought I would come to let you know, so you can be ready and prepared, so to speak." "Sure," said Joe "Anybody can visit. We are well ahead of schedule." "The area will need to be cleaned up," said the admin guy, "Make everything presentable." "But this is a building site!" said Joe. "You can never have a clean one." "I realise that, but we can make it a little more presentable." "When is the visit planned for?" "26th March, Monday." "The day before I go on leave," said Joe. "Well mister Tully you have four days, then you, myself and others will accompany him and explain the various items of equipment." After the admin guy had left Joe spoke to Les, "Make sure the access to the office from the main gate is clear and tidy up in the suite, particularly in the engine room." "Right Sir, leave it to me." On the morning of the 26th, there came to site what Joe would describe as a bloody carnival. At 7.30am two cars full of senior officers with a dozen outriders arrived. They went all over the site with a fine tooth comb. "What's the idea?" said Joe "We have work to do, you lot are stopping the whole show." "We must make sure the place is secure and safe," answered one of the officers. Les took Joe by the arm, "Steady Sir," he said. Joe looked at Les, who looked genuinely afraid. "OK, OK, turn the bloody place upside down if you must, I'm in my office if anybody wants me, but a full report of any damage caused will be sent to Akeja Construction ." Joe went to his office, followed by Les who said. "These people are the law. It is the military, they have the power of life and death, you just don't interfere. If they decide to knock a wall down, they will knock it down, we have no say in the matter." "Very well Les, we will just sit back and let it happen, we can always put it right afterwards I guess." At that Joe went to the adjoining wall and banged on it with his fist, which was the signal for the tea boy to bring in tea. At 9.0am they arrived, first the top boffins from Akeja Construction , they came into Joe's office all of a splutter, "Is everything ready Mr Tully?" "Of course," he said, as a big black Limousine came into the compound with at least two dozen outriders. The leading pair were literally kicking objects and people out of the way as they rode by on their bikes. Four of them came into Joe's office and positioned themselves. It was the same in Les's office, even the tea boy was promptly thrown out and scarpered quickly away, Christ knows where. The limo stopped and the doors were opened by an outrider. Then out got the President, who was large and elderly. He was all smiles as he came into the office. The admin guy went over to him bowing and salaaming. All this was new to Joe, who had been persuaded to wear a shirt with collar and tie, and trousers instead of the old T shirt and shorts. "This is Mr Tully Sir, the engineer managing the site." The President offered his hand Joe took it, saying "How do you do Mr President?" "I hope the workers are satisfying you, and Akeja Construction are looking after you," said the President. "Yes Sir, the workers are doing a first class job, we are well ahead of schedule, and I am very happy with my treatment. I have no complaints. "I would prefer you to show me round if you would be so kind." "My pleasure," said Joe, "I think we should start with the nearest point, the engine room, which is also the area of most interest." "Excellent!" said the President. Joe took him across. All the machinery was in position. Four skilled fitters and their mates were working on the pipework to the water chiller's. The men looked round from their work wondering where to run. They were scared by the occasion. Joe entered and said "It's OK fellows, no panic, whatever you were doing carry on, you will not be disturbed." This seemed to reassure them and they carried on. Joe then explained the climate changer, the 'S'-mat filter arrangement, the water chiller's and the multi-motor panel and controls. Joe was surprised by the interest shown by Chief Elido, and he could tell the interest was genuine. They then went into what was to be the President's office, Joe explained the way the air would be delivered and returned. He then explained the controllable light switch to give dim or bright illumination. He spent two hours taking the Chief round the site, answering a lot of questions. Then they went back to the office where Joe went through some of the drawing to illustrate some of the answers he had given. He was surprised by the knowledge shown by the Chief, he must at some time have had some engineering training, thought Joe. Joe asked whether the President would like some tea or coffee. "Tea would be nice," said the Chief, to everyone's surprise except Joe's, for he saw nothing unusual in offering a man a pot of tea and it being accepted. Joe went over to the wall and banged on it as usual. The tea boy wasn't there of course, but Les heard it and went through to Joe's office. "The tea boy isn't there Sir, he's gone on an errand," lied Les, can I get you something?" "Yes," said Joe, "Tea for everybody, but first Les will you come here please?" Les went over, a little apprehensively. "I would like to introduce my foreman Mr President. It was his idea to use the automatic light illumination switch in your office." The President offered his hand to Les who took it and bowed, you are a very bright foreman, Les," said the Chief. "He is," said Joe, "He is my right hand man, I couldn't do without him." "I hope the company appreciates your worth," said the Chief. "Yes Sir," said Les, who was totally overwhelmed by this episode. "I'll get the tea if I may Sir." "Of course, please do," said the Chief. The Akeja boffins were somewhat surprised and put out by Joe introducing Les to the President, things like that just do not happen, but Joe, unlike the others in the office, had no fear of the President or the military. This of course all relates to where one is brought up, and the kind of society they are brought up in. Joe had been brought up in a land of freedom, whereas the others in the office had been brought up to be subservient. "I suppose you wonder, Joseph, why I have my new office in this particular area." asked the President. "It did cross my mind Sir, it is a little out of centre of things." "Yes, at this time, but the main Torridor Road runs across the back of the complex and no doubt you have noticed some of the most beautiful countryside is out from the Torridor, going North for as far as the eye can see. This is the residential area of Akeja, and I intend to build my military academy here, on similar lines to your Sandhurst academy, I was there you know, Joseph, I was studying engineering. Then the war with Germany broke out so I went to Sandhurst and got my commission in 1941 and I fought with Montgomery in the Africa campaign. Does that surprise you Joseph?" Everybody in the office was amazed at the way the President would talk to Joe about his personal life which was all news to them. "Well, I've wasted enough of your time Joseph, I will leave you to carry on the good work with my suite. I think, in fact I know I will have you build my military academy, if you will, that is." "Of course Sir," replied Joe. The President then left with his entourage and rigmarole. Joe was glad that was over, now he could plan tomorrow.

He was going home and was booked on the 12-45am flight to arrive at 06.30am. He arrived at the check in desk at 11-15pm and went to passport control and put his passport on the desk. The passport officer just folded his arms and stared at Joe. Joe then took out his wallet, removed a five pound note and put it on the passport as it lay on the desk. The officer picked up the fiver, stamped the relevant page of the passport and gave it back to Joe. "Thank you Sir, have a pleasant journey." Joe went into customs - in Ligeria you go through customs going out as well as coming in - he walked up to the customs table with a five-guinea note rolled up in his fist. The customs man asked "Which is your case Sir?" Joe pointed to his case with the hand that had the guinea note in, the customs man slipped the note out of Joe's hand and chalked the case. "Thank you Sir, please move along." Joe went into the departure lounge, got a beer and sat down thinking about Jane and the children, it was fantastic going home, if everybody was as happy as Joe Tully there would be no wars, no terrorism, no crime, but there was only one Jane Tully, he figured that must be the reason.

His leave was just as ecstatic as his last leave, but again, it was over too soon. He was going back. He had hugged his two children and said his goodbyes. Now he held Jane, her stomach visibly swollen with his child and, just as before, he was too choked to speak. Could he ever get used to saying goodbye? Joe arrived at the airport and checked in and boarded the plane for the thirty five minute flight to Heathrow. When he arrived he checked in at the Ligerian check in desk and thought how orderly it was compared with Bakra airport, where nobody ever bothered to form a queue. It was always a matter of scrum down and do the best you are able.

He boarded his flight and sat in an aisle seat on the centre row. Next to him sat a pretty young woman about twenty years old with her twin half caste boys of about three years old. Their father, Joe thought, must be Ligerian. The girl started to make conversation. She was asking Joe about Ligeria as she had never been there. In fact, she had never been out of England before. She was from Middleton near Manchester. She went on to tell Joe how she met her husband at the cotton mill where she worked. He had been on a course for Courtaulds and had stayed for two years and was now a big man in textiles in Bakra.

She was rabbiting on about how they got married in a registry office, how her father and two brothers were against her marrying this man, but, as she put it, she had to get married as she had become pregnant. Joe thought she was a really nice girl but a bird brain. Her boys were bonny lads, all happy and laughing. They were enjoying their flight. When they arrived at Bakra Joe got her through immigration and customs, as she would have stood no chance on her own.

When they got through to the foyer area Joe saw God Bless waiting for him, then he saw the girl, Lucy, waving to someone in the crowd. He realised she must have seen her husband in amongst all the chaos. She said goodbye and left with her twins.

Over the next two months they made good progress and Joe figured it would be completed and handed over inside ten months. Chief Elido paid another visit when the rooms were in the process of being decorated. The big dome ceiling in the President's office, complete with plastered sculptures and magnificent chandelier made from fine crystal, was very impressive.

The engine room was complete and all the equipment was wired and operational.

Joe had met Steven Sandies, whose father was one of the directors of Akeja Construction and the Ligerian ambassador in London, on the Chief's previous visit. Steven was a captain in the National Guard who, having spent a number of years in England, could talk to Joe about general matters concerning both countries and their ways.

During the time they were having tea, Chief Elido said to Steven, "Why don't you take Joe on a visit to one of our field units, let him watch a little gunnery practice. Would you fancy that Joseph?" Joe was pleased at the invitation as it offered a chance to do something other than sit around the club. Steven also invited him to their indoor rifle range to try their new AK 47 automatics rifles, and Joe said he would love to.

"Good," said the Chief, "You are our guest, you must visit our places of interest."

Five days had passed since the Chiefs visit when the daily courier arrived from head office of Akeja Construction with a letter from Jane and an invitation to Joe to attend a cocktail party. The party was being given by the President at his home on Saturday June 23rd. Joe was pleased about that, it would give him something to write home to Jane about.

Later that morning, Steven Sandies rang Joe at the site office. "Do you fancy a trip to the rifle range today Joe? Will you be able to get away this afternoon?"

"Yes" said Joe.

"Good, I'll pick you up this afternoon at 2-30pm.

At noon, Joe called God Bless into his office. "We will need to go into town to get some throw away type filters, the ones we have in now need changing.."

"Will we have to go to an agent Sir?"

"Yes, if we know where he is," said Joe.

"Les will know Sir."

"Then go find Les and we will be on our way."

They collected Les and drove off to Lepapa. As they approached the city they turned off the main road into a side road. The area was in a very dilapidated state. There was just one multi storey block of flats and rubbish thrown out of the upper floor flat windows was piled up so high that it passed the window sills of the ground floor.

The roads were in a terrible state of repair, and the stench was vile, It was, Joe thought, similar to the area where the beggars were. Then he spotted a woman washing clothes in a bucket at a stand pipe. As they approached he noticed that it was a white woman.

"Slow down God Bless," said Joe, "Stop, please."

Joe got out and walked slowly towards the woman, who looked up. It was Lucy, the young girl he had met on the plane.

She was dressed in rags. The hair, that had been so beautifully styled, was now just rats tails, it was hard to credit. "Hello," he said, "Do you remember me? We met on the flight out here." She had stopped washing and was looking at Joe with a look of apprehension on her face. "I won't ask how you are doing, I'm not blind." With that she started to cry.

Joe went to comfort her, but she pulled back, "No!" she croaked, "If anyone saw us he would kill me." She went on to tell

Joe how they lived with his brother and wife and their 3 children and his father, whose age they guessed to be seventy five. Ten people in one room, 10 foot by 10 foot square with no water, no light, no power and no toilet. Her husband now shared her with his brother. She was just a skivvy and her two sons were shunned by her husband's family because they were half caste. She had been to the British embassy, who had said they are helpless and could do nothing. This is Ligeria not Britain, she had been told. Here, the husband has total control over his wife and divorce is out of the question unless the husband agrees. Her husband had found out she had been to the embassy and he had beaten her almost to death. She was battling on for the children's sakes. Just then, one of the twins came running over, "Mama! Mama! Come quickly!" She grabbed her bucket and was off. Joe was about to follow but she shouted, "No! please, if my husband sees us he will kill me."

The girl ran round the block of flats to the dwelling places. One could hardly call them houses. They were made from packing crates, corrugated iron and mud, and with an open sewer running down the street, hence the stench.

Joe looked at Les, "Lets go." he said. They got back into the car and drove into the city. Joe was finally beginning to understand what life was like for the common people in the third world.

At a crossroads, a military policeman was on point duty, Joe was somewhat amused at the way they do point duty in Ligeria. Instead of giving positive signals with their arms, this policeman had his arms by his side and was giving the signals with his fingers. Joe's car was first in line and stationary, when a mammy wagon went straight through, apparently against the signal. The policeman went mad, blowing his whistle and shouting, then he ran over to Joe's car, jumped in the back with Les and told God Bless to follow the bus. God Bless was off like a shot and Joe was just about to object when God Bless interrupted, "Yes Sir, we always help the military. Oh yes Sir!" Then he pursed his lips, looking at Joe and holding his index finger up in his lap as a warning. Joe got the message and sat back to just let it all happen. They were gaining on the mammy wagon.

"Faster! Faster!" screamed the red-cap. God Bless was already breaking all speed limits, but out here, speed limits, traffic lights, they were all arbitrary anyway. They drew up alongside the Mammy wagon. With the red-cap leaning out of the window screaming at the driver to stop. It pulled over and stopped. The red-cap got out and ran to the bus, opened the drivers door, grabbed him and pulled him out of the cab and struck him with a tremendous blow to the jaw. The driver went down and, as he landed on the ground, the red-cap took a short run and kicked him in the head with his big heavy army boots. The driver was flat out on his back unconscious. Joe was again about to protest when God Bless grabbed his arm. "No Sir! Say nothing, do nothing - big trouble if we interfere! The military is the law here." God Bless was obviously afraid and Joe could see this.

The red-cap got back into the car looking satisfied, leaving a bus full of people with an unconscious driver. God Bless turned the car round and drove back to the crossroads. The red-cap got out, all smiles, shaking hands with Joe, then God Bless, then Les, who hadn't spoken a word during the entire incident. The red-cap then held up all traffic to allow God Bless to be on his way. Les then leaned over and said to Joe, "In any situation involving the military police you do exactly as they say, they are the ultimate law and they cannot be wrong." Joe just sat there quietly thinking and recapitulating the events he had witnessed during his short stay in Ligeria - dead bodies by the road side, just being ignored, policemen beating up drivers who happen to infringe traffic regulations. He could just imagine the situation in Britain if a body was found by the road side. The police would be out in force. The area would be cordoned off and the best forensic experts would be brought in. No stone would be left unturned until they had all the answers. But here in the third world. Just dig a hole, roll it in and cover it up. Life is cheap. Joe had had just about enough of the so called third world - little did he know.

EVENS CHEMICAL CORPORATION (ECC) LONDON

At the usual monthly board meeting of ECC, a major multinational company, the chairman and managing director, Mr Charles Johnson, was speaking, "Gentlemen, you have all had a copy of the prospectus with the findings of the exploration carried out by our colleague here. As you can see, there is Uranium in the Olantika mountains in Ligeria, on the border with Cameroon. During the 12 months since the discovery, two business delegations have been to Ligeria and during these visits private meetings were set up between our sales director James Clegg and the President. The meetings were set up by my brother-in-law Simon Denning, the British Ambassador to Ligeria, who has been a great help during the entire exercise. However, so far we have been unable to get permission to mine the Uranium. The President will not hear of it. He has never given a detailed explanation for the rejection, but claims that the oil exploration caused such upheaval and degradation that he will not put up with it again.

He is fully aware that the revenue from the oil is vital to his countries economy, but will not allow exploration to start again. I need not tell you, gentlemen, just what it would mean to each one of you in this room, to the company, to the share holders and to Britain as a whole. I personally have spoken to the Energy Secretary, who has told me to do everything possible to get the concession, but neither he nor the Government can get involved unless the Ligerian Government makes representations to them. That gentlemen is how the situation stands. President Elido came to power in a military coup 4 years ago and since then has been promising to hold a general election to elect a civilian government. Gentlemen, with a little help - financial that is - from us, that situation can be helped along."

"What do you intend to do, finance another coup?" The meeting quickly degenerated and other, similar comments were bandied around.

"Gentlemen, this is a board meeting not a gathering of rabble."

The financial director was angry at the behaviour of the board members, he was the type who like things orderly and proper."

"Thank you, Leonard," said the chairman, "No, I can assure you I plan nothing so drastic as that. However, there is a man some of you know, a Mr Unico Sandies, the former Ligerian Ambassador here in London. He lived here for some years and was the ambassador under no less than four different military leaders. He is the founder and unofficial leader of the National Socialist Party.

They have the organisation and members, and should democratic elections come about he would lead the party in those elections. When he does become President, and at this time there is no alternative to the NSP, he will give us the mining rights. Simon Denning confirms this with the unofficial discussion he has had with senior members of the party."

"Mr Chairman, you mentioned a little financial help, well how much is a little?"

"Good question, Leonard, I've had a series of dicussions with Unico Sandies and Simon and I am assured that half a million pounds Sterling will guarantee the Uranium mining rights. That may seem a great deal of money, but not when you consider the potential. That sum, plus the eighty million pounds to mine and process the Uranium, will be petty cash by comparison."

"Mr Chairman."

"Yes Ian,"

"Eighty and a half million pounds is a great deal of money, and I'm sure Edward would agree that it is not possible to determine with accuracy that Uranium is present without mining and processing a considerable amount of ore. I personally am not sure that I go along with the idea."

"I agree with Ian in part, so I think Edward should give his view on this matter." Edward Lang was the companies geologist and chief chemist.

"Well gentlemen, Ian has a point, but I've spent 6 months in those mountains and I can assure you there is Uranium there, now there is not time to go into the technical detail, for obvious reasons. You know the first oil wells to be drilled in both Saudi Arabia and Kuwait found only water, but I knew there was oil there and kept the pressure on the consortium to carry on the exploration. I led the first exploration team back in 37, then after the second world war I led the British and American consortium in 48 and we found oil. Now I am telling you there is Uranium in the Olantika mountains. Thank you gentlemen."

"Could you enlighten the meeting as to cost, Edward?" Said the Chairman.

Edward didn't like board meetings at the best of times and to try and justify his findings to a lot of morons was to Edward very exasperating, and usually the chairman would watch out for this, but whatever his reasons, he seemed to be dropping Edward in it this morning.

Edward spoke, "The cost of 80 million will cover all mining and processing and that is the outside sum. In other words it will move the whole bloody mountain if needs be, thank you gentlemen."

"That figure was worked out by Edward and myself," said the Chairman, "It could well be two thirds of that. The other half a million is to guarantee the mining concession by sponsoring the Sandies in their election campaign. That is the total sum, taking into account every conceivable setback. What I would like to do now gentlemen is vote whether or not we advance the half a million pounds to the NSP."

"Mr Chairman."

"Yes Leonard?"

"I am all for initiative and calculated risk, where the outcome is worth the risk. I didn't put that very well, did I?"

"We all get your meaning, Leonard." Replied the Chairman.

"Thank you. Well like I say half a million pounds for an election campaign is rather high."

"Ligeria is a big country with a big population Leonard," said the Chairman.

"Well, I think that I would like more details before I am asked to vote."

"Nonsense!" broke in the Technical Director, "It is all cut and dried as far as I am concerned, the pressure is being brought to bear on the President. He has got to call elections soon, the whole country is rumbling with discontent. We dare not stall any longer, I say we vote."

The Chairman got to his feet.

"Very well, I call for the vote. Do we advance the half a million pounds to the NSP."

All hands except that of the Financial Director voted in favour. One abstention was recorded in the minutes. "Thank you gentlemen."

NIGHTMARE

Steven called at Joe's office as arranged, at 2.30pm, "Are you ready Joe?" he asked.

"I'll be with you in a minute Steven. Hand that envelope to Captain Sandies please Les," said Joe, pointing over to Les's left hand. Les picked up the envelope and handed it over to Steven, who opened it and read the invitation. "I'm not surprised Joe, you really impressed the President and rightly so, I'll see you there."

The two men walked out, Joe threw his keys over to God Bless, "Take the car home for me please." They drove out into the bush. It took them 2 hours. They saw a small unit training on mortar fire and rocket launchers. Joe was introduced to a Lieutenant Nigel Lapengio. They shook hands, Joe thought he was a young man who really looked mean, Nigel smiled and walked on. "He is a one man fighting machine," said Steven. He was of medium height and good build, similar to Joe but maybe an inch or so taller.

On there way back Steven asked, "Do you ever do any hunting back home Joe?"

"No, there is nothing to hunt in my part of the world."

"We hunt occasionally for bush rat, they are quite nice really," said Steven.

"You're joking of course!" said Joe.

"I'll show you if you like but it will mean a little detour."

They branched off from their homeward route and went deeper into the bush, it was beginning to get dark now. They stopped and waited in the cab in silence. After a minute or so several of these rats appeared, their body size was that of a large cat with short legs. Steven started the Jeep, and the rats were off at tremendous speed.

"You eat those things?" asked Joe.

"Of course! They are delicious roasted!" Joe pulled a face, and Steven laughed.

Darkness was falling fast now. They both heard a horrendous screaming. Steven stopped the Jeep and switched off the engine, putting his index finger to his lips. The screaming came again. They both got out and moved silently across a small clearing. From the end of the clearing it appeared to be dense bush. As they entered they could hear voices and laughter, then once again the screaming, mingled with a thudding cracking noise. Steven then parted the dense vegetation and they both peered through.

What they saw was a sickening sight. A squad of red-caps were training their AK 47s at a small group of men huddled together on the ground. The prisoners were all bound hand and foot. One of them, stripped naked, on his hands and knees, his hands stretched out wide apart in front of him and with his wrists tied to wooden stakes driven into the ground, was pleading for his life. A red-cap, a very big man with an enormous club, was swinging it at the man's head as the unfortunate victim tried to dodge the blows, without success. His skull cracked open, spattering blood and brains all over the place. There were already two men slain. The other prisoners moaned in horror as they witnessed their own fate. Although there were about a dozen red-caps involved in the grisly murders, Joe knew he had to do something. He was just about to leap out at the perpetrators of this heinous crime, when a large black hand was clamped over his mouth and he was flung on his back, with the weight of Steven's body on top of him.

Steven restrained him and, when he stopped struggling, whispered fiercely, "Joe, calm yourself! If I let you go not a sound or we will join those wretched people. I've no desire to have my skull caved in." Steven moved his hand from Joe's mouth, and indicated that they should move back the way they had come. After some distance Joe began to vomit. He was motionless on his hands and knees, his head bowed. Steven stooped by his side, "Come on Joe, there is nothing we can do here, let's go, come on Joe, Joe! don't you understand we are in grave danger!" Steven got Joe on to his feet and they started walking. They quickened their pace until finally they were running.

They got to the Jeep. Steven pushed Joe in, then leapt in, started the engine and moved off. They drove quickly, bouncing over the undergrowth. They were both silent. After an hour or so they broke out onto the Macadam roadway, and were now on the outskirts of Akeja. Steven looked across at Joe, who looked to be in some kind of trance.

"I don't believe it!" he said, as he leaned over to vomit again. "Good God!" he said, "I just witnessed a bloody nightmare. I don't understand, for Christ's sake man don't just sit there! This is your bloody country, what's going on?"

"Steady Joe, I'll explain as far as I know, I'm just as shocked and sickened as you are, please don't shout. We are in an open Jeep and we are coming into town now so be calm and reasonable, for Christ sake!" Steven was beginning to get agitated now but managed to control himself. He pulled over to the side of the road and stopped. "Look Joe," he said, in a calm voice, "Please don't go off half cocked, let me take you home and we will talk then, do you agree?" Joe looked at him with what could be described a determined, or defiant, look, Steven couldn't quite make out which. Joe's shock was now turning to anger. Steven thought the situation could become delicate. They drove on in silence. They arrived at Joe's bungalow, Joe opened the door and they walked in just as Lucky came out of the kitchen. "Ah Mr Tully, you are very late!" It was 9-0pm.

"Go home Lucky," said Joe curtly. Lucky was just about to explain what he had got for dinner. he was holding a plate towards Joe when Joe snapped again. He knocked the plate upwards out of the startled Lucky's hand "Go home man, leave it! Leave everything! There is the door for Christ sake, go home."

He had never spoken, or behaved, like that to the inoffensive Lucky before. It frightened Lucky and he just stammered out a quick, "yes Sir," as he turned to leave, hurriedly taking off his white jacket and throwing it over a kitchen chair on his way out. Steven went into the living room and poured two large whiskeys. Joe took the whisky and sat down. He took a large gulp, let his head drop back on to the back of the chair and gazed at the ceiling. Steven said, "OK, Joe. Are you calm enough? Is your mind coherent enough to appreciate what I'm about to tell you?"

Joe took another gulp to finish his whisky.

"Yes," said Joe, "I'm sorry, I'm being childish, forgive me." He looked at the door "I've never spoken like that to Lucky before, he is really a splendid little man, he deserved better, Joe sighed and shook his head. "What I did just then was unforgivable."

"But understandable under the circumstances," said Steven, "Now Joe you must forget everything you saw tonight, forget it ever happened, and don't ever breathe a word about it to anyone, do you understand? To do so would mean your certain death. What you witnessed was a political crime. You cannot go to the police, they would be helpless, the army is the law in this land. For you to report it would mean your disappearance and death, nothing can be done yet, but it will soon change. I've known about such atrocities for a long time, but this is the first time I've witnessed it."

"What is it all about?" asked Joe.

"Not now," said Steven, "I promise I will explain everything in detail, but not now. You couldn't possibly take it in, you are not fully in control of yourself. Tomorrow, after a nights sleep, the immediate shock of horror will have passed and you will accept what you have witnessed as an act of premeditated murder, that can be thought out rationally. You cannot think in a rational manner now. Your treatment of Lucky proves that." Joe nodded and passed Steven the empty glass, he filled it and passed it back. I'll stay the night Joe, just to be on the safe side."

"That won't be necessary," said Joe "I'm alright now."

"Promise you won't go to the police."

"I promise," said Joe.

"OK" said Steven, "Don't leave this house tonight, go to bed now, don't go to site tomorrow, say you're ill or whatever, I'll be here in the morning, OK?"

It was after 10pm when Steven left. Joe got the whisky bottle and went into his bedroom. He filled his glass and sat down on the bed, looking across at the picture of Jane smiling out at him. How he needed her just now. Would he ever be able to relate what he had witnessed this night to any civilised person. He had been in Special Forces in Malaya, and in Borneo and the Middle East, and he had seen actions and killings and woundings that had shocked him. But never had he seen the sort of gruesome slaughter that had been so casually perpetrated by those red-caps in the bush tonight.

Whatever possessed him to take this bloody contract and leave his lovely Jane. Even three months is a life time without her. He topped up his glass and eventually fell asleep on the bed, fully clothed, having drank virtually a bottle of whisky, a drink he never touched at home.

Next morning Joe awoke with the sun beating down on his face, for he hadn't drawn the curtains the night before. He swung his legs off the bed and sat with his head in his hands. Lucky slipped into the room in his bare feet as usual and put a pot of coffee on the side unit by the bed, then slipped out again, he had been watching for Joe to awaken, but wouldn't take the chance to wake him.

Joe looked at the clock. It was 7-30am. God Bless had called as usual at 6-30am, but Lucky had told him Joe was sick. Joe walked into the shower and let the hot and then the cold water awaken him, and then sat on the bed and started on the coffee, Lucky then looked into the room.

"Come here please Lucky."

"Is there anything I can get you Sir?" The nervousness in his voice was apparent.

"No thank you Lucky, I would like to apologise for my unforgivable behaviour last night. I had some very distressing news and wanted to be alone, I do hope that you will forgive me, it will never happen again I assure you."

"That's all right Sir I had forgotten all about it." Lucky lied diplomatically.

Joe smiled and stood up. "You are a good man Lucky."

"Can I get you some breakfast Sir?" Lucky asked, less nervously this time.

"No thank you. I will have another pot of coffee if I may please," he answered, handing Lucky his empty pot, "It's excellent."

Joe got up and started to dress. Lucky came in with the coffee.

"Is there anything special you would like for your lunch Sir?"

"No Lucky I'll have a sandwich at the bar as usual."

"Then I will just go and get the fish for the evening meal Sir, it will be fresh in this morning, but by lunch time it would be gone."

"Very well Lucky thank you," Lucky liked working for the English man, as he called him, he got Saturday afternoon, Sunday and every evening off, but when he had worked for the Asians or Ligerians, it was every day, virtually 18 hours per day.

Steven arrived just as Lucky was leaving, "Good morning Sir,"

"Good morning Lucky, is your master in?"

"Yes Sir, in the kitchen." Steven walked through. "How are you feeling this morning Joe?" he asked.

"Just a slight hangover, that's all, it's nothing, I am sorry for my behaviour out in the bush Steven, I guess I was in shock, thank you for saving my life."

"And my own!" replied Steven,

"Are we alone Joe?"

"Yes. Lucky won't be back for at least two hours. Would you like a coffee?"

"No thank you. About what you saw last evening. They were political killings. There are undercurrents of unrest amongst our people with our system of government. Chief Elido has ruled since his military coup four years ago, and although the situation to the outsider seems stable, it is kept that way by terror and death. The fact that I am telling you this would mean my certain death if Elido found out, yours also, I might add. Everybody knows that to stay alive they must say nothing, do nothing. The man in the street cannot take on the military, you never ask questions of the people you work with, you never ask for their opinion of Elido or his government, because there are spies everywhere. It is not only your life but mine also, that is what you would be risking. Just leave well alone and stay safe. It may be as well if you were to say your wife is having difficulty coping without you, and she wants you home right away, then resign. Go home, forget your nightmare. We will understand, there would be no question of your running away from problems. It is our suffering. Our problem.

"Oh, I've thought of that, believe me nothing would please me more than to go home and forget it. This is not my country and I don't want to be involved. I've only got maybe seven weeks to do before job completion, then I will have completed my contract, I will be well in with my agent, plus I'll get my bonus which is worth a lot of money to me. If I quit now I will have failed, and I need the money. I'm staying Steven. Like you say this is a Ligerian problem not mine. I say nothing, ask nothing, I'm a foreigner minding my own business."

"Very well Joe, when you go into work tomorrow just say you were not feeling well, but now you are fine, then work and behave as normal. If Chief Elido pays you another visit treat him as normal, he thinks a lot of you and considers you a friend. I will be honest with you Joe, I never thought I would witness such horror as we have, I have always known that intimidation and torture went on, but not on that scale, that was beyond my comprehension, I'm just a small cog in the military Joe, I'm not privileged to government policy. I was educated in England. I got my 'A' levels there and then went on to Sandhurst where I got my commission, I respect and believe in the British system. I'm a product of it, my sister Paula is at London University taking her BA in political science and economics. She has just taken her finals and is awaiting her results. My father was the Ligerian Ambassador in London, he has always brought us up to respect the British system of democracy, which we are striving to achieve for our people here. One day we will change things for the better. There are many others who want to put a stop to Elido's state terrorism. We are not alone, but we can do nothing yet. We must bide our time and try to avoid attracting the attention of the red-caps. That is why it is imperative that you say nothing. You must come to our house and meet my father, I'm sure you will like him."

Joe felt a sense of relief at his young friend's words. It was encouraging to know that there was opposition to this ugly regime that was responsible for such appalling poverty and inhuman atroci-ties. "Don't worry, I won't say a word about last night to anybody, or about anything else you've told me, I'll go to the site now. I'm over it, honest Steven I'm OK."

Steven smiled and extended his hand to Joe. "You must come to our house and meet my father. I'm sure you will like him."

"It'll be a pleasure." Joe said grasping this young idealist's hand. He walked Steven out to his jeep and waited until he drove away. Then he got in his own car and drove to the club to get a sandwich and a beer before going on to the site.

Everybody was glad to see him back and looking fit. The afternoon went well, the main construction was completed that day as was the commissioning of the President's and the Secretarial offices. It was now just a matter of finishing the balancing of the rest of the office block. The furniture was beginning to arrive, the two main offices were carpeted with the best axminster imported from Britain. The computer was also on site but it needed to be installed. Then, on completion, it would need commissioning, but that wasn't Joe's province.

"Let's have a walk round the site Les." said Joe. They went to the engine room.

"The 'S' mat filter was groaning this morning, one of the nylon bearings had come adrift, but we fixed that and everything is now operating as it should, would you like to see the furniture that arrived this morning Sir?" asked Les.

They both walked round to reception of the Presidential suite, the workmen were placing the luxurious furniture.

As you entered the main door, immediately on your left was the reception desk which was like a large bar going almost the entire length of the wall, at the end were the large double doors that led to the rest of the office complex. Across the foyer was the big office, the President's, the door to its right was his secretary's.

The rest of the reception area was fitted out with the most luxurious furniture, hide three piece suite's and teak tables, the centre piece was an indoor fountain with circular pool beneath it full of various types of the most colourful tropical fish, and the entire area was fitted with the best axminster carpet.

Joe went into the President's office, both men taking off their boots before entering. The decor was splendid, the air- delivery grilles, situated 8 feet from the floor in the wall opposite the door, were flanged to match and blend with the raised patterned plaster, so they were not noticeable unless you knew they were there.

The crystal chandelier was magnificent, the room temperature was 75 degrees F, with 50% relative humidity, "Conditions are holding," said Les.

"And they will," said Joe. There was no natural light in the office for there were no windows, for security reasons. Joe was satisfied the Presidential suite was complete, it was just a matter of the furnishing. The secretaries office was smaller with a flat false ceiling it also was a very attractive office, with the best axminster carpet and furnishings.

Both men went outside and put on their boots and then walked round the front garden, all the flower beds had been laid out and the best quality turf had been laid. The centre garden fountain was operational, the front main gate pillars were erected and the wall was almost complete, the back and rear sides were still in a rough state though.

They both went back to the office, Joe banged on the office wall and sat down, two minutes passed before the tea boy brought a large pot of coffee for Joe. Les asked for a pot of tea. "The job is drawing to a close Sir," said Les.

"Yes, do you know where your next contract will be?"

"No Sir not at this time." God Bless came into the office all smiles, Joe knew that when God Bless came in uncalled it was time to go, "Is it time we were off?" asked Joe.

"Whenever you are ready Sir." he replied.

They moved out of the office and into the car and drove off.

"Call at the supermarket please I need some writing paper and envelopes," said Joe, they arrived at the store and parked in the car park.

"I won't be a minute," said Joe as he got out and walked into the store. Joe selected a lined writing pad, for he had never mastered the art of writing without having lines to follow. He paid at the cash desk and walked out of the nearest exit. As he walked round the building, a wee girl of maybe 4 or 5 years old jumped out at him shouting "dash master! dash!" (dash being the operative word for tip or something for nothing). She was tied by a loop of cord from her left wrist to the right wrist of a very old blind woman, they were both in rags and their feet were bare, "dash master, dash!" she would shout and jump forward stamping her tiny feet. Her mouth was hard and her eyes cold, just a tiny infant who should be cuddled and spoilt.

This sight above all others disturbed Joe as he went to bed that night with the infant on his mind, his first conscious thought the following morning when he surfaced was of that infant out begging. There but for the grace of God goes my daughter, he thought.

Life is cheap here in Ligeria, but what can one individual do, a foreigner in a land of 100 million. This situation made him think, he had signed this contract to improve his situation back home, now he realised that he already had everything that mattered, it couldn't be improved on, he and his family wanted for nothing, yet he had wanted more.

Have people in the West become obsessed with material wealth? Is it beginning to take precedence? Was Joe's education now taking on a new dimension? When he was a child they were poor, they had nothing from a material point of view but they were happy, they had full bellies and there was love. Bitterness was as foreign to them as Chinese, yet he had seen only bitterness in the eyes of that infant.

He arrived on site and got hold of God Bless to go on some errands. On a side road that led onto Torridor road there were two men having a debate, trying to reach an agreement. Around their legs were about 8 goats tied to a stake driven into the ground, and there were children playing around and with the goats. The two men then reached agreement and the owner stood over one and grabbed its nose and jaw, pulled its head and slit its throat with the knife in his right hand. Then all in one movement the hand with knife grabbed the goats front legs, tipped it on its back slit it down the middle and was peeling its hide, as it was still kicking in its death throes. The entire exercise had taken only seconds. The last thing Ligerians would bother about are abattoirs, but even the goats fared better than those poor wretched men in the bush. Joe realised he'd had a belly full of the third world, it was one bloody thing after another. They completed their errands and went back to site.

With the exception of the computer room all was complete, there were some tests still to be carried out, the computers were now installed, a heat loud test was required and the computer commissioning engineers were due to arrive on August 1st, the project was weeks ahead of schedule.

The President and his entourage had paid another visit, and the President had decided to move in, it was now Saturday June 23rd, time for the cocktail party. Joe had recovered from the bush nightmare, he had convinced himself that it was none of his business, what people and governments do in their own country was their own affair, nobody else's.

Joe arrived at the President's home at exactly 2-30pm, he was dressed in his grey light weight safari suit. As he entered the house he was shown through to the entertaining room by the servant. The Chief was talking to several men and women, he saw Joe and came over to him. "Hello Joseph! So nice to see you," they shook hands and the President took him over to introduce him to the other guests.

"What will you have to drink Joseph?"

"A beer please if I may." They walked over to the bar that ran all the way down one wall. The double doors that led out onto the patio and garden were open, so while the Chief got him a beer Joe walked out onto the patio, then walked over to the lily pond and wandered over to its edge to admire the various floating plant life, when suddenly he jumped back with a gasp. Immediately below him in the pool a crocodile opened its massive jaws, at this Chief Elido laughed as he brought Joe his beer.

"What is the matter? Did my pet Clarence startle you!"

"Startle me! It frightened the life out of me!" Said Joe "Is it safe?"

"Yes, of course, the water is too far below the edge for him to climb out and he is well fed - he wouldn't be hungry. Joe took a long drink and made his way back into the bar, the bar room was large with beautiful expensive occasional furniture, with low level settees along one wall opposite the bar. They both walked through the lounge area, Joe was saying "I'll go back inside, I believe in the old saying safety in numbers!" At that the Chief laughed and they both walked in, the Chief with his arm around Joe's shoulders.

The lounge was L shaped, with an archway between the two areas. The buffet was arranged in the smaller area, there were all kinds of meats and fish - prawns, crayfish and lobster, all kinds of salad with beef pork and caviar pate, fruit, cream, ice cream, and of course, all the best wines - "this is some spread," thought Joe.

There were three waiters, three waitresses and a chef, all in spotless whites ready to carve and serve whatever the guests asked for. From the archway leading to the buffet area came a very large individual dressed in a black dinner suit, he was at least 6 feet tall with shoulders that would fill a doorway, and a belly that would shame a pregnant buffalo. On his left was Captain Steven, he was an inch or so shorter with shoulders as big, but slim with it.

The Chief saw them, "Ah, Ambassador! How pleased I am to see you!" he remarked as he walked over to them. He grabbed the big guy and took him in a bear hug, then shook hands with Steven. "Come I want you to meet a friend of mine, he led them over to Joe. "This, Joseph is my good friend Unico Sandies, and his son Steven. You know Steven, of course." He continued. "This is Joseph Tully an Englishman building my new office suite."

"Installing the services actually," said Joe.

"Unico is our Ambassador in London." Joe shook hands.

"How do you do," said Joe. Unico spoke excellent English, without a trace of accent, as did Steven.

"What will you have to drink?" asked the Chief. A Ligerian in a white coat was now behind the bar.

"Whisky and water," said Unico.

"The same for me," said Steven.

"I'll have a beer please," said Joe. They were all now sipping their drinks and making small talk. Steven was telling Joe that he had received his consignment of new AK 47 automatic rifles, and asked if perhaps he would like to try one out on the rifle range.

"Yes I would like that," said Joe. The National Guard was the crack regiment of the Ligerian armed forces of which Steven was a captain, but he was Sandhurst trained, which must account for his being a captain so young.

Then everybody stopped talking and all eyes went over to the buffet. Standing in the archway was the most beautiful black girl Joe had ever seen. She spotted them and came over. She was small and beautifully proportioned with classic features. Her nose was small and slim, her lips full and her eyes large and black. She was smiling, her teeth were even and white, and contrasted perfectly with her very black skin, she wore virtually no make up, her hair was negroid but trimmed and full at the back of the neck. She was wearing an off the shoulder cocktail dress that came just below the knee, she wore a diamante above the left ear, she was indeed an eyeful, Joe thought.

The Chief threw both arms out wide.

"My dear, how you have grown!" he then took Paula's tiny hand in his, which were more like shovels by comparison, he shook her hand warmly then kissed it.

"You are a beautiful sight to gladden an old mans heart." he was looking at her with fatherly affection in his eyes, Joe was finding it difficult to comprehend his involvement in the bush massacre. Her father then went to introduce her to Joe, who took her small hand in his and said, "The President's remark was an understatement - you are a sight to gladden any man's heart, you are indeed very beautiful."

"Thank you Sir," she said, her voice was as beautiful as she was, again perfect English without trace of accent.

The Ambassador then said, "My daughter has now completed her education, gaining a first class honours degree in political science and economics, at the London School of Economics.

"Congratulations," said Joe, "You are obviously as clever as you are beautiful."

"Come let us eat!" said the President, they all walked over to the buffet.

Paula was asking Joe which part of England he was from, "I knew by your accent it was North but I couldn't just decide Lancashire or Yorkshire." She asked about his family, and he proudly told her of his wife Jane and their children Elizabeth and Jonathan.

"I love England very much," she was saying, "I have spent 14 of my 23 years in England, I love and respect her and her wonderful people, it will always be my second home, the English will always be dear to my heart. But Ligeria is my country and she must have the benefit of my education and knowledge." Joe could tell these words were spoken with sincerity, if not modesty.

At the buffet Paula got prawns with salad Joe got lobster with salad, they both walked back to the lounge and sat at an occasional table to eat their food. Joe then returned and got two glasses of white wine. Just then another white man entered the lounge from the buffet area. There were about 30 people at the party and until this moment Joe hadn't noticed that he was the only white man present, the colour of people hadn't registered.

"Who is that guy?" Joe asked Paula, "do you know him?"

"Yes, I'll introduce you." They walked over, her father and Steven also walked over, Paula said, "Hello Simon, I would like to introduce you to a friend of mine and a fellow countryman, Simon this is Joe Tully, Joe this is Simon Denning, your Ambassador in Bakra."

"Hello," said Joe. "A pleasure to meet you," said Simon, "It's nice to see you again, Paula, looking as beautiful as ever." At that Chief Elido and party arrived on the scene, they all shook hands and engaged in conversation, the Chief explained that Joe was doing the suite of offices etc etc, at that Paula and Joe moved off to mingle with the other guests, until at 5-0pm people started to leave.

Joe was going home tomorrow so he decided to make a move, he said his goodbyes to the men, then went over to Paula.

"I must be leaving now, I go on leave tomorrow so I must go and sort myself out, I've really enjoyed this afternoon it has been most relaxing in such delightful company."

"I hope we meet again," said Paula.

"Me too," said Joe and then left.

The following morning Joe checked in for the 8-40am flight to London, he was excited as usual, as always feeling great going home, and at a low ebb coming back. He arrived at Heathrow, got the family their presents, then got the 3-30pm flight to Manchester. Joe's two weeks were as usual great, the children were always so pleased to have their Daddy home with them, no more overseas contracts he had promised himself.

It was Sunday 8th of July Joe was sitting in the lounge at home listening to Chopin's Etude No.3 in C minor, it was one of his favourite pieces of music. Jane came in, she had been getting his gear ready for morning.

"The children are both fast asleep," said Joe.

"Yes," said Jane, "they are no trouble, they really enjoy having you home Joe."

"Well Jane my petal this is the last time I will be going back, next time I'm home for good."

"Joe I notice you seem troubled. I haven't said anything because most of the time you are being your own self again, just as daft as ever with the children, and I don't want to stop it. I can't explain it, but I know you, and something's on your mind."

Joe got up and went over to her and sat down beside her, he took both her hands in his. "Jane love, I've seen a lot of things living in that country, it has added to my education far more than I could ever learn from a book, education about life. I want you to know that I love you, far more than I could ever express in words, I would need to be a scholar or a poet to do that. This job will be complete in a matter of 3 or 4 weeks then I come home, finished, I shall burn my passport and that's it, I'll take a mundane job, and if this is it, if this is our lot, well all I can say is we have wealth beyond the imagination of millions of people in the third world. As long as we have each other we want for nothing, we love care and bring up our children so that they grow up strong and stable, understanding and accepting justice and equality."

"I love you Joe, I love you so much, I don't ever want us to separate again ever." and those were Joe's feelings exactly. The time came when Joe arrived back at Bakra airport, and went through the palaver of dash clearing customs, God Bless was waiting for him, he first drove to site then on to his home. Good Luck was waiting to greet him and dinner was prepared.

The next two days went well. On the Wednesday morning the phone rang Joe answered, it was Steven. "Did you enjoy your leave Joe?" he asked.

"Yes it was great as usual."

"Well I'm ringing because tomorrow I'm on the rifle range, would you care to join me?"

"Yes why not." replied Joe.

"Good, I will pick you up at 3-30pm."

"Fine I will be ready and waiting," said Joe, Steven hung up. The following afternoon Steven called at site for Joe who threw his keys to God Bless, "Take the car home for me please." he said.

"How are your at snap shooting?" Steven asked,

"Fair I guess" replied Joe, he did well at snap shooting during his own army days, Steven handed him an AK 47 and explained its operation, "On auto when the target comes up you have 3 seconds to aim and fire then it goes down again."

"Let's go," said Joe. The target appeared. Joe raised the automatic, aimed and fired, and hit the wooden man right in the chest.

Steven was impressed.

"Now on repetition from the hip." The wooden man appeared and Joe almost cut it in half.

"Very good! You are a real marksman." said Steven, as they made their way home.

"I will just have to call home Joe, I need to collect some things. I'm working late tonight so I will just make a quick call and you can say hello to Paula."

When they arrived Steven showed Joe into the living room, Paula was there playing chess with her father,

"Hello Paula, hello Sir," said Joe. Paula was dressed in a floral dress with white sandals, she looked so tiny without her heels, she couldn't stand more than 5 feet 2 inches at the most, just the opposite of her father and brother.

"Who's winning?" asked Joe.

"Oh, there is a long way to go yet," replied the old man. "Do you play Joe?" he asked.

"Not very well I'm afraid." Steven came in, "You ready, Joe?"

"Yes," Joe replied.

"Paula my dear, I'm afraid I will have to cancel our date tonight, I'm needed at headquarters all night."

"But Steven, you promised."

"Well I'm sorry, it can't be helped."

"What do think of a brother who breaks his promise to take his younger sister out Joe?"

"Well, I... I..." Joe was tongue tied. Steven broke in, "Joe, will you do me a favour?"

"Yes, if I can, of course."

"Well," said Steven, "There is this new restaurant opened in Akeja called the 'Mandarin', would you mind escorting my younger sister there for me, otherwise she will never let it drop!"

"Of course, it will by my pleasure. I know the 'Mandarin', I've been there. What does your younger sister have to say about it?"

"Less of the younger sister bit! I'm happy to accept," she then went over to link arms with Joe, "and Joe isn't a big hulk like you!" she said.

"Thanks Joe, now I owe you one."

"I will pick you up at eight."

When Joe arrived for Paula, the house boy showed him in. Paula was just getting small items out of the sideboard drawer, and putting them in her evening bag, which was made of the same material as her dress, a maroon silk. The dress itself was an off the shoulder fitting, it fell about 2" below the knee. She had a solitary ruby pendant on a long gold chain, that fell some way down her chest, ruby ear rings and a diamante above her right ear. She walked over to Joe and stood right under his nose. He looked down at her and he could not help his eyes being drawn to the cleavage of her ample breast, then he caught her eyes and they seemed to be laughing at him, for she knew where he was looking.

"You look very beautiful," he said, stepping back and offering her his arm. They went outside to the car. Joe opened the door, and as she sat down her dress ran up her thigh, giving a very generous display. She was not quick to push it back down.

They arrived at the restaurant parked the car, went in and

crossed the foyer which was very elegant with the best quality carpet, at the entrance to the restaurant proper they were met by the head waiter.

"Good evening Madam, Sir."

Joe answered, "Good evening. Table for two, Sandies."

"Yes Sir, this way please." The place was decorated with splendour, exquisite period wallpaper, and excellent parquet floor and crystal chandeliers. At the centre of the far wall there was a small bandstand and a musician was playing romantic music on a grand piano. On each table there was a request pad for the patrons to request the music of their choice.

The head waiter seated them at the table and gave them each a menu. The table was round and in the centre there was a second tier which could be revolved, Joe said, "You order and whatever you have I'll have the same,"

"Very well," said Paula. She ordered sweet and sour pork with prawns and crayfish pieces and rice. The food was brought in on steaming hot stainless steel dishes, and placed on the second tier in the centre of the table, along with all kinds of additional dishes such as diced fruits and nuts. The waiter then gave them both a preheated plate.

Paula got what she wanted from the first dish, then turned the centre tier and helped herself from the second dish, and Joe was doing the same until the centre tier had been round 360 degrees, by which time they both had their meal before them. Then Paula started with her chopsticks, with which she was, as Joe expected, expert. Joe tried them and had food flying all over the table, much to her amusement. "That's it!" he said, and put the chopsticks down and picked up a knife and fork.

"Oh you are a square Joe, you are just like my father and Steven, no sense of adventure!"

Joe wrote several requests on the request pad and gave them to the waiter, who took them over to the musician. Both during and after the meal, Paula asked Joe if he would mind going into Bakra tomorrow with her to get some material for some drapes she was making, as she didn't like going to the industrial estate on her own.

49

"I would be delighted to," said Joe.

"Good, I will pick you up at your site tomorrow at 9-0am," said Paula. After the meal they had coffee and brandy.

"I cannot drink spirits," said Paula.

"You know," said Joe "I never drank spirits until I came out here!" Paula laughed at that.

"Do we drive you to drink then Joe?" she said, and with that she grabbed and squeezed his thigh. He was just a little taken aback by this, and his red blood corpuscles started to race. She chuckled happily. "Better to drive you to drink than to drive you to something else, eh Joe!" she said, and this time when she squeezed his thigh he felt her fingertips press into his groin. He was now beginning to get hot under the collar, which he was not wearing.

They spoke of many things - Paula was very knowledgeable regarding England - they talked and they laughed, and the evening wore on very quickly. When he felt it was time to go, he called over the waiter. "Check please," he said. The waiter smiled. "One moment Sir," he said and then walked away. The head waiter then came over. "The check has been taken care of, Sir, by Captain Sandies."

"Oh I see, thank you." replied Joe. The waiter smiled and left.

"Steven needn't have done that," said Joe.

"Oh that's alright, Steven can afford it. I am glad Steven was tied up this evening, I love Steven very much, but I prefer your company!" at that she squeezed his thigh again, sending his adrenaline racing again.

"Shall we be leaving, Paula? It's getting late." She smiled and got up, Joe threw a couple of Guineas on the table and they left. They went outside to the car and Joe opened the door. Paula got in showing ample thigh again, Joe got in and they drove off, again talking about England.

"Do you miss your wife Joe - or is that a silly question?"

"I miss her very much," he replied. At that she moved closer and rested her head on his shoulder,

"You are so easy to grow fond of Joe." she said, and with that she started to stroke his thigh, once more. Oh God, thought Joe, what could she possibly want from him? Every female he had been in

50

contact with in Ligeria whether it be the hotel receptionist, or the ones from the various companies he had dealt with, even shop assistants, had seemed to be trying to get him into bed. If you were white then you were rich and had influence, and their one idea was to win your favours by sleeping with you. Every one of them seemed to be willing to go on the game for something or other. But what could Paula be after? She wanted for nothing.

He stopped the car outside her front garden and opened her door. "Well, Paula," he said in his usual easy going manner "Thank you for a very pleasant evening, it really is a joy to dine with you."

"Aren't you coming in, Joe?"

"Well, it is getting very late."

"Nonsense! You will have to say good night to father, he would think it very odd you not coming in." Joe's mind was now racing. "OK, why not. I'll just get my keys." He went round the car, got his keys and locked the door. He escorted Paula into the house. The old man was in the living room, sitting at the chess board, alone.

"Hello father," said Paula.

"Hello Paula, Joe. Did you have a pleasant evening?" "Yes, thank you, it was great," Joe replied. Paula kicked off her shoes and poured two brandies, gave one to her father then went over to Joe, closed right up to him and gave him his brandy. They made a little small talk, then Joe said, "Well I must be going, it is getting late." He got up and shook hands with the old man. Paula came to him and said "I will show you out." They walked to the door. Joe opened it and stepped down off the step, leaving Paula just inside the doorway, which brought them nearer in height to each other. Paula then said, "Thank you, Joe, for a lovely evening." Before he could answer she threw her arms around him and kissed him full on the lips, then she broke away, said good night and closed the door. Joe walked to the car totally bewildered, it just did not compute.

Back in the living room, Steven was there with their father. "Have you got him, Paula?"

"I don't know, I can't understand it, unless he is afraid because of who I am. But he seems very much in love with his wife, and he's a very shy person, that's a fact. But I have other plans."

Joe drove home put the car in the car port and went inside, it was 1-30am as he went into the bedroom, stripped off then went into the bathroom. He came out and sat on the bed looking at the photo of his Jane. "Jane," he said "I'm in a mess, but two maybe three weeks at most and I'll be away from this bloody circus." He then kissed his finger and touched it to the face in the photo.

Next morning a letter came for him from Jane, and one from head office, confirming to him that the computer engineers would arrive August 1st, so after their heat load acceptance test on August 5th, the building would be handed over. Just 4 weeks to go thought Joe. There was also an invitation to dinner from Unico Sandies. With it was a hand written note - 'Dear Joe, I hope you can accept this invitation, as I have some very happy news to announce, best regards, Unico.'

Sent by the old man himself. He wondered if Paula had any-thing to do with it, anyway I suppose I'll go, he thought, can't come to any harm if the old man is there. A lovely family, the Sandies, but he wished that Paula would abandon this come-to-bed attitude, for it was beginning to disturb him.

It was 9-0am and Paula arrived for him as arranged, God Bless was fussing around her to make her welcome and comfortable. She was dressed in a pale blue sleeveless dress with flat open toed sandals with a pink varnished toe on display. Joe thought she looked, as always, delightful.

"Hello Paula!" he said, as he took her small arm, "shall we go?" Paula said "I'll drive!" and walked over to a red Chevrolet convertible. Expensive, thought Joe, as he opened the door. Joe climbed in and she started the car and sped away. The girl obviously has no respect for speed limits, thought Joe to himself.

"You like fast cars I see?" said Joe.

"No point hanging around, life is too short as it is!" she re-plied. She glanced quickly at Joe and smiled.

They arrived at the industrial estate. Joe recognised it he had been on several occasions for various materials. She drove down between two of the warehouses and stopped the car. "Here we are," she said, as they walked in. There was some kind of service counter about 2 metres from the door. She said nothing to the old man sat on the opposite side of the counter, but walked to the right hand side of the counter, lifted the flap, pushed open the gate and walked into the warehouse proper.

"You obviously know your way around," said Joe.

"I have been here many times with my father whilst on holiday," she said. They walked over to a small office and went in. There was another old man sat behind an even older, dilapidated desk, Paula spoke in a tribal language that Joe could not understand. This girl never ceased to amaze him. Then she turned to Joe. "Excuse me Joe, I don't want to be ignorant, but although English is the first language in Ligeria, it has not always been the case, and some of our elderly people still have difficulty with it. This man doesn't know how old he is, but it is a fact that he is over 100 years old, so we speak in our tribal tongue which is Mausa. It makes life easy."

"Well, naturally, I understand," said Joe.

"My father arranged with this man for me to come down here to select some material for some new drapes that I am making for our home."

"I see," said Joe, but all he could see were sacks stacked from floor to ceiling. The old man led the way out, he was very badly stooped. They went over to another warehouse situated between two bigger ones, this one was much smaller, but it was built of breeze block as opposed to corrugated iron. The whole area was a mass of warehouses.

The old man pulled out a keyring, selected a key and opened the door to a low building and walked in, followed by Paula and Joe. They walked over to another door, the old man selected another key and opened it. He nodded towards them they followed him in. This room was clean with a tiled floor and plastered walls. Against the walls were wooden pallets stacked high with rolls of material, cloth of every type from clothing to curtain fabric.

Paula went over to a particular pallet and inspected the various rolls and asked Joe, "What do you think?"

"Very nice," he said looking at the various rolls of a maroon velvet-type material. She then went on to the old man, in their native tongue, for quite some time. The old man kept nodding, "OK shall we go?" she said and they left.

"Is that it - have we completed our errand?" he asked.

"Not quite, I would like you to meet a couple of friends of mine." She then drove over to the Akeja country club. "I know this place, this is where I spend my weekends," said Joe, as they drove into the car park.

Paula walked right through the restaurant into the cook house, out of the back and into a long corridor that ran parallel with the bowling alley. This was new to Joe he knew only the restaurant, bar and games room. At the end of the corridor they stopped and she knocked on a door and as it opened they went in. This was the room that used to be living quarters of the steward who ran the club, it now looked like a snug of an English pub.

Two men, both Ligerian, were sat at a table, drinking. Paula greeted them both warmly then introduced Joe.

"This is Doctor Tony Daniels."

"Mister," corrected Tony.

"And this is Mr Jibil Peters, an attorney of law."

"Was," he corrected.

"Nice to meet you, Doctor who isn't and attorney of law who was, it takes all sorts I guess," joked Joe.

"Let me explain please," said Tony.

"No," said Paula. "What will you have to drink Joe?"

"A beer would be nice," Tony went and got Joe a beer, then went over to a percolator and poured Paula a coffee.

"Well, now I will explain," said Paula. "Tony was a doctor practising at Bakra Royal Infirmary. He was the senior house surgeon there, until he helped a man brought to his home who had two broken arms, a broken jaw, a missing right eye, and various other injuries. The two men who took him said he had been in a road accident. The Doctor, being the kind of man he is, set the mans arms, wired up his jaw and did all he could, in his own home. Tony then told the men he would go to the hospital with them. However, when the Doctor and the injured man were in their Land Rover, they didn't go to the hospital but drove deep into the bush to their hideout, where the doctor cared for the man as best he could. The injured man was, in fact, an outspoken critic of President Elido who had been arrested and beaten half to death, in order to get from him information about an opposition group, which at the time didn't exist."

Joe then put up his hand, "Paula, why are you telling me all this?" he asked.

"I'll explain later, please let me finish. Following the Doctor's release by these so-called rebels after 6 days he was invited to police headquarters - military police. They wanted him to inform on these people and their whereabouts, but the Doctor could tell them nothing for he knew nothing. The following week the Doctor was arrested on a narcotics charge where the prosecution claimed he was a drug pusher peddling drugs on the street. He was brought to trial and Jubil here defended him. The trial was rigged from the start, but Jubil produced some damning evidence against the authorities. If you like, a lot of dirty linen was washed in public. The Doctor was convicted and spent 2 years in jail, and Jubil was disbarred. The hearing was held in camera so nothing was made public. The Doctor now works at his brother's textile mill,"

"Where I run the medical room" Tony put in.

"Yes," said Paula "The men still go to him when they are sick, they also take their wives and children, all of which means the Doctor is taking a terrible risk. Jubil works at the British embassy as a courier.

"OK," said Joe "I sympathise with you guys, but I don't see why I should be told."

"Joe, all this happened 28 months ago and since then the tortures and killings go on."

"Paula I think I shall be going," Joe had had enough, life was tough, everybody had problems, why should he be burdened? They shook hands and left. In the car driving back, Joe said to Paula "Why are you telling me all these things?"

She smiled, "Joe I would like you to do just one more thing for me. Will you have a day off tomorrow?"

"I guess so. I'm the boss and I am well ahead of schedule."

"Good I'll pick you up at home at 5-30am sharp," said Paula.

"That early?" he said.

"Well we have a long journey ahead of us," said Paula "and we are going deep in the bush, so dress accordingly." Paula then drove Joe back to site, "Thanks Joe, you are special, I mean that,"

"Sure," he said and smiled, as he got out of the car.

She drove off blowing him a kiss, Joe was mystified. He went into the office and sent for Les and explained what he wanted, and that he would not be on site tomorrow. At 5-30pm he left site, God Bless drove him home.

Next morning Joe was up and showered and shaved at 5-30am, when he heard a car horn, He went out wearing a tee shirt, denim trousers and boots, Paula was there in the Land Rover.

"You have quite a range of vehicles Paula," he said.

"This belongs to Steven actually, but we always share things."

"Its the only way," said Joe.

They drove off and headed for the network of bridges that led to the city of Bakra.

"I thought you said we were going deep in the bush."

"Yes," she said, "But first we have to collect something." she drove to the industrial estate and in the same way as before, went into the same office. As they went in Joe noticed the same old fellow with two young ones, Paula spoke in her tribal tongue to the old man, who got up and beckoned the two young men to follow.

"What now?" said Joe.

"Tea!" said Paula and started to pour tea into two cups on the battered old desk, from a thermos flask.

"Not for me thank you." Some 15 minutes passed, then the men came back.

"Lets go," said Paula and they walked out with the old man following. The Land Rover had now been loaded with various sacks from the warehouse, from those that are stacked from floor to ceiling, Paula made a quick check then went into the shoulder bag she was carrying, and pulled out a wad of Guinea notes, she gave them to the old man who stuffed them in his pocket, nothing was said and nothing was counted.

Paula was dressed in similar fashion to Joe but she looked

better in it.

They got into the Land Rover and sped away, Joe thought this girl sure drives fast, then he said, "I just wish I knew what was going on."

"We are going to a refugee camp to feed the starving Joseph," she said, "I have bought sacks of maize, powdered egg, powdered milk and flour, also blankets, this is all part of the aid that was sent during our civil war with the Ibo tribe. It never got further than the warehouse as you can see, the aid came from all over the Western world, but President Elido decides it expedient to feed the rats, not the starving millions, the only way it is ever released is by buying it. Yes it can be purchased, if you are in the know, then sold to the starving for whatever possessions they may have, with Elido taking his cut. Steven and I keep one particular camp supplied, we cannot possibly keep them all because we are not wealthy people Joe."

"I see," said Joe, "Well, I must say you surprise me." They drove deep into the bush in the four wheel drive vehicle, after 5 hours they had covered about 90 miles and came to a small clearing close to a stream that fed a water hole, here was the refugee camp.

It was a series of mud huts with corrugated iron, packing crates and anything that could be utilised to form shelter, there were also tents, Paula drove up and stopped in front of a large open ended tent and packing crate, it was really quite remarkable what could be made in the way of shelter with all manner of things.

They got out and went over to an elderly white woman, Paula introduced Joe.

"I would like you to meet a friend of mine Joe. This is Miriam Gaskel, Miriam this is Joe, an engineer working in Akeja and a friend of the family. Miriam held out a rather frail hand. "How do you do Joe welcome to our little community."

"The supplies are in the truck Miriam," said Paula, Miriam then started to shout instructions to some of the men hanging around, who started to unload the vehicle, stacking the goods at the rear of Mrs. Gaskel's open fronted tent.

"You are very kind my dear, I don't know what we would do without you." She went on to explain to Joe how the camp housed

237 people, mostly Ibo, but a few stragglers from other tribes, nobody was ever turned away. Mrs Gaskel had been in missionary work since she was 19 years old, she was now 68. Her only aim in life was to see an end to the refugee problem, all peoples with homes and regular living standards, but she was afraid she would never see it.

Maybe if she had another 50 years she might, and realise her life's aim, but as things were that was not possible. "We grow a little food and the men hunt bush rat and the like, but we have no proper equipment, and the men only have their home made bows and arrows, but we survive with a little help from Paula."

"I think you do a remarkable job Ma'am," said Joe, "If I can be of any help I will do whatever I am able."

"Thank you Joseph, I know you mean well but there is nothing save a miracle at this time."

Miriam then took them into the clinic tent, where the children were being cared for, they were suffering from acute malnutrition. Joe thought it was all a pathetic sight, people back home would never believe it, it was all so bloody unbelievable. Paula then got out the hamper basket and they all had a sandwich in Miriam's tent.

"We had better make a move," said Paula, so they said their goodbyes and started off on their journey home.

Joe was driving and during their discussions going back, he said, "I am going to ask a question I've asked before and never got an answer to."

"Yes?" said Paula.

"Why are you showing me all this? This is your country not mine."

"Well I suppose I just want someone in England to know what it is really like in Ligeria, someone I know and trust, I don't know Joe it is all so very sad, I've lived for so many years in Britain, and there, as in the West as a whole everybody is so stable, so caring, so just, I just want your people to know what there is to be done, because if they don't know, as you didn't before you came, it will go on and on, but I intend to do something about it. I have my education, my knowledge and, I understand after 14 years living there, British know how. Thanks to your people Joe it will not be wasted."

"OK, that is all very well, and believe me I feel for you Paula, and the situation is all very tragic, but I don't understand why you are involving me, I am just a visitor, simple Mr average Englishman, an engineer paid to do a job," Joe was beginning to get himself all worked up now, "I'm no politician, I know nothing of these ways and I will be going home soon, in just a matter of 4 weeks." (Joe couldn't know of the nightmare that was about to envelop him.) "I sympathise with you, but that is all." Joe was getting concerned. This was not his problem, and he didn't want to know, so what had they got in mind, why were they involving him? And why the ploy to get him here?"

"Please forgive me Joe, I have no right to tell you these things, no right to burden you," said Paula.

"Your not burdening me with anything." replied Joe.

"Well let's forget it and go home Joe."

They now drove on in silence, Paula was deep in thought. She wasn't getting the response she wanted from Joe, she was hoping for some kind of commitment or promise to do whatever she asked of him, and she knew how to seal that kind of promise, but she couldn't possibly know the kind of man she was dealing with in Joe Tully.

Never mind, she thought, it was early days yet.

Joe was deep in thought, he was very sympathetic to their lot, he was fond of Paula, he liked everybody he had met so far, but the one nagging thought, he prayed to heaven that she wouldn't use the method that seems to be inherent with every female he had been in contact with in Ligeria. That 'my knickers come off for you white man' method for whatever it is they are after. It wasn't money with Paula - so what was it?

They arrived back at Joe's house, "I hope you are feeling better now Joe."

"I feel just great," said Joe.

"I do apologise for the whole episode," she said, noticing the ironic tone of Joe's reply.

"Forget it Paula, I have." Joe was in is old easy going manner again, she said goodbye and drove off.

He let himself in and went to the cocktail cabinet and poured himself a small whisky, Good Luck came in from the kitchen, "Are you ready for dinner Sir?"

"Give me 10 minutes Lucky," Joe then had a shower. He felt sure the whole exercise had been engineered, but why? To hell with it he thought.

Joe had dinner then he went to the country club had a few pints and a game of darts with Ray and his colleagues. Sunday he wrote to Jane, then spent the afternoon by the pool at the club.

The next week dragged, Joe was kicking his heels, almost all of his men had been transferred to other sites. Monday 16th July Steven made an official visit to site with the usual entourage. "President Elido will be moving in on the 23rd, next Monday." Steven told Joe.

"That's OK, all paths and the front wall are now complete, the front garden landscaping is finished, this rear area will be clear before I leave in three weeks time." explained Joe, "The President will only ever use the front entrance anyway, and as you can see it is all complete."

"Very well, as of next Saturday Akeja Construction security will be withdrawn, and the military will take over all guard duty 24 hours per day."

"That's fine, thank you for telling me, but that isn't my business anyway."

Time was beginning to drag for Joe, it was now Saturday 21st. He was waiting patiently for the computer engineers to arrive then he could pack up and go home, it couldn't come soon enough. On site now he just had one plumber, one electrician, and God Bless his driver, all the others were on other sites, his office was still on site, and the bared wire fencing was still around the back and sides.

The site was now patrolled 24 hours a day by the military, it was for Joe now a big bore.

There was one entrance at the rear to let in site personnel, where the prefabricated military guard room was situated. The front entrance was for the President and his staff only, all beautifully landscaped. Joe called it a day and went home, where Lucky was preparing a salad.

"I'm dining out tonight, I did tell you this morning."

"Just a little salad Sir, these people never dine before 9-0pm Sir, it's only 5-0pm now."

"Just coffee please, I'm not in the mood for eating."

Joe went to his bedroom, his blue suit was laid out on the bed, Lucky had brought it back from the cleaners. Joe took a shower, then wrote a letter to Jane."

ASSASSIN

The invitation was for 8-0pm, Joe decided to arrive a little late to see who else was there. When he arrived there were three cars there with their front bumpers up against the low white fence, one of them the official British embassy car, Joe parked on the end and then walked round the others up the path and rang the door bell. The door was opened by the house boy in his immaculate white coat.

"Good evening Sir." He showed Joe through to the study and Joe walked in amongst the other guests.

The British Ambassador was talking to Unico Sandies who saw Joe and came over immediately, hand outstretched.

"Good evening Joe."

"Good evening," said Joe.

"I would like you to meet some friends of mine," said Unico, and he took Joe over to two Ligerians who were talking together with two women.

"Gentlemen this is my good friend Joe Tully, this is Ely Lentoy," Joe shook hands, "and his wife Pursa." They then moved over, "This is Ibrahim Buhari and his wife Gertrude," they shook hands. "Are you enjoying your stay in Ligeria Mr Tully?" asked Lentoy.

"Yes thank you," he replied, "And please call me Joe." Then he thought to himself I wish I'd never heard of the bloody place. Paula then came over dressed in a royal blue evening dress off the shoulder fitting, ankle length, a split off centre reaching almost to her groin, she had a blue sapphire pendant on a golden chain and a blue diamante above her right ear. She came over to Joe and held out her hand. "Good evening." she said.

"Good evening Paula, you look as beautiful as ever, beautiful and radiant is the only way to describe you."

"Thank you Joe you are very gallant." The boy waiter came over with a tray of glasses containing Champagne, they all took one, Joe took one and handed it to Paula, then took one for himself. They were all making small talk when Steven walked in wearing dress uniform, Joe noticed immediately that he had a majors crown on his epaulette, instead of the three pips. His father walked over to him.

"Ladies and gentlemen I have a small announcement to make, before we sit down to dinner. I called this little celebration to honour Steven's promotion from Captain to Major, it has been on the cards for some time, and 4 days ago it came through. Thank you." Everybody went over to congratulate Steven.

"Shall we dine?" said Unico. They all went into the dining room, Unico sat at the head of the table, on his right sat Steven, on his left sat Simon Denning. On Steven's right sat Paula and on her right sat Lentoy and his wife Pursa, on Denning's left sat Joe, on his left sat Buhari and his wife Gertrude.

There were dishes of caviar with small toasted biscuits for hors d'oeuvres following these the waiter served soup followed by the wine. After soup dinner was served and to Joe's surprise it was roast beef and Yorkshire pudding, with boiled and roast potatoes, carrots and cauliflower and gravy followed by fruit salad with cream then coffee with brandy.

At the end of the meal the host said, "I trust everyone enjoyed our simple meal," Joe commented, "Give my compliments to the chef, the meal was excellent."

"Compliment her yourself, you're sat directly opposite her!" said Unico, Joe looked across at Paula.

"You are indeed a remarkable young woman Paula."

"Thank you," she said, "You are too kind."

"Shall we retire to the lounge and let the staff clear away?" said Unico. Everyone got up and moved to the lounge, it was a large very attractive room thought Joe, there was an imitation fire place with a teak mantle piece, on it was a Capi de Monti clock and two figurines, one either side of it. Joe thought one of the Sandies has taste.

A portrait hung above the fire place, at first Joe thought it was Paula, but as he studied it he realised the face in the portrait was more mature, it could be Paula in ten years time he thought. He moved with a start as Paula moved up beside him,

"My mother," she said.

"She was very beautiful." he replied.

Steven was attending to peoples glasses. There was champagne, or a liqueur, in fact whatever anyone wanted. Joe was drinking Scotch.

The house boy came in and said something to Steven. Steven quickly left the room with the boy in tow, some ten minutes passed then Steven came back and whispered something to his father, Paula then walked quickly over to them, there was a low murmur of conversation between them, and Paula put her hand on her fathers arm.

He nodded to Steven who went out again, the old man disengaged himself from Paula and walked away from the fire place and began looking out of the large French window. Joe thought he could see what could well have been a tear in Paula's eye. There was total silence, everyone sensed there was something very wrong, it was magnetic. A few minutes passed then Steven came back in, closed the door and stood with his hand resting on the door handle.

The old man walked over to the fire place and stood with his back to it.

"Ladies and gentlemen, I have some very bad news, I'm afraid. I have just been informed that the refugee camp in Ofiki has been destroyed, and all 237 people men, women and children have been killed, including a very dear friend of mine," with this his voice broke but he recovered, "Miriam Gaskel."

At that Paula rushed over to her father and was in his arms. She looked so small, like a child embraced by such a big man. Paula was sobbing. Nothing was said and nobody moved, then Unico, very gently holding Paula's shoulders disengaged himself and looked at Steven, who then left the room, Joe looked across at Paula, her head bowed with her hands held between her breasts and she was kneading them together.

"Is there anything we can do Sir?" Joe asked. Paula looked across at Joe, her eyes full of tears.

"Not now Joe, later, we will have to act quickly before Ligeria destroys herself," said Unico in a strained voice. Steven then came again.

"The staff have all been dismissed Sir, we are now alone."

"Thank you," said the old man, "Gentlemen I have something of great importance to say and now is the time. They all looked expectantly at him, there was absolute silence, you could have heard a fly walk, but even they were still.

For some years now we have talked, hoped, and worked for the day when we would have democracy here in Ligeria, with a government elected by the people, for the people, all of our peoples." Joe noticed the emphasis on the plural.

For many years now we have been governed by one military dictator after another. I know, I have served under the last 4 as ambassador in London, where I gained my knowledge of democratic government, and where my children have been educated, lived and been brought up to know and understand and accept the meaning of a democratic process and justice. Well gentlemen, this dream will now become a reality, for we now have the financial backing for our campaign." At last Lentoy leapt to his feet and embraced the old man, Buhari shouted, "Hear Hear!"

"Please gentlemen, let Unico finish," said Denning, Lentoy then went back to his seat, and the old man continued.

"We now have the finance to drive ahead and put our National Socialist Party in power..." At that the British ambassador Denning broke in.

"Yes, £500,000 Sterling is now at your disposal, half a million pounds is a great deal of money, which I know will be well spent. Thank you gentlemen."

At that Joe spoke, his tone seemed somewhat bewildered. "Excuse me Sir, are you saying the British government is involved?"

"Not directly no, but they will be glad to see the end of this mad man Elido," said Denning.

"Mad man!" gasped Joe, "he is a lovely old man, shrewd yes, but." at that Paula jumped in.

"How dare you, you English man you...you." she was struggling just a little for the correct phraseology. "How gullible you English can be, you have led such sheltered lives, you see only your own thoughts, the good guys and the bad guys, of your fairy tales you watch on your television screens and cinemas, your celluloid world, well this Mr Tully is the real world!" That was the first time Paula had ever used his surname.

"The world of corruption misery and death. Yes death! Steven told me of what you and he had witnessed out in the bush, and you saw Mrs Gaskel." At that she choked, the tears were beginning to flood her eyes again.

"The man who was behind all that," her voice was choking on every word now, "Your lovely old man," at that she gave up and let go she sobbed she cried, Joe was lost. He wanted to go and hold her comfort her, but he was rooted to the spot.

Paula turned to her father who took her in his arms. Everything Joe realised was true he had led a sheltered life, as do all in the Western world, sheltered by democracy equality and the justice of civilised society, that had been carved out of life by their parents and their parents before them and so on back through hundreds of years, where as in the third world it was just the beginning.

"I am sorry I didn't know, everything you say is true I guess, but I am what I am, what can I say?" Joe's voice was very strained, as though he was ashamed.

"I think I should go Sir!" at that he stopped, there was nothing he could say, he was in a situation unprecedented in his life, a situation totally foreign to him and he was lost.

"Joe," said Steven "Don't go just yet."

"No," said Ambassador Denning, "Please Joe sit down." He then got a clean glass from the cabinet and poured Joe a whisky. Paula stopped crying and pulled away from her father, and with his handkerchief wiped her eyes her face, blew her nose, screwed up the handkerchief in a small ball and held it in her tiny hand, then she walked over to Joe and stood in front of him. He looked up and their eyes met and held each others gaze, for what seemed like an age.

"Joe," she said, "Forgive my outburst it was inexcusable." He raised his hand to stop her, "You were right," he said. "What I say, what I do, is done in ignorance. I would say nothing to offend you or these people." With that he gestured with his hand to the other guests.

"Joseph," she said, "I have just lost a very dear friend in

Miriam, she was like a mother to me, she saw good in everyone, and now she is gone, she will have died in the most appalling way that you could imagine. She has died Joe on the orders of that monster you call a lovely old man."

"My ignorance," said Joe.

"Yes I know that, it is that which makes my outburst unforgivable, that is my ignorance, my weakness. Please, I ask you forgive me and forget." Joe stood and took her hands in his, even the one holding the screwed up handkerchief fit easily in his she was so small.

"I will forgive you anything. I realise your pain, if I could wipe away all your hurt I would."

"I know you would." she said, as she pulled his hands up to her face and brushed them to both her cheeks and kissed them.

She turned then and walked to her father.

"Carry on father." she said, Joe sat down and finished his whisky.

"Ely, could you enlighten Simon as to the situation?" asked Unico.

"Of course. The machinery is all set, we have the party organisation, we have people in radio stations, in broadcasting house, at TV headquarters and their sub-stations. It is now a question of finance to buy broadcasting time, we have vehicles to move the famine relief supplies to the refugee camps and villages. Steven has got the National Guard ready to organise and police the convoys."

"Well," said Joe, "what are you waiting for? Now you have the finance you can move immediately."

"Not quite," said Simon Denning.

"That's right," said Unico, "Not quite."

"Then what?" asked Joe, looking perplexed.

"President Elido will have to go, to be killed."

"Killed?" gasped Joe.

"Yes," said Simon.

"Then, said Unico, "There would be rejoicing in the streets, the armed forces would be relieved. Oh he has his sides and their men but believe me they will run for cover when Elido goes, and Steven who is the President's adjutant would automatically take over until the elections. Then all relief supplies sent to us from all over the Western World would be sent to those in need, refugee camps would be a thing of the past, new villages would be built."

"Yes," said Denning. "All kinds of trucks, tractors, low loaders, will be supplied at ex-works prices, I can assure you of that I have my connections."

"You've been busy Simon!" said Joe.

"Unico, you will want for nothing, the people providing the finance will see to that." Steven then came over and stood with his father and Paula.

"Joe," he said, "This is where you can help."

"If you don't mind I must be going now," said Simon.

"Of course," said Unico, "How is Mrs Denning's sister? I wasn't aware that she was seriously ill and she had rushed home to be near her."

"Her sister is out of danger now fortunately, she is under the finest surgeons in London, Margaret will be phoning me tonight that is why I must be going."

"Well give her our best regards," said Unico.

"I will, thank you." Simon then went over to say his good nights to the rest of the guests, and went to Paula. "Good night my dear, I know all will work out for the best."

"Thank you." she said, "Thank you for everything."

He then crossed over to Joe, and shook his hand.

"This will all seem strange to you Joe, but that is the way it is in this kind of political climate, all will turn out for the best believe me, I've been in government for more years than I wish to remember, just you go along with the Sandies they are good people, Ligeria needs them." Joe said nothing.

Steven then said, "As I was saying Joe, this is where you are needed, you must assassinate President Elido! You are the only one who can do it, the whole of Ligeria depends on you!"

At that Joe went cold, he couldn't believe what he had just heard! He looked round the room. Everybody was looking at him. "But that is insane!" said Joe, "I could not kill anybody!" Joe was struggling looking for an analogy to express the impossibility of it.

"I could no more kill a man, than I could stick a feather up my arse and fly home!"

Joe then rose. "I'm off! You must be completely bloody mad!" Paula then said, "Joe! Please hear us out." She then went over to him and stood so close that he had to sit down, Paula's mind was now racing, searching for the right phrase.

"Joe you're a Christian, you believe in Christianity because you know it is the only thing that has held people together otherwise it would mean survival of the fittest, the strong always the winners, just as the heathen, it is your belief. Well Joe it is similar with us, oh we are all Christians in this room, but we are also Mausa. We are the biggest tribe in Ligeria, and an Mausa can no more kill a fellow tribesman than he can fly." She omitted the comment of the feather, "To do that would be to go against everything we believe in and a curse such as you could not imagine would befall the killer, and his family and children, and children's children, for all time. Total damnation, so you see Joe you must do it for us. For Ligeria, if it wasn't for that curse I would do it, gladly do it, for Miriam, Joseph do it! Do it for me!"

"Paula you are asking me to do something I am incapable of doing!"

"That is not altogether true is it Joe?" He looked up quickly at old man Sandies. "In 1954 you were stationed in what at that time was called the canal zone in Egypt, with the infantry, were you not?"

"Yes." replied Joe.

"You were also hand picked and trained with eleven other men by a Major Hall. You were known as Major Hall's commandos. You all were expertly trained," Joe said nothing, he was looking transfixed at the old man, "On one particular occasion there was sniper fire into your temporary camp from a derelict village on the opposite side of the Treaty road. Major Hall and his commandos went in to route out these snipers, and directly outside a derelict police station a sniper stepped out and fired at the Major ripping one of his epaulette's and causing a wound to his shoulder, he promptly rolled out of his jeep taking cover behind it.

You Joseph were several feet behind the Major and close to

69

the buildings so you couldn't be seen. You fired and the sniper who ducked back into the police state. You, Joseph, then lobbed a grenade through the glassless windows. The grenade exploded killing five snipers, you were highly commended by your Major and your commanding officer, but there was nothing official because you were all acting illegally, as her Majesties forces were in fact guest of the Egyptian government, so the whole thing was hushed up."

Joe was flabbergasted. He was speechless, and again he was lost.

"But that was war!" said Joe.

"No it wasn't," said the old Man, "You were a guest of the Egyptian government, and therefore acting illegally. The correct thing to have done was to have reported the incident to the Egyptian authorities and let them deal with it. But you took the law into your own hands, and you killed 5 men, and that is a fact. Now please don't misunderstand I also commend you for your prompt action, you did the right thing, and you will do the right thing by us now. You will assassinate President Elido because it is the right thing to do. You are the only one who is able."

Joe didn't speak, he reached for his glass but it was empty, Paula read the situation and got the decanter of whisky and handed it to him.

"I'm sorry if I distress you Joseph," said Unico, as Joe was taking a long drink of his whisky.

"But this has got to be done and we have got to know who we are dealing with, and we know that you are the man for the job?"

"How could you possibly know what you do?" asked Joe.

"Denning!" Joe said as an afterthought, "he is the only man who could get such information."

"As Simon said your government will be just as glad as we will to be rid of this man Elido. Also Joseph you will not go unrewarded. The sum of £25,000 pounds will be deposited in a Swiss bank account for you, this will be done and confirmed before you do the job. You see Joseph we trust you, you and your family will always be welcome here. You would be afforded the freedom of Ligeria for the rest of your lives. You will find that we will be a fine country to live in under a National Socialist government."

Joe just sat there looking into his empty glass, "How could I get myself in such a hell of a mess?" he thought.

"All that was such a long time ago," said Joe in a quiet strained voice. "Such a long time ago."

"A leopard never changes," said the old man, "You have always been a fighter Joseph, and you have always fought for money, money was always the outcome." Paula walked over to Joe who sat with his head bowed and cradled his head in her breasts. "We are sorry Joe, we would not wish to distress you for the world." I'm fond of you Joe you must know that, but this has got to be done. The whole Nation is depending on us, and on you Joe." She then took his face in her hands, looked at him with longing eyes, then kissed him full on the mouth, her cunning plan had worked, Joe nodded, "I'll do it, he is a murdering bastard anyway."

Joe was driving home when it was very dark, the roads were deserted. "Well Joe." he thought, "you are in one hell of a mess, but there is no point in getting excited, the situation is bad so it is going to need a lot of thought, controlled calm thought, you have always said the greatest power on earth is thought, without it nothing ever gets done, you have got to hand it to the Sandies, they have done their homework, that bastard Denning is behind it all. He must be. 25 grand is not to be sneezed at and Paula as a bonus. The cradling of the head the kiss full on the lips, it is synonymous with these women knickers off will get them anything, or so they think. They may be able to make a killer out of Joe Tully, but they will not make an adulterer out of him. Janie's worth more than the whole bloody lot of them, and their confounded country, she is worth more than life itself, Jane and their children were his symbols of everything in life that is wholesome and good. They above all else must be protected, and he is the only one who can do this, if he doesn't go through with it now, he will never leave Ligeria alive, that's a fact, but would they also take their spite out on his family? He couldn't know one way or the other and he couldn't take the risk, so he has to go through with it.

If he does the job nobody would care, nobody would know

who did it, the new government would be installed, the British government would be pleased, there would be no scandal, he would go home and never set foot out of England again, and fuck the third world and all the politicians.

He parked his car in the car port and let himself in, it was now 2-0am Sunday 22nd of July. He sat on the bed and looked at the photo of his Janie, he just sat there looking at the photograph, "Well I might as well get some sleep, I've got to think and act positively."

The next 5 days went routinely, Joe was kicking his heels. Steven arrived at site on the 27th July.

"Do you fancy a trip to the range Joe?"

"Yes, why not?" he said. When they were in the car driving to the range, Joe said to Steven, "This is what I want, I need a hand gun with a silencer, a good one."

"You can select your own," said Steven.

"Good," Joe replied.

"Here's how it will be done, I've been watching the guards patrol the compound. Now as you know the front entrance has two guards, one on each of the pillars, across the front of the garden you have the wall that is almost complete, from this wall down to the back of the site we still have the barbed wire fencing. The entrance at the rear is about 20 yards or so from my office. Each night at 6-0pm two guards leave the guard house or shed as it is at this time which is situated at the rear entrance.

The two guards then go in opposite directions they prowl along the perimeter until they reach the front gate, then they return the whole thing takes one hour there and back. They do it twice then change guard, are you with me so far?"

"Yes," said Steven, "That is usual, 2 hours on 4 hours off, but go ahead forgive the interruption."

"This is how we do then I will need an accomplice, whom I must meet and brief in the next couple of days."

"Whatever you say," said Steven, Joe then carried on.

"We wait on the opposite side of the road at the rear of the site on a level with my office, as the guard leaves the guard house, it takes them each 20 minutes by which time they are travelling down each side of the site and for 20 minutes they are out of site of the rear, and more importantly the rear is out of their site. That is when we rush to the fence and get through, and then into the building, my accomplice then goes back into the bush."

"How do you get through the wire do you cut it."

"No," said Joe. "I've made a jack specially for the job, it is the jack that comes with the Chevy." Joe had cut two steel plates 3 feet long 3 inches wide and an inch thick, he had then welded one to the base of the jack and one on to the head, to separate the scrolls of wire, he explained all this to Steven. "What if the wire snaps?"

"Then," said Joe, "We have a problem but it won't. This particular exercise will take 30 maybe 40 minutes, my accomplice keeps his eye on the rear of the building. When he sees my signal from my pencil torch, that is on off, on off, he immediately runs to the fence jacks it open and lays the piece of hard board across the bottom scroll of fencing, by then I will have arrived there and I will dive through, we then dump the jack and the hard board in the bush and each makes his own way home. Elido as you know always works late on a Thursday night because of some game park he is setting up on a Friday. He will not be missed at home until at least 6-0am when his staff start their duties, or when the cleaners arrive to give the office a quick clean over. It is possible that a servant could come looking for him but I doubt it, they are normally off duty by midnight, unless otherwise instructed. The hit is next Thursday 2nd of August, 1 leave Ligeria on the 5th, any questions?"

"Just one, how will you make the hit?"

"That's my business," said Joe, "It will be done."

They arrive at the range.

"I'll need a hand gun and silencer a revolver say a 38", Steven got what he asked for, then he dismissed the Sergeant.

"We can manage Sergeant," said Steven.

"Very good Sir." replied the Sergeant, and went back to his office.

Joe put the silencer down, then brought the target forward by winding it in, and set it 4 paces from the butts, Steven was a little puzzled by all this, but Joe said nothing, he knew that when Elido was sitting at his desk his head would be approximately 4 feet from the ground, his desk was 10 feet from the wall, and the air diffuser was 8 feet up from the floor. From the diffuser to Elido's head was an approximately 30 degrees therefore the distance was a little under 11 feet. Joe aimed the revolver at the head of the target in a standard manner using both hands, he hit the neck so he made the necessary corrections and most times he hit the head in the centre, then he pulled the gun back to his face holding the heel of his left hand to his shoulder and looking down the gun as when aiming a rifle, Joe was a left handed shot. He fired from this unusual position until he was consistently accurate, Joe would practise like this because when he actually made the hit he would be lay cramped in 18 by 18 inch square duct work, firing through the supply air diffuser with the gun close up to his face.

He then put the silencer on the gun and making the necessary corrections, he practised like this for several hours, until he was as near perfect as possible.

"I don't suppose you will tell me if I ask you why all this?" asked Steven.

"Correct," said Joe, "I won't tell you, that's it for today same again on Monday, then Wednesday." Steven then drove back to site office, Joe had now adopted a serious attitude, it was the same procedure on Monday.

"I must meet my accomplice on Wednesday Steven to brief him."

"Right," replied Steven, "at my home say 8-0pm."

"That will be fine I'll collect a new 38 revolver and silencer at the same time," said Joe. They arrived back at site, and as Joe got out of the car.

"Joe," said Steven. "Yes?" said Joe, looking back into the car, Steven had a puzzled look on his face.

"Yes?" Joe repeated.

"Oh nothing," said Steven and drove off. Joe went into his office and sat down, "I have got Steven puzzled he thought, it must be my change in attitude to one of seriousness." Yes Joe was now acting more like a professional than just Mr average. It was now

Wednesday evening 7-50pm as Joe was driving over to the Sandies, the target practice that day like Monday was faultless, he stopped the car outside the front garden of the Sandies house, walked up the path and pushed the bell push, the door was opened by the house boy, who showed him through to the study knocked and opened the door, Joe walked inside.

"Good evening" said Steven walking across to Joe, I would like you to meet Lieutenant Nigel Lapengio." A young soldier dressed in jungle greens stood up from his chair, the man Joe had met at the field unit, the mean looking one.

They shook hands neither man spoke, Joe pulled up a chair and sat down as did Steven.

"OK Nigel we meet at the intersection of Torridor road and Pupil road, the road that runs down from the back of the site, at
10-30pm." Nigel nodded.

"We walk down in the bush parallel with Pupil road until we are level with my site office. Then we watch and wait until the guards start their tour and within 20 minutes they will be out of site of each other, and at this time they will not be able to see our activity. Now we have 20 minutes to run to the barbed wire and jack it open with my jack." Joe then gave Steven his car keys. "Would you get the jack from my car Steven and bring it in." "Sure," he said and went out. "Then I lay this sheet of hard board on the bottom scroll and dive through, once on the inside you remove the jack and hard-board then run back into the bush with them, I will have crossed the yard by then and entered the building, and you will then Nigel keep your eye on the back of the building. When I am ready to return," he then took out his pencil torch. "I will give this signal." and he demonstrated on off on off, "When you see the signal you run to the wire and jack it open use the hardboard I will be there by that time and I will dive through the wire, and we will dump the jack in the bush and the job is done, any questions."

Nigel shook his head. Steven then returned with the jack and Joe gave them a demonstration. "I figure with luck I will be out of the building in 30 or 40 minutes." Steven then went to his brief case and unlocked it to remove the 38 Smith and Wesson revolver, and silencer, and handed them to Joe. They were wrapped in a Chamois leather Joe unwrapped them to inspect them they were spotless and loaded. Steven then got Joe and himself a whisky.

"Well that's it gentlemen that's simple enough eh?" said Joe. Nigel got up shook hands with Joe, Steven showed him out, "He doesn't say much does he?"

"No," said Steven, "but he is the best Joe, believe me everything you have told him he carry out to the letter." Joe had noticed that he didn't have a drink.

"Well I will be going now."

"No don't leave just yet my father returned from London today and he would like to see you." Old man Sandies walked in.

"Joseph I'm glad to see you I have a letter for you." he said handing Joe an envelope, it was sealed and a Swiss National bank motif on it, it was addressed to Mr J. Tully Ligerian embassy London.

Joe opened it and read it, it was a letter from the bank informing him that an account had been opened for him for the sum of £25,000 pounds Sterling, wishing well and thanking him for the sample of his signature.

"How did they get a sample of my signature."

"Simon got it from the embassy, as you know when you register as a British citizen resident in Ligeria you complete all necessary documentation, well Simon took it from there."

"He is a shrewd man." thought Joe. "Well, said Joe, "Now I'm worth a bob or two."

"You see Joe we trust you I know you won't let us down."

"By 6-0am Steven," said Joe, "You will be in the hot seat as the new President, I trust you have all the news media ready, breakfast news etc."

"Yes Joe everything is ready. I will be the first one to be contacted when they find the body, then I will contact Lentoy by phone, he will have radio breakfast news make the announcement that Elido is dead and Major Steven Sandies is the new acting President, Lentoy's people are in constant radio contact with Benine Illorin Kasunu and all other major states and cities, it is all cut and dried."

"You know something?" said Steven, "you surprise me Joe by the way you are handling things. As though you were a real professional, not a Mr Average."

"I am a professional," said Joe, "A professional engineer, you see everything that is properly done is engineered whether it be a suite of offices or an assassination. Whatever it is, it takes a professional."

"Yes of course," said Steven, "I'm glad your on my side."

"Well I better be going, good night." "Good night," said the old man. "And good luck."

Joe arrived home and let himself in and went to his bedroom, took down his suit case from off the wardrobe opened it, and put in the gun and silencer locked it, and put it back on top of the wardrobe. Then he took a shower and retired. His alarm clock went at 6-0am, he leaned over to mute it, "Today is the day," he said to himself, he wasn't feeling too good, he had felt better, but he told himself that he was the good guy and Elido was the bad guy, but it didn't help, he would just have to get the whole thing over with, then go back to work hand over the suite to Akeja Construction , and go home. With the blessing of the new Ligerian Government, or so he thought, little did he know that this was far from the truth. For it was to be the beginning of a nightmare that would be beyond the realms of his imagination.

The day was the usual nothing to do day, at 5-0pm he called it a day. God Bless drove him home, parked the car in the car port said good night and went on his way. Joe let himself in went into his bedroom then had a shower, he then ate dinner in his bath robe, Lucky had made a chicken casserole. After dinner Lucky did the dishes and then went home, Joe got dressed he put on his dark blue roll neck shirt, charcoal grey trousers black socks black pumps and a black beret to cover his grey hair. Now he was ready, he sat on his bed looking at Jane, he could tell her he won the money on the Bakra lottery, and they transferred the money to a Swiss bank, but that would be telling her a deliberate lie, but at the same time he could not inflict the pain of the truth on her, he would just have to learn how to live with the lie.

What a mess what a confounded mess. He took his suit case down from the wardrobe unlocked it and took out the revolver and silencer, he put the revolver in the waist band of his trousers then covered the revolver grip with his shirt, he put the silencer in his pocket, and went out to his car, reversed it out of the drive, and drove out to the intersection of Torridor road and Pupil road.

As he approached he ran just off the road into the bush, got out and crossed over the road at the intersection and went into the bush. At exactly 10-30pm a car approached then stopped, he heard a door snap shut then the car drove away. Nigel appeared walking towards him, dressed in his jungle greens, Joe thought to himself this is the most un-Nigel looking man you were ever likely to meet. At his left hip he wore a ghurka knife. They walked down in the bush parallel to Pupil road. When they were level with site office they stopped as close to the road as was safe then waited. It was now almost 11-0pm, and the two guards approached the guard house. They checked in and then came out to start on their second tour, the first guard passed the site office and stopped at the end of the perimeter fence, then turned at 90 degrees and started down the second leg, the second was now out of sight. After a further 5 minutes the first guard was out of sight.

"Now!" said Joe, they ran silently and quickly across the road Nigel had the jack in and was pumping quickly. "He's fast." thought Joe, who then laid the hardboard on the bottom scroll and dived through, he was on his feet and across the yard, and the whole exercise hadn't taken two minutes. Nigel removed the jack and board and ran back into the bush to wait.

Joe unlocked the engine room door and went in, closed the door and stood with his back to it. After a few seconds his eyes were familiar with the situation, the run lights in the multi motor panel gave off enough light for him to see his way about. He went over to the tool cupboard unlocked it and took out a torch, a screwdriver and a pair of pliers, he then moved over to the multi-motor panel and switched off the main supply fan. He then got the small aluminium steps, went to the inspection panel down stream of the 'S' mat filter and opened the inspection panel door. He went in and let the door close gently for there was quite a bit of suction on it, as the return air fan was still in operation. He walked down the duct until he came to the 90 degree bend, there the 18 by 18 inch duct branched off the top of the larger duct, it went up 7 feet from the base then turned 90 degrees and ran down the wall of the two offices, the President's and his secretary's, the bottom larger duct ran at floor level then rose into a builders duct to supply the rest of the office complex.

Holding the torch, Joe placed the steps against the inside of the duct, climbed up and put the torch in the smaller section, so that it illuminated the inside of the vast duct which ran down the side of the offices. He then leaned at full stretch and using the pliers he removed the bolts that held the 18 inch volume damper blade to its shaft. He then lifted the damper U bolts and nuts and placed them together on the floor of the duct in a tidy manner.

He then went out of the main duct through the inspection door, and taking the screw driver he climbed onto the main duct, reaching up he released the screw that held the quadrant handle in position and withdrew both it and the shaft, which he then placed carefully on top of the duct. After removing this he went back into the main duct, stood by the steps and took the revolver from the waistband of his trousers and the silencer from his pocket, and attached it to the gun.

Then, holding the revolver in his left hand at eye level he climbed the steps, leaned into the duct then using his left forearm and his legs he inched and wriggled along the duct, his shoulders across the diagonal, it was tight but he moved his way slowly, he could see the light from the chiefs office reflected through the supply grill, when he reached the first grill he could see the President clearly working at his desk. He opened the damper blades of the supply grill fully with the fingers of his right hand.

The vertical slats were on one- inch centres, thus a 38 calibre bullet would pass between them with no danger of catching them, Joe brought the revolver to his face and looking down the barrel he drew a line of fire on Elido's left ear. His mind suddenly went off at a tangent, he couldn't believe he was actually going to kill a man, his mind now began to fight with itself, he couldn't do it, but if he didn't then he was a dead man, and there was his family to consider, he didn't know what reprisals would be taken against them.

He had to do it, he held steady just as on the rifle range, gently he squeezed the trigger, there was a pop and a slight kick, the bullet entered Elido's head just above the left ear, he collapsed across his desk and as he did so his hide chair slid back on its casters, so that Elido fell to the floor on his back, head facing Joe, who could see that when the bullet left Elido's head on the right hand side, it took part of the skull with it, covering the right side of his face with blood and brains.

Joe then returned the damper blades to their original position, and started on his journey back down the duct. When he felt the end of the smaller duct with his feet, he wriggled and turned so that his legs bent at the knees going downwards, he then wriggled again turning as before on his stomach, when his feet found the steps he got down removed the silencer from the gun and put it in his pocket, and put the gun in the waistband of his trousers at the small of his back. He then went out of the duct, climbed on top and replaced the volume damper shaft and quadrant, then he returned to the inside of the duct, switched on the torch and retrieved the damper U bolts and nuts, climbed the steps leaned into the duct, placing the torch so that he could see to work, and assembled the damper blade to its shaft.

He now took the steps and the tools out of the duct, put the steps back where he found them, climbed onto the duct, and reset the quadrant handle and locked it in position as before with the locking screw. He then returned the tools and the torch to the tool cupboard, and locked it put the key in his pocket. He then switched on the main supply fan, everything was exactly as before, Joe looked at his watch by the light of his pencil torch it was 11-50pm, the exercise had taken 50 minutes.

He cracked open the engine room door and looked out. The guards were just returning, and would change at 12 midnight, so there was nothing to do but wait. At 11-55 the two guards went into the guard house at midnight two fresh guards came out. In 20 minutes time they should be out of sight. That 20 minutes seemed like two days to Joe, he didn't now feel too bad, it hadn't sickened him as he expected, because now he was too preoccupied with his escape,

20 minutes had now elapsed.

"Here goes!" he thought, and gave the signal, he then counted 3 and moved out, locked the door and made a run for it. As he ran he was hoping Nigel was awake. As he approached the fence. Nigel was there with the jack in position and he was pumping like mad. The hardboard was in position and Joe just dived as he would dive into a swimming pool, he hit the hardboard and slid through the barbed wire, and was on his feet and grabbed the hardboard and was off. Nigel in the meantime lowered the jack just enough, gave it a snatch and was off as quickly as Joe. The hardboard was then flung into the bush followed by the jack, which landed in clump of dense bramble and disappeared. They both then looked at each other without speaking, then started on their walk back to the intersection. Immediately to their right the ground sloped away downward from them, where in the rainy season it becomes almost a river. Joe had an allergy irritation that came behind his ears, and this irritation was active just at this time. Just at the moment when Joe reached up with his left hand to rub his ear lobe between finger and thumb, Nigel flung a garrote around Joe's neck, lucky for Joe his left hand foiled the attempt, and his right hand instinctively came up to the garrote, and fortunately for Joe Major Hall had trained him well, he arched his back and coming up on tip toe, he suddenly dropped back, his right leg stretching back to Nigel's rear, as far as it would go, at the same time smashing his backside into Nigel's midriff and let his right hand slide over Nigel's head to grab his neck, and just at that moment Nigel's foot stepped into some animal droppings as they were struggling and he slipped just enough, Joe pulled with all he'd got, Nigel came flying over Joe's head and came down, the small of his back landing on the sharpened stump of a cut down tree, his spine snapped like a dry stick.

Joe went down on top of him, for Nigel still held on to the garrote around Joe's neck, Nigel's grip released when his back snapped, and Joe came up grabbing the Ghurka knife as he straightened, then he crashed back down plunging the knife into Nigel's already dead body, the knife entered just below the left side of the rib cage going up at an angle of 30 degrees and entering the heart.

Joe stayed in that squatting position for some time, trying to gather his faculties. He then let go of the knife and fell back in terrified exhaustion. He lay prostrate beneath the shadows of the warped shapes that loomed over him like ghoulish guards with their grotesquely twisted limbs silhouetted against the darkness of the nights naked sky.

How can one think when the mind is being raped with illustrated events that had just passed, and those that were yet to come, it could only end in death or total insanity, these were the immediate thoughts on Joe's mind.

"Get a grip man!" said Joe out loud, "You got yourself into this mess, now you do the best you can."

He then got up, it was now 2-30am so he must have been lying there a couple of hours, he went to his car, took the revolver out of the waist band of his trousers and threw them onto the passenger seat and drove home. He parked the car and let himself in, went to his bedroom stripped off and threw his clothes in the wash basket, went in the bathroom and took a shower, letting the hot water sting him, he then treated the wound in his neck made by the garrote, a long deep burn around the right side of his neck, the blood had congealed and was dirty. He bathed it in dettol and covered it with lint and adhesive tape.

It was dinner at the officers club for the Sandies. Simon Denning was there as an honorary guest, it was a dinner to celebrate Steven's promotion, all very cleverly engineered to give the Sandies an alibi, not that it was particularly necessary, for with Elido gone they were the power anyway, but the Sandies liked everything tidy. At 1-30am Steven said, "I think we should go now, all will have been taken care of."

"I agree," said Denning, "I will join you if I may."

"Yes do," said the old man.

"I hope everything went as planned," said Paula.

"It did, you can bet on it, Lieutenant Lapengio is the best, so we have achieved everything," said Steven.

They bade their farewells, it was now 1-45am and Denning told his driver to go to the Sandies residence.

Steven was driving the old man's Mercedes limousine, they arrived home and the old man opened the door and went inside. Denning was making small talk with Paula. There was a splutter of feet on the hall floor and the house boy came rushing in, fastening the buttons on his white jacket.

"That's alright boy you can go," said the old man, as they all went into the library, Steven half expecting Nigel to be there. He called the house boy back.

"Did Lieutenant Lapengio call at all Shoto?" asked Steven.

"No Sir," he replied, "No one called."

"Very well boy you can retire." The boy turned and disappeared into the kitchen.

"I don't like it," said Paula.

"We will give it half an hour," said Steven.

"I think I'll go under the circumstances," said Denning.

"Not yet!" said Paula, "We wait and see what the situation is."

"Lets have a drink," said the old man.

2-30am came and no word.

"Are sure of the details?" asked the old man.

"Yes, said Steven," The motor bike was delivered as agreed on the West side of Torridor Road at the intersection, I drove Nigel there myself to his rendezvous with Tully, the job should have been done by 11-30pm or midnight at the latest, Nigel was to see to Tully and report back here. On the bike it is only 20 minutes the way Nigel drives."

2-45am, then 3-0am came.

"I think we made a mistake," said Paula.

"So do I," said Steven.

"How do you mean." asked Denning, sipping his gin and tonic.

"Well," said Steven, "I think I got to know that Tully guy, and he is a professional in every way, in everything he does, but I'm sure he couldn't get the better of Nigel."

"I knew I was right!" said Paula, "It was a mistake to try and get rid of Tully, if we stuck to the original plan all would have been normal this morning as far as Tully was concerned, he would have

83

gone back to England and all would have been well."

"But," said Denning, "Knowing that I had been implicated in the assassination of the President, who knows what or how he could have used that information in the future."

"And that would never do would it!" said Paula angrily. "You and your knighthood!"

"Stop it!" said the old man, "We should think, not bicker!"

Steven said, "I will go and check on the motorbike at least, all of you stay here."

Steven left, got into the Mercedes and was off like a shot. He pulled in at the intersection, crossed the road and went into the bush, the bike was still there. Steven looked around but could see nothing. He crossed over and walked into the bush, the way it had all been planned, about 15 minutes in he came across Nigel's body with the knife still buried in his chest. He had slipped down the slope a little and lay at a grotesque angle, displaying the obvious broken back.

"Tully!" he thought, and a cold shiver shook him. He stood there several seconds, it was difficult for him to comprehend how this situation could have developed the way it did. He turned and went back to his car and drove home.

He parked the car and let himself in. Steven then looked at each one individually, he then said in a strained voice.

"Lieutenant Lapengio is dead. He had been killed with his own knife, and his back had been broken. I would not have believed that was possible, not with Nigel he was the best individual fighting machine in the National Guard."

"Come now," interrupted Denning, Steven became very tense and walked slowly over towards Denning.

"Nigel Lapengio was a karate black belt 4th dan, he had also trained with the best terrorist organisations in Libya, I'm telling you the Devil himself couldn't have done what was done to Nigel." Then in a whispered voice, "Who is this man Tully?" He then turned quickly, addressing his sister and father. The situation now as it stands is this, Elido is dead. By 6-0am at the latest his body will be found, I'll be the first one contacted, Lentoy and Co. will be informed by me on the phone and their party representatives will be contacted by radio, they have been in constant radio contact since 6-0pm this evening, all networks have been open, every newspaper and radio station will be informed. By 6-30am the whole of Ligeria will be aware of the situation, I will head the caretaker government until the elections, we will have some dissensions from the Elido loyal supporters, he was, after all, a much loved and respected leader.

The dissenters should not be too much of a problem, as I see it we have only one problem" ..... "Tully!" said Paula.

"Yes," said Steven, "We tried to double cross him, and we all know what them means. Paula, Father you go nowhere without an escort of two National Guardsmen each. I'll put the best at your disposal, I'll put guards around the house. Denning, get out! Back to your embassy, and make an official request for guards, but nothing can be done until tomorrow, after Elido has been found and the announcements have been made, so Tully still has two hours or so, Paula, father go to your rooms try to get a few hours sleep, lock all doors and windows I'll stay here in the lounge armed."

"But he may be watching the house now waiting for me to leave, he ...." at that Steven interrupted. "No" he snarled. "And that is a chance you will have to take."

"You have brought it on yourself," said Paula, "On all of us."

"Come," said Steven, "I'll see you to your car, and on your way."

Steven then removed his 38 revolver from his waistband under his coat, and escorted Denning to his car, and saw him drive away. He then returned to the house, Paula and the old man had retired. "Damn," said Steven to himself, I could do without this added problem of Tully, the situation will be tricky as it is.

Joe figured he had 24 hours at least, the Sandies he reasoned couldn't put an all points out on him, because they like everybody else would have to be taken by surprise shock and fake distress. But he couldn't stay, the National Guard would have him and see him off, he set his alarm clock so he could get a couple of hours sleep, the alarm woke him at 5-30am, he got washed shaved and dressed.

Put on his denim trousers and pale blue roll neck shirt, he then put a couple of pairs of pants and socks, and his shaving gear in a small holdall, he then got his £500 pounds in travellers cheques, all unsigned, £100 in cash and the 250 Guineas.

He then picked up the photograph of his Janie, and stood looking at it. "I love you Jane my darling." he said out loud, then put it back on the cupboard quickly paused and walked away.

Joe went outside and got into the car, he then picked up the gun and looked at it, he put it in the holdall, and drove into town once there. He pulled into a super market car park, sat there for a few minutes going over his plans, such as they were, he could get himself a decent motorbike, that would allow him to travel through the bush, a tent for shelter, and some food.

What he couldn't do was book into a hotel, to do that you need your passport and very soon there would be an all points out on him, not as a killer, but as a missing person, Akeja Construction and the British Embassy would see to that, and once he was found the Sandies and the National Guard would see him off, and he wouldn't give them that pleasure.

The thing to do was hole up somewhere, and figure out just what to do. He left his car locked it and walked away. He went into a cafe to get a coffee and some breakfast of eggs and bacon, people in the cafe were asking each other had they heard the news, President Elido was dead, assassinated, and to Joe's surprise they were all genuinely upset, the proprietress then broke out in tears, Joe just couldn't understand it.

He then paid and left, he just walked around town to kill time, he went to a car and motorbike show room, he saw the bike that would do the job, a 500cc Honda at 700 Guineas, that would be ideal thought Joe. It was now 8-30am and the show room opened at 9 so he went to another cafe, buying a newspaper before he went in. The assassination was a full page stop press, and again people were in tears at Elido's death, it had Joe completely bewildered, he had seen people murdered on the orders of Elido and yet people were grieved to see him dead, it just did not compute. He went back to the show room and talked to the owner, he checked out the bike it was sound so he offered the owner £300 Sterling in unsigned travellers cheques, Joe knowing full well that he could get a sight more than 700 Guineas for them on the black market. A deal was struck for £350 Sterling, all this of course is illegal, for all hard currency is recorded at customs coming into the country, and can only be changed officially through a bank.

However a deal was made, Joe then drove around and found a sports shop where he bought a small tent a collapsible camp bed a compass a map and a small primus stove. He then went to the supermarket and bought in the main tinned food stuffs, it was now lunch time. He stopped at a small cafe for a sandwich, the evening papers were out, he bought one, "Elido assassinated!" was the head line, Joe reasoned he would have to leave town. His description would soon be circulated and a white man amongst a nation of black men would soon be recognised. He could hardly disguise himself with a false nose and dark glasses.

But he reasoned he could grow a beard and darken it with Grecian 2000, then he remembered the man who sold him the motor bike was bald, and you don't see many bald Negroes. That's it he thought he would shave his head bald, then he would be a bald man with a beard, and a black beard at that, his description now would be a clean shaven grey haired medium sized white man, and in disguise he would be a medium sized bald man with a black beard.

That should do it he figured, he then went to a pharmacist and bought a couple of tubes of Grecian 2000, a pair of scissors and a mirror, he then headed out of town heading North the Macadam Roads soon started to branch into secondary roads and tracks, Joe was now 30 miles North of Akeja and he noticed a small range of mountains to the East. In one section there was an enormous boulder stood on end, which looked as though a small push or wind would topple it.

Using that as a land mark he headed through the bush, he was now heading North North East, he arrived at the mountain range where there were several small clearings which had been used to make camp, but he reasoned other people might head for this particular land mark, so he headed due West for a couple of miles, then stopped at another small clearing.

This thought Joe would be an ideal place to make camp, it was close to a river, the water of which was clean and sweet. After

7 days he had a reasonable 'full set' so using his mirror and scissors he cut off his hair, then he heated some water lathered up and shaved his head, then for the Grecian 2000.

In 10 days he had a black full set his disguise was as good as was possible.

It was now 6 weeks since the assassination, and every 3 or 4 days the bald headed bearded man would go into town, using the same route going to as coming from, to keep himself familiar with it. He kept up with the news, Major Sandies had now formed his government, but things were not going well for him, also Elido had been the most loved and respected leader of modern times, the slaughter in the bush and that of Mrs Gaskel and her refugees, had all been planned and stage managed by the Sandies, there could be no other explanation for it. Paula was one hell of an actress, but why Denning?

A great many staunch Elido supporters had been arrested, some had fled and some of the military had gone deep into the bush, and were making guerrilla attacks on strategic military targets, the senior minister in Elido's government who had been arrested, had been broken out of jail by an armed gang, and it was believed that he was bringing in white mercenaries, to wage his own civil war.

*   *   *   *   *

September 14th London. Friday 9-0am.

Board Meeting ECC

"Well gentlemen, I've called this meeting today to give you the latest developments with the Uranium project, and the events taking place in Ligeria. As you all know President Elido was assassinated, and the now acting President Major Sandies, has given us his pledge that he will give us the mining concession for the Uranium. However since the people of Ligeria are shocked saddened and angry, it is considered expedient for us to wait until after the elections or for a period of 6 months.

It is a foregone conclusion that the National Socialist party will win the elections, and as you all know Unico Sandies the father of the acting President, who is leader of the NSP will himself be President, and he has already given us his written guarantee to the mining rights. The period of 6 months is to allow his people to recover from shock, apparently Elido was a much loved leader, are there any questions?"

"Yes Mr Chairman, I have a question," it was the financial director Leonard Oakes.

"Go ahead Leonard."

"Well Sir I have given this a lot of thought since I read of the assassination, and I'm sure you all agree this has come following our granting of half a million pounds to the NSP Now from what I've read this assassination must have been carried out by a top class assassin, so I ask myself and now this meeting, was any of this money used to pay for this assassination? The people claim that it was the devil himself brought in to do the killing, which is ridiculous, so it must have been an assassin of very high calibre and therefore very costly."

"Well Leonard," said the chairman, "I'm shocked to think you consider such a thing. I personally would have nothing to do with such an act, I know I speak for everyone present when I say that." "Here Here," came the mutter.

"Oh I know that Sir, but I feel the NSP should give us an account of their expenditure so far."

"Yes Leonard, that is reasonable, I'll get on to Simon Denning first thing in the morning, I feel sure everything will be in order. Any other business?

The general feeling of the Elido supporters was that it was a military coup, planned by the Sandies, who had paid a million Dollars to a Mafia assassin to kill Elido, it still wasn't known how it was done. Nobody had entered the building and nobody had left the building, the place was surrounded by guards, yet Elido had been shot.

Major Sandies now had the problem of stabilising the situation, he was doing this by promising elections as soon as possible, as soon as the climate was right.

Joe could read the papers until he was word blind, try as he might to reason things out, it all came to the same explanation, the massacre of the refugees, the atrocities committed in the bush were all engineered by the Sandies. It had all been a macabre blind to induce him to kill Elido, but why him? Why Joe Tully?

That was a question he may never get an answer to, and he couldn't spend the rest of his life in the bush, but he resolved to make the bastards pay, if it was the last thing he ever did he would put the Sandies in the ground. He decided to reconnoitre the Sandies property, what had he got to lose? He rode out of his camp into town, and along the main road heading towards the Sandies residence.

He then turned off the road heading West, and came to the beginning of dense bush, deepening into a forest, he could remember at the back of their house was a garden about 20 yards long surrounded by a low white fence, from the fence the back lands were open, sloping steadily downwards for about 100 yards, then it banked up to the North, and from the top of this rise it was open bushlands with desert brush of various kind, until it came to a dense forest which was about 300 yards from the rise, a total distance from the house of 400 yards.

The Sandies next door neighbour was a shipping magnate.

He could see between the houses, he could see the comings and goings, from his vantage point with the binoculars he purchased on one of his visits to town. Joe had shown a lot of patience on this exercise, for he knew he had to be right first time, this would be a one only chance, he would never get a second, there were guards patrolling all the time.

There were two guards at the rear, and two at the front with a quad vehicle parked up the road a little, with the rest of the guard contingent. The two guards at the rear would stand and talk for a couple of minutes, then each would turn in opposite directions and walk to the side ends of the garden.

The garden was so laid out, there was a path of one metre square paving stones, leading down from the double French windows in the centre of the garden, to the white fence at the bottom, and there were two similar paths leading off from the centre path to each side of the garden, one of these paths was half way down, the other was at the bottom, the idea of this was to allow maintenance to be carried out on the flowering bushes without disrupting the garden. These bushes Joe thought were beautiful, and over hung the white fence at the bottom. There were quite a few bushes throughout the garden, some tall and some just shrubbery. Each time Paula and Steven went out together, the lounge light would come on when they returned, the lounge opened out onto the garden by the French windows, the study light was invariably on, that was where the old man spent most of his time.

Joe was back in camp reading about some army general from Ghana who was paying Ligeria a visit, and he would be shown around the National Guard and there was to be a dinner dance celebration on Saturday 29 September, that is when he would hit the Sandies.

Saturday 29th Joe was about to make the Sandies pay, lots of innocent lives had been lost to put them where they were, plus the destruction of Joe Tully, the name he was using now was Jake Cross, Cross being the name of the agent who got him the contract in the first place, and Jake? Well it was the nearest to Joe he could think of.

Joe was sitting on his camp bed listening to the sounds of the forest, "What a bloody mess!" he thought, "living in a tent in the middle of a forest with no hope, no future, just living now to get even with the people that put me here, and if he died in the attempt so what he thought. Getting the guards at the back of the house would have to be done silently, and he was no knife fighter, "A bow and arrow" he thought, he had seen them in the archery section of the sports shop in Akeja.

On one of his visits to town he spotted a shop that sold old English furniture, a lot of Edwardian stuff, an old cross bow, plus a ball and chain, old armaments, maces, a complete arsenal from old England. Joe went in to enquire about the cross bow because it was small and that would suit him better than a bow and arrow, they were large and cumbersome, the cross bow was in working order and had three bolts, "we are in luck," thought Joe, he bought them that was the last of his cash. The last 250 Guineas was now gone, he had just £50 pound Sterling in cash left.

When he was back in camp he tried out the cross bow at close range on a tree, and at close range it was deadly, then this particular exercise would have to be done at close range, for his plan to work.

Filling in time living in the bush as Joe was, took a lot of patients and self discipline, there were times when he thought he would go out of his mind, what was keeping him going, was his determination to get even with the Sandies, they would pay and they would pay the ultimate price, and that's a fact. Joe made himself a cup of tea on his primus, sat on his camp bed to read the paper he had bought in town.

The rebel forces now claimed to be led by General Adejumo, who had been the senior minister in the Elido government, were now bringing in white mercenaries, causing the Sandies government a great deal of concern, this pleased Joe he would try to join them, it was his only chance.

At 7-0pm Saturday 29th Joe left his camp, and rode down into town heading for the Sandies, he detoured off heading West as he had done previously, heading for the forest, then he turned North and rode on for about 100 yards without lights, he left his bike under a bush of some kind and walked to his vantage point.

From here with his binoculars he observed the residence, the place was in darkness, the guards were patrolling as he had observed them on previous occasions.

It was now 11-30pm, he figured he had a long wait, this was his go for broke effort, he had to get these murderous bastards, then if he survived where would he go from here? His total wealth was £50 Sterling and he couldn't get far on that. He would have liked to have got Denning, but that was too much to hope for, if he survived this his only hope was to join the rebels.

Finding them would be like finding a needle in the proverbial haystack, there was thousands of miles of wilderness, and he didn't know where to start.

South was out that direction led only to the ocean, so all things being equal he would go North, but on balance he didn't really care now whether he lived or died, all was lost now anyway. Jane would have been informed exactly as it read in the Sunday Times Bakra,

Joe Tully the British engineer who was responsible for the new Presidential office suite was abducted by the President's assassins and presumed dead.

His thoughts were interrupted then by lights, it was Stevens Limousine, Joe watched through his binoculars, the drivers door opened and Steven got out, walked round and opened the door on the passenger side, Paula got out looking as gorgeous as ever, the door closed and he looked back at the two guards, who were patrolling the rear garden as Joe had observed previously, it was now time to act.

He went back to his bike and got the cross bow and three bolts, then returned to his vantage point. The two guards were patrolling as before, they were patrolling the bottom path, they would meet in the centre, say a few words then turn and patrol to the side outer ends of the garden. The lights in the lounge came on. Moments later, Steven opened the French windows and walked into the garden. The senior guard stopped abruptly, turned and marched over to Steven. The guard stood to attention and saluted. Steven returned the salute and spoke for a few moments to the guard before returning into the house, and the guard returned to his duty.

Joe then ran east and waited until the first guard was nearing the centre, then he ran towards the house, then ran back West to the corner of the white fence where he was obscured by the flowering bushes.

In his crouched position, he loaded the cross bow and watched the approach of the guard through the gaps in the branches. As he appeared at the end of his circuit, he turned and as he did Joe fired and stood up. He was actually no more than a yard from him point blank range the bolt slammed into his chest and he never saw what hit him, as the bolt struck Joe grabbed the guards shirt front to guide his fall into the flowering bushes and he finished up hanging over the fence.

He then reloaded the cross bow, and ran silently in a crouched manner to the centre of the fence, then went a little further on to where there was a gap between the bushes, there were numerous gaps and Joe selected one, as the guard approached Joe stood and fired, the bolt struck the guard in the chest, and with a dull thud he fell back in the garden. Joe dropped the cross bow leaped over the fence, went to the second guard and took his AK automatic rifle and a spare magazine, putting it in his hip pocket, he then checked the magazine on the rifle it was full he then ran silently to the French windows, and gently put his hand on the door handle, and very gently pressed. The door handle moved, when it had finished travelling Joe pushed, "Here goes," he thought, he pushed gently and the window moved, then very quickly with his right hand opened the window wide and stepped inside flinging the curtains open at the centre with the AK rifle, and closed the door. Stevens hand went inside his coat.

"Freeze!" said Joe, "Or you die without knowing why?" Paula stood in a state of shock. Steven let his hand fall to his side.

"Who the hell are you? And what do you want? Where are the guards?"

"Dead," said Joe, "You mean you have forgotten your old friend already?" said Joe in his easy going manner. Joe was pleased with his disguise.

"Joe Tully!" said Steven.

"No!" gasped Paula.

"Oh yes!" said Joe, "You at least owe me an explanation."

"I can explain everything," said Steven.

"It was Denning." broke in Paula, "He was worried about having an English man back home knowing the truth of his implication,"

"And it was Denning," broke in Joe, "who slaughtered those poor devils in the bush, and wiped out the refugees?"

"That," said Steven, "was expedient, expediency is common practice in politics."

"Not where murder is concerned," said Joe, "Not in my book."

"It never was planned to kill you Joe, you were to do the job on Elido go back to work, then go home £25,000 pounds the richer. What is done Joe is done, we can make amends surely?"

"Tell me then why did it have to be me, to kill Elido?"

"Because," said Steven, "Everybody at the right level is Mausa and you know that situation, anyway any other man of another tribe that had the guts to do the job, would also have the guts to blow the whistle on us, and to bring in a hit man would require a cover, and we are military, not industry. Then you came on the scene, we did our research on you and find that you are a man who has had a thorough training, if that had not been the case we would have trained you, once we had your agreement to do the job. May I ask a question?" said Steven, Joe nodded, "How did you get the better of Lieutenant Lapengio?"

Joe had asked himself this question many times, and the answer was luck sheer unadulterated luck, but he wouldn't tell Steven this. "You mean that little boy Nigel?" said Joe, in his easy going manner. "Well Steven, you know you should never send an amateur to do a professional job." Steven looked puzzled.

"Who are you?" asked Steven.

"Just a simple English man who wants justice."

"Joseph," broke in Paula, "We.." Just then there was one hell of a racket outside. Orders were being shouted and there was the sound of heavy footsteps running up the garden path. Just at that time Joe was momentarily distracted, Steven went for his gun, but he wasn't fast enough, Joe opened fire on repetition, the bullets smashed Steven to the wall, blowing his chest apart. Paula looked on in horror, then she turned to Joe hands held out in front of her, as if she was trying to stop the bullets. Joe swung the AK round without taking his finger off the trigger, as the gun traversed the bullets spewing out disintegrated the cocktail cabinet, then they lifted Paula against the wall, and all but cut her in half, she fell to the floor staring into space but seeing nothing.

At that moment the French windows came crashing in, with three National Guards men. They were met with a hail of bullets, Joe was elbowing his way past them as they were falling dead or dying, Joe dropped off the step outside changing the magazine, in is minds eye he caught a glimpse of more guards coming round the right hand corner of the house, he spun round in a crouch firing. The guards went down, Joe then started running down the path, holding the AK rifle out at arms length, pointing back the way he came from, and the bullets were just going any where, but it was having the desired effect. What guards there were left ducked for cover.

The magazine emptied he dropped the weapon and jumped over the fence, and ran across the bush as fast as he could, with what guards there were in pursuit. He reached his bike kick started it and was off bouncing over bracken in a very erratic manner. But he was moving and moving fast, he then picked up the main trunk road and driving with the throttle wide open he headed North. Joe knew that they would soon be mobilised, but it would be some time before road blocks were set up, he had a full tank and a spare can containing an extra 2 gallons, he figured he could stay on the road for 50 minutes at least.

He had been on the main road now for 40 minutes, he pulled off onto a secondary road that did eventually peter out into a track, that passed through some derelict buildings housing refugees and squatters, the track had virtually run out but this suited Joe, the terrain was more like desert with wild brush, his compass showed him heading North, he could see in the distance as the sun came up, it was dense bush, or that is how it appeared, but he had no choice, and it would be just as bad for his pursuers.

He hit the bush, it wasn't as bad as he thought it would be, but it slowed him down and he was travelling between 15 and 20 miles per hour.

* * * * *

Sunday 30th

Denning had just got up, and gone down for breakfast, the house boy gave him his newspaper, he ordered bacon eggs with coffee, then he switched on the radio. The newscaster came on. "Good morning listeners, this is the Bakra news read by William Gendo. Major Steven Sandies the acting President and his sister Paula," (at that Denning looked up and fastened his eyes on the radio) "were both gunned down in their home early this morning, both died instantly their bodies riddled with bullets. The slayer, a white man, also killed 7 National Guardsmen who were guarding their home.

He escaped on a motor bike with National Guard in pursuit, we will keep you informed of developments."

"Tully!" Denning said to himself, "That damn confounded Tully."

He then went straight to the phone and called his secretary at her home. "Good morning Enid, I hope I didn't wake you."

"No Sir," said Enid, "I was just about to get up when you rang. What is it Sir?"

"Book me on the first available flight to London, as soon as possible."

"Very well Sir I hope nothing is wrong."

"No no, nothing is wrong everything is fine, but something has come up. I must return to London immediately."

"Very well Sir I'll phone you at home with the arrangements."

"Thank you Enid." he hung up.

"I'm next. If he can get through the Sandies guard, Tully will have no trouble getting through my sloppy lot." he said to himself.

It was now midday Sunday 30th, Joe stopped. He was exhausted, he drove the bike at 5 miles an hour into a dense thicket, then stopped, got off the bike and sat down, leaning back against a tree. He fell asleep out of sheer exhaustion, he awoke at 6-0pm, he had slept for 4 hours. He felt better and now he assessed his situation, he was already into his spare petrol, so he figured he had 80 miles or so more, with what he had in the tank, he still had the revolver with 4 bullets and his Stanley knife. "Not a lot," he thought, "to take on the whole Ligerian armed forces."

He moved off, still heading North, the bush was now thinning out, with great stretches of barren desert scattered with patches of bush. Darkness came, there were times when he could clock up 40 miles an hour and other times he was doing 15. Dawn broke and he was now making better time at 20 miles an hour. The bush was now in patches of maybe 80 or so square yards, he stopped at the end of a small section, the time was now 10-0 am.

In front of him lay open brush lands, wide open, no cover, does he go or not? Once out there he is just an open target, he didn't know where his pursuers were but they were there somewhere.

He couldn't stay there for the rest of his life, he thought, "so here goes, I go until the petrol runs out then we take it from there." It was now midday the sun beat down mercilessly. He was making good progress doing 30 miles an hour, in the distance he could now see clumps of bush, another hour passed.

The area now turned to pretty dense bush, the terrain continued like this for some distance. At times the bush was quite dense and then it would be just desert, then he heard it, "A bloody helicopter!" He said to himself, as he came up to a relatively small area of bush and drove right into it, fell off the bike, switched it off and lay still, the helicopter hovered for some time then moved off, Joe got up and started the bike, "I can't stay here forever," he said to himself, and moved off, again he was making good time, in front of him now was open desert, to the east he could see nothing. It was either ocean or he was on a plateau, then he heard it again, "Damn, what a time for that bloody fool to come back!" he thought. There was no cover, he was driving like a mad man, across the sun baked ground and bracken, bouncing as if out of control, he was travelling in a direction he knew not where, just trying to avoid the helicopter, it swooped and fired its machine guns and its cannon, it was a gun ship, the blazing sun beat down its scorching rays mercilessly upon him, the sweat ran down his forehead into his eyes, blinding him, the gun ship swooped and fired, then excruciating pain enveloped his entire body, he became airborne floating through time and emptiness on and on through space, then the nightmare exploded.

When consciousness returned he was drifting below the surface of the river, the current was strong. The blood from his wounds was soon dissipated by the fast flowing river, it was as though he were in a gigantic tropical fish tank, and the events of the last few minutes returned to his now conscious mind, he could see the reeds rising to the surface, he swam to them, he could feel them thrashing about him as went deeper into them, then he looked up. He could see the surface where the reeds broke through to open air, as he approached the surface he held on to the reeds, and head held back allowed his face to break the surface, he gulped a lung full of fresh air, as the reeds pressed on and around his head and body, reaching high above him swaying gently in the winds.

He could hear the gun ship searching for him, but he knew he could not be seen. The gun ship would then fire bursts of machine gun fire into the river, after what seemed an age the gun ship moved on. There was silence, just the sounds of nature, that of the river and its inhabitants the bullfrog the crickets all carrying on with their uncomplicated lives, Joe never thought he would see the day that he would envy the bullfrog, such was the intensity of his nightmare.

The pull of the current was strong so he moved out slowly from the reeds with gentle side strokes using his left arm and leg to move down river with the current, he could see the land over to his right about 20 feet or so. As he pulled towards it he could feel his feet catching the bottom of the river bed, when he could he stood, then limping and dragging his injured leg he made it to the bank, pulling hard on the sparse reeds that grew by the river edge.

He collapsed and lay there, he passed out, the next thing he knew it was dark, and had started to rain, the thunder was heavy and the fork lightening was horrendous, "The story of my life," he thought, his body was numb, totally without feeling, he couldn't move, yet his mind was clear, for the first time in ages he thought of Janie and the children, they would be on their own now, for their Joe died a long time ago, he died the moment he accepted £25,000 to commit murder.

Jane would have the £30,000 insurance money that he was covered for on this contract, so that would give them a start. Jane was young and attractive, she would find someone else, some nice guy who played tennis and didn't drink, Joe Tully would go down as an innocent engineer who had been kidnapped and murdered by the Elido assassins or rebel forces, or whatever bloody lies would be expedient at the time he guessed.

"Where did it all start?" the mind asked, the rain pounding on his face and body. He was at peace, he had no weariness, no pain, as if the mind was outside the body, looking down at the unreality of the whole thing. A nightmare developed from torment of his own making.

* * * * *

Tuesday October 2nd.

A Board Meeting ECC

"Gentlemen, I've called this meeting in rather a hurry, to make you all familiar with the situation now prevailing in Ligeria. Early Saturday morning Major Sandies the acting President of Ligeria and his sister Paula were both murdered in their home. Most of you will have read about in the Monday papers. I, however, was informed on Sunday night by the British ambassador Simon Denning as he arrived back at Heathrow airport.

Therefore it goes without saying that any signing of the agreement relevant to the mining of Uranium will be delayed. I should, as you all know, along with Barry here, have flown out there on Thursday of this week. The NSP are as committed as we are to this project and all Major Sandies' senior ministers are likewise committed.

Now as you know we have at this time got our Geologist Edward out there with the engineers, and there is a consignment of the most advanced geological testing equipment, and earth moving and mining plant, and trucks of one kind and another. I would like to get your feelings gentlemen on whether or not to halt that consignment, assuming of course that it isn't too late, it may have already been shipped.

This consignment has a nett value of nine million pounds Sterling. Plus the hiring of agents to supply the necessary labour force."

The financial Director spoke. "Mr Chairman Sir,"

"Yes Leonard," said the chairman.

"Personally I am not, and never have been happy with the situation, we did ask that we were given an account of how the half million pounds we invested was being spent by the NSP, I never received anything relevant to it. Now that there is, it would appear, an on going situation of assassinations, I personally would like to see the whole project shelved, and our people brought home, we all know there are opposing rebel factions waging Guerrilla warfare, which could possibly lead to a full scale civil war, the whole project could prove to be a financial disaster. Those are my views Mr Chairman."

"Thank you Leonard," he replied.

"Mr Chairman" it was the technical director,

"Yes Barry," said the Johnson,

"I believe we should carry on with the project, whatever the outcome of these assassinations, tragic as they are, for what is left of the Sandies government and the incoming NSP are all committed to the project, let us face the fact that there is no opposition to the NSP and the economic value to Ligeria goes without saying, there will never be an end to tribal conflict in Ligeria, or Black Africa as a whole for that matter. I say we carry on with the project."

"Thank you Barry. Well gentlemen there are two views, both of which in their own right are sound, so I propose we all think on these views, at least until I've spoken to Simon. Each of you has a complete report on the situation prior to the Sandies demise, I will arrange a meeting with Simon Denning and get his views on the political situation. We will meet again on Friday the 5th.

Tuesday October 2nd

"Sir William will see you now Sir."

Sir William Glover was the foreign secretary to the British government.

"Good afternoon Simon it is good to see you, I must say I was somewhat surprised to receive your resignation, which I found on my desk this morning, and you returning from Ligeria on Saturday without any warning whatsoever, this is so irregular, and if I may be so bold, improper, what is it Simon?"

"Well Sir, my health has not been so good for some time now, and I've been over working, I realise that is inevitable with the situation as it is, but the pressure is too intense so I feel I should step down, and give a much younger man the opportunity. I feel I am unable to serve you as you have the right to be served."

"If I were to offer you a reliable assistant would you reconsider?" asked Sir William.

"No Sir."

"You realise then," said Sir William "That you could never be considered for the honours list, and you did look set for a Knighthood, but to resign at this time with unrest as it is in Ligeria, would obviate that probability."

"I know Sir, but that is my decision."

"Very well Simon, I unhappily accept your resignation."

Four hundred and fifty miles North of Bakra, encamped a group of rebels, led by a Scot mercenary, Major Adam Campbell, who had been a regular soldier with the British army with the rank of sergeant major, now earning a living as a mercenary, a big heavy set man, who had been in the army since he was a boy, it was what he did best.

A runner came into the majors tent,

"Sir a platoon of National Guard with a helicopter gun ship, were spotted by our reconnaissance party, they were just 11 miles West of us Sir, by the Kasunu river near Mushishi. They shoot into river Sir, so do gun ship?"

"Why I wonder?" said the Major "We thought we could hear shooting. What the hell were they doing this far North?"

"Our reconnaissance party also say that the Sandies family were killed on Saturday morning, by a white man who escaped heading North Sir."

"Did he now?" said the Scot, "did he indeed?"

"I know the Kasunu river Sir, it is very big river it joins up with Ligeria river and goes down as far as Port Hardbury, but in the Mushishi area it is only very small river Sir, but it could swell. Last night we have heavy rain, it come early."

"OK let's have a look." they went outside.

"What is all the excitement Adam?" said Doc,

Doc was also a mercenary. He was an Englishman named Trevor Reed, "I don't know Doc, apparently a contingent of National Guard were active last night and maybe still are, 11 miles east of us, so I think I'll take a look. Care to join us Doc?"

"Sure," he replied the Sergeant came over and saluted.

"You sent for me Sir."

"Yes, we will take a look at whatever it was the NG were interested in last night. Mobilise the men Sergeant, we move out immediately. Don't strike camp, leave 10 men, we will be back, we will take two Range Rovers.

The rebels reached the river in a little over an hour, they left the vehicles and went on foot. Slowly the 10 men moved out to the rivers edge, the runner pointed.

"There Sir just at the end of the mountain range, they fire into the river, and the gun ship too."

"Well," said the Major, "I don't see anything Sergeant, take 4 men across the river and work your way North, we will cover this side. If you see anything let us know, the river is no more than 9 feet wide at this point, and gets smaller the further North you go."

The runner then spoke. "The river is very shallow over the ridge Sir, about two miles North, we can go round and work South."

"OK you know this river, take two men and lead off, we will follow.

The three leading men set off at the double, they crossed the river at the ridge where it was about 3 feet deep. At this point they found Joe, just where he lay when he had pulled himself out of the river. The runner then headed back to Adam and his party. He came to attention and saluted.

"Sir we find dead man a white man Sir."

"Are you sure he is dead?" asked Adam.

"He is dead Sir, yes he is dead."

"Are his eyes open or closed?"

"Closed Sir!"

"Lets go Doc," said Adam, they set off at the double, with two rebels carrying the Doc's medical bag and equipment.

They arrived at the prostrate figure of Joe, Adam felt for a pulse in the neck.

"Can't feel any pulse Doc, but he doesn't feel dead."

Doc then retrieved his stethoscope from his bag. He tore open his shirt and tested on several points on Joe's chest,

"He's alive Adam, but only just." He then went back to his bag.

"Get rid of his shirt Adam!" Adam immediately got his knife out and cut the shirt off Joe's body without moving him, Doc in the meantime removed a phial and syringe and gave Joe an injection. He then started to clean and stitch the wounds in Joe's neck and thigh, the bullets having gone clean right through.

"Now," said Doc, "we are going to have to turn him over, it would appear he has a wound in his back, going off the state of the grass. What he needs is blood which I don't have with me."

"I'll give him some," said Adam.

"We don't know his blood group and I don't have with me what I need to test it."

"O negative same as me Doc," said Adam "According to his medallion around his neck." Joe wore a St Christopher medallion, and on the back of it, it stated his allergy and his blood group.

Adam noticed it when he was searching him for identification, which of course he didn't have.

"Great!" said Doc, "I'll take a pint Major." He then with the equipment in his bag made up a line for the transfusion, then he turned Joe over gently, Adam sat down next to Joe and Doc connected them up.

"We will time it Major, I guess a pint will hold him until I get him back to base." The men now had a fire going to enable Doc to sterilise his knife.

"The bullet will have to come out," said Doc "His neck and thigh were no trouble, the bullets went right through, here the bullet has gone through the shoulder blade." The neck wound was just at the point where the neck joins the shoulder.

"Can you get the bullet out Doc?" said Adam.

"Well it isn't the ideal operating theatre, but we will just have to make do. He is in a coma state but we will give him a local just to be on the safe side.

Doc removed the transfusion line.

"That should do it Major," he then opened Joe's back. The bullet had come to rest just behind the shoulder blade just short of the lung. Doc removed the bullet and stitched him up, he then dressed the wound.

"You know Doc there are a few questions I would like answers to, if this guy did do the Sandies, what is a civilian doing taking this kind of job? Is he a professional hit man? I guess he must be to pull off this kind of job. I hear according to our reconnaissance party that he took out 7 NG to boot. So he is good, bloody good, what I would like to know is, who hired him? It wasn't us that's a fact."

"How do we get him back to base, Major, that is the only question I'm interested in right now," said Doc. "It will take two days at best in the Range Rovers."

"I will contact base and get them to send the chopper," said Adam.

Adam went over to the radio operator who carried the portable transmitter receiver set, the operator set the frequency dials then started calling.

"Able calling control, how do you hear me, over." The reply came.

"Control calling Able, loud and clear over," Adam took the mike, "This is Major Campbell I want the chopper sent immediately to the following coordinates, longitude 6.1 degrees latitude 9.6 degrees comply over."

"Control to Able one moment please, out." Adam then gave the mike back to the operator, saying, "Call when he returns." He then went back to Doc.

"Any luck?" asked Doc.

"They have gone to check with the Colonel, he won't like it, but he will send it when I have spoken to him." Seven minutes passed the operator called, "Major Campbell Sir," Adam went over took the mike, "Campbell over."

"Why the chopper over."

"We have a package of great value, but the package is spoiling I wouldn't ask if it wasn't important over."

"This is Pike, will comply, out." Adam handed the mike back to the operator and went over to Doc, who was checking Joe.

"How is he Doc?"

"Well believe it or not he is getting stronger."

"Its the Campbell blood Doc, does it every time!"

"When I get him back I will give him more blood and put him on a drip feed, I think he will make it. But this guy has the luck of the devil. If either the neck or the back wound had been half an inch one way or the other he would have been a goner."

"How do you mean Doc?"

"Well if the neck wound would have been half an inch higher the jugular vein would have been severed, with the back wound half an inch lower or to the right the lung would have gone."

"What are his chances?" said Adam.

"In hospital, 70-30 in favour, in my bush clinic 50-50."

"That's good enough Doc, he will make it, the Campbell blood will see to that. You know Doc he gets himself all shot up he comes off the cliff which is all of 60 feet, he then manages to avoid all they throw at him from the cliff and gun ship, he gets 100 yards or so down river climbs out and waits for us, quite a character eh Doc?" Doc got the men making up a stretcher from the vegetation.

"How long Major before the chopper gets here?"

"3 hours give or take," said Adam. True enough 3 hours later the chopper arrived, the men signalled it in, and it landed between the small signal fires. Doc got Joe settled in while the pilot had a cup of tea.

"I will see you in a couple of days or so Doc." Adam then spoke to the pilot.

"I want a fast smooth flight, the cargo is very important, is that understood?"

"Yes Sir Major no problem." the pilot was just one big smile, Adam knew and liked him. He knew the stranger would get a good flight.

The pilot got into the chopper, Joe was on the made up stretcher at the back of the seats, Doc sat next to the pilot, they moved off.

The pilot was in contact with base, there were plenty of eager hands waiting to help Doc get Joe out and settled in the clinic, Doc set up a drip feed and a blood transfusion. The clinic was a 6 bed construction made from corrugated iron and timber. For its primitive surroundings it was pretty well equipped. Joe remained unconscious for two days. On the morning of October 5th he regained consciousness, he lay there looking around as best he could.

Joe realised he was in some kind of makeshift medical centre, he could see two empty beds adjacent to his, and three opposite, a black man came walking over to him, Joe watched the man as he came over without taking his eyes off him, he had a big grin on his face,

"Well look here then!" he said, "If masser hasn't awaken! How are you feeling friend? Can I get you something, food, tea? You name it and it's yours, the Doc says when you wake you can have light food and plenty to drink."

"Where am I?" he asked.

"Well now, it's not my place to be telling you that, but I will get you a nice cup of tea." The man went away grinning from ear to ear.

He soon returned with a pot of tea and a plate of scrambled eggs. The man then went over to the office, shortly afterwards Doc came out went over to Joe.

"Good morning my friend, it is nice to see you with us, do you have any pain?

"I ache all over," said Joe, "but no pain."

"That's understandable under the circumstances," said Doc.

"My name is Trevor Reed. But you can call me Doc, everybody else does." Joe nodded, "Thanks Doc. Where am I?"

"You are at the headquarters of one of General Adejumo rebel units. We control this particular area, 250 miles East of Kasunu, we found you the day before yesterday 460 miles North of Bakra. You were in a sorry state, but you will mend OK. Who are you anyway?"

"Cross," said Joe. Jacob Cross." that being the name he used when buying the motor bike.

"Well Jake welcome." He offered his hand and Joe took it.

"I have now got the medic making you some broth with mince meat, once you are eating you will be fine." The medic brought Joe his broth and a pot of tea, they got extra pillows to prop Joe up with, he winced with the back wound.

"I guess I pulled a stitch," he said, "What was the damage

Doc?"

"Bullet wounds in your neck, back and thigh." Joe just raised his eyebrows made no comment and started on his tea, Doc went back into his office, then in a few moments came back with a syringe.

"This will ease your aching without sedating you," said Doc who then lifted the bed clothes and gave him the injection in his hip.

"Thanks Doc, I guess I owe you."

"Not at all," said Doc. "It has been a pleasure!" then he grinned. He then went back to his office leaving Joe with his meal. The medic then placed a tray across Joe's thighs and gave him a spoon.

"Can you manage Sir or should I help?"

"No thanks." he said, "I can manage, thank you and my name is Jake." He was enjoying his broth, it was the first food in 4 days, after he had finished the medic cleared away the tray and bowl. Doc came back very pleased.

"I'm glad you ate your broth, your only problem now Jake is weakness, but now you are eating you will be on your feet in no time. The wound in your neck badly tore the muscle, so your right arm will not be fully active for a time, the thigh wound is the same, you will need a stick for a spell and you could have a limp for a short time. But the muscles will all heal, and you will be as right as rain, the back wound well you were very lucky the bullet went through the shoulder blade, therefore it stopped just short of the lung, else you would have been a goner."

"What day is it Doc?" he asked.

"Friday October 5th."

"Blimey I must have been out a couple of days, yet all of a sudden I'm tired.

"That's OK, its weakness," said Doc, "Try to sleep now. When you wake up you will have some dinner, your weakness will soon pass now you are eating, you will be fine in a day or two, in a couple of weeks you will be your own self."

Shortly after noon Adam arrived back at base, he called at headquarters,

"Colonel Pike has gone to Kasunu." the Sergeant told Adam,

"The Colonel left just after your message for the chopper, he said he should be back on Saturday or Sunday." Adam left and went across to the clinic.

"Hello Doc," he said as he walked in, "How's the package?"

"Very well actually Adam, he surfaced this morning, had a bowl of broth with plenty mince and a pot of tea."

"Can you talk?" asked Adam.

"Yes but not to hold a conversation," replied the Doc, "he is extremely weak, by tomorrow he will be fine, after a few light meals you will be able to quiz him all you want, I don't think he is ready for it just yet."

"You're the boss Doc, I'll just say hello if that is alright, do we know who he is?"

"Well," said Doc, "He says Jake Cross, and he has no reason to lie."

"That sounds reasonable, I thought we would have a John Smith!" said Adam laughing. They went into the ward, Jake was still propped up on the pillows in a sitting position with his eyes closed. As the two approached his eyes opened.

"Jake?" said Doc, "This is Major Adam Campbell, Adam, Jake Cross."

Adam smiled and offered his hand, Jake took it.

"It isn't everyday one meets his own blood brother, eh Doc?"

Jake looked at Doc with a puzzled look on his face, "What Adam means Jake is, you are both the same blood group, so Adam was able to give you a blood transfusion, when we found you, and that saved your life."

"Very commendable of you Adam," said Jake "I guess I owe you, but you would probably have done me a favour, and yourselves one too if you had left me dead." At that his words trailed off and he closed his eyes.

"Well we couldn't do that could we Doc, and you a fellow Brit, anyway get some sleep we will talk tomorrow." At that Adam and Doc left him and went back to the office.

"Like I say Adam, by tomorrow when his brain and body have been fed nutriments, he will be able to answer all your questions." "Thanks Doc, you do a good job."

"Its what I'm paid for Adam, what I'm paid for."

The rebel camp was mainly standard wooden sheds, with tents as the living quarters, the headquarters were two wooden sheds constructed into one. The clinic was similar it had a 6 bed ward and an office, there were electric lights and a refrigerator, with 4 small diesel generators for the power. All the rebels lived in the tents except Doc who had a cot in the clinic office.

The showers consisted of 8 shower heads in a corrugated iron canopy type shed, with a screen across the front, the toilets were similar in construction, but inside there was a pit 18 feet deep with an elongated box over it, the box had holes in the size of the standard size toilet each hole had its own lid, and there were corrugated partitions between the holes for some measure of privacy. The officers had a separate set up from the rest of the rebels. There was also a toilet at the back of the clinic. They had there own bore hole with submersible pump, which supplied water to a 800 gallon tank on a 14 feet gantry that supplied the water gravity feed to the clinic the mess cook house and numerous stand pipes throughout the camp. The total compliment of the rebel camp was 62, the nearest village was Yoruba tribe and they were friendly with the rebels.

There was little chance that government troops would venture this deep into hostile territory, and they wouldn't know where to start anyway, in total there were 11 such contingents throughout the Northern and Eastern provinces, this was the second largest, the largest being the one led by the General himself, in the North, the one here was led by Colonel Pike who had been a Colonel in the British army, decorated in the second world war

'D S O and Bar' and during his service with the British in the Palestine police he got the 'M.C.' a formidable opponent for any government to face was Colonel Pike.

That evening in the mess tent, over the evening meal Adam asked Doc.

"How's the patient coming along?"

"Fine Adam he had scrambled egg and bacon for his evening

meal, and for breakfast tomorrow he will have pineapple followed by porridge, followed by scrambled egg."

"What are you running Doc, a clinic or a bloody five star hotel?" said Adam laughing.

"Seriously Adam, he is eating well and that is all to the good." After the evening meal Doc went back to his office, just as the medic came dashing in, "Come Sir, quickly!" They both ran into the ward, Jake was out of bed hanging onto his locker.

"What is this then?" asked Doc.

"I want to go to the toilet, and don't give me none of this bed pan nonsense."

"OK Jake steady, get me a crutch Clarence," that being the medics name, he got the crutch.

"OK here you are now, steady, take your time." Jake, with the aid of Doc and the medic, made it to the toilet at the back of the clinic, they waited outside, Jake coped OK, then he said, "I can manage without aid." he got back to the ward and went to the sink at the back, washed his hands and splashed water over his head and face, he now had a 6 day growth of grey hair over his head looking through the mirror over the sink at the back of the ward, Jake then started to laugh.

"What is the joke Jake?" asked Doc.

"Well," said Jake "My bald head now has a 6 day or so growth of grey hair to go with my full set which is black, I guess I blew my disguise."

Doc saw the funny side of it and started to laugh, along with Jake. He then walked with the aid of the crutch back to his bed.

"How we doing Doc?" he asked.

"Very well," said Doc.

"Then I will just try another lap!" he said, as he turned and started back up the ward.

Next morning Jake had two slices of pineapple then a bowl of porridge followed by scrambled egg, then he was up walking about on his crutch, doing laps of the ward, Adam then came in, "Hello Jake, it is nice to see you up and getting about, what do you think Doc?"

"All I can say it is a remarkable recovery."

"Do you feel like talking Jake?" said Adam.

"What do you want to know?" Jake replied.

"Well for starters how did you get yourself all beat up the way you did?"

"It is a long story," said Jake.

"We have plenty of time," came the reply from Adam, "I want the whole story, from beginning to end, the whole bloody story."

"Well," said Jake, "I hit the Sandies," Jake went on and told the whole story, from the time he observed the Sandies residence, then the strike at the time of the dinner dance in honour of the visiting General, the killing of the Guards with the cross bow, he left nothing out.

"But why?" asked Adam.

"Because they destroyed a friend of mine."

"Can you be more specific?"

"Well we discovered by accident that they were committing atrocities in the bush to discredit President Elido, unfortunately they got on to us with a vengeance they tried to kill me, garrote me." He then showed them the scar left by the garrote, it looked almost like a tattoo that went from the right side of his Adam's apple round to the back of his neck.

"And your friend?" said Adam.

"He is lost for all time I guess, he's dead. Like I say they tried to garrote me but I am still around, so I fled out into the bush, I disguised myself by shaving my head bald and growing a full set and darkening it with some cosmetic.

"I couldn't leave the country - Sandies and his National Guard would see to that, I decided I had nothing to lose so I'd make the bastards pay, and they did, there is only old man Sandies left, and if I live I'll get him too.

"So, Adam, you have three choices regarding me."

"And they are?" asked Adam.

"You can let me join your rebels, you can dump me back where you found me, or you can kill me, one way or the other makes no difference to me, the choice is yours I just don't care and I mean it."

"I don't run this contingent Jake, Colonel Pike makes all decisions it is up to him. But nobody is going to kill you, we fight and people do get killed, but we don't commit murder. The situation Jake will be discussed with him when he gets back from Kasunu.

In the meantime take care." Adam and Doc then went back to the office, what do you make of that Adam?"

"How do you mean Doc?"

"Well when he was giving you the three choices his look was deliberate and his voice positive."

"So?" said Adam.

"Well he meant it, he doesn't give a damn whether he lives or dies, he has problems Adam and they're not his immediate injuries."

"I see what you mean, yes," said Adam, "but we will leave that with the Colonel."

The following morning after breakfast, Jake wandered out of the clinic on his crutch and was having a look round. He looked in on Adam's tent who was studying a map, Jake put his head just inside the tent flap which was pulled back and said, "Knock knock."

Adam looked up and smiled.

"You should use the bell Jake, but come in anyway." Jake walked over to Adam saw the map and said, "Do you mind?"

"No" said Adam, "look all you want." Jake looked at the map.

"What's it all about?" he asked.

"Well I'm not sure I can tell you just at this time, we don't know if you are one of us or not."

Jake smiled, "You're careful, I like that, but what have you got to lose? I can't go anywhere, I don't even know where the bloody hell I am, I know we are surrounded by bloody jungle and I'm no Tarzan, and with a bit of luck I hope to be joining you."

Adam pointed to the map.

"See that Jake, at one time it was a live sea mammal research establishment. As you can see, it is a horse shoe type enclosure which looks out over the ocean.

The sea bed falls very steeply just a short distance from the beach, and the only way onto the beach either side is 3 miles away, unless of course you climb down the cliff, so they could study sea life, whales, sharks, you name it. Well now it is an ordinance depot, and we are thinking of hitting it." Adam was grinning all over his face.

"What is your strategy for that kind of strike?" Jake asked.

"Well to be honest I'm not much on strategy, I leave that to the Colonel, I just lead the attack, that's my field so to speak." Jake was studying the map.

"Do you have a boat Adam?"

"What the hell do we want with a boat?"

"Oh nothing," said Jake, "I was just thinking out loud."

"Come on now Jake you asked a question, you must have a reason."

"Well," said Jake, "Whenever I do anything I engineer it, that way it gets done properly."

"You mean planning? I leave that to the Colonel."

"Well you can't plan without strategy," said Jake.

"OK show me."

"Well," said Jake, "If you hit from the sea, saying as you did because of what it used to be, there are probably no perimeter barricades or barbed wire, so a relatively small party can bombard it from the North side to draw their attention, then launch a full scale attack from the beach, that would be the last thing they would expect, and you could run all over them, but of course to do that you would need a boat."

"I like it," said Adam, "I like it. There are about 150 men in the depot, they store all the National Guard armaments and equipment, and our intelligence tells us they have just received their latest consignment of the latest rocket launchers, mortars and we hear, AK 47 automatic Russian made rifles."

"The National Guard are about 20 miles away North West of the depot aren't they Adam?" asked Jake.

"Yes, why do you ask?"

"Well, during the first assault they may radio for help."

Just at that time they heard vehicles enter the camp.

"That will be the Colonel," said Adam as he got up and made

to leave. "I'll see you in the clinic later." he said as he was walking out.

Adam went in to headquarters, Colonel Pike was at his desk, Adam walked up saluted and then they shook hands, Pike was a tall man with a slight stoop his hair was greying at the temples, he was in his mid fifties. The two men then went into a deep discussion.

"You know Adam I've been thinking. The base at Kasunu have received a delivery of 6 gun ships, I would like one of them, a gun ship in our hands would be devastating."

"I agree Sir, but hitting that kind of target with what we have at this time would be damn near impossible, they would scramble the ships and see us off in no time Sir."

"Yes, this will need a lot of thought. Now what is this package you brought back with you Adam?"

"He is a civilian Sir, he is the man who hit the Sandies, he was hurt pretty bad, but he is making a good recovery." Adam then told Pike the story, exactly as Jake had told him. Pike then went into his briefcase and took out several newspapers, he gave them to Adam, "According to the papers, the white man, who was bald and wore a beard, had a contingent of more than 50 rebels with him on the hit."

"No Sir he was alone."

"Yes, the General knows that, none of his men were involved, that story is to save face."

"Well Sir, like I say he was shot up pretty bad, he was all but dead but Doc works miracles sometimes, and now he is on the mend. And he wants to join us."

"Well Adam let us analyse his actions from the story. First he observes the Sandies residence so he knows their every move, exactly where they will be at a particular time, then he takes out the guard with a crossbow, that shows professional cunning. Then he gets into the house when he knows he will get the Sandies in that particular room together, that shows planning, then he blows them apart using the guards own automatic rifle, alerting the rest of the guard that has been guarding them since the Elido assassination. He then takes on the guard and kills 5 of them, that shows he can fight, he then escapes on a motorbike and makes 400 miles or more before they catch up with him. The exercise shows planning, cunning, tenacity, courage, and madness. A chance in a million Adam and he pulled it off."

"Well like I say Colonel, he wants to join us, he is quite a strategist too Sir he has given some ideas for hitting the ordinance depot."

"OK Adam let us have a word with him. Sergeant go bring the stranger we have in the clinic."

Now Jake had studied the map a little deeper when Adam had gone out, and he had formed a plan as to how he would deal with ordinance depot then he went back to the clinic just as the Sergeant arrived. He then followed the Sergeant back to headquarters. Jake was stripped to the waist, and covered in bandages, he had on a pair of Doc's old slacks and a pair of his sandals.

Jake walked over and stood in front of the Colonels desk, Pike stood and offered his hand, they shook hands.

"How are you feeling?" said Pike.

"I'm fine Sir, give me a couple of days when Doc has taken out my stitches, and I'll be able and prepared for whatever you decide to do with me."

"Well Mr Cross Major Campbell tells me you want to join us."

"That is right Sir." replied Jake.

"What military experience do you have?" asked Pike.

"Five years in the Para's" replied Jake.

"What rank did you attain?" asked Pike.

"I finished as a Sergeant. You see Sir, I was picked as one of a specialist group of twelve men, we were trained by Major Hall of the Special Air Service and we were known as Major Hills commandos. We were trained in ambush and anti-ambush general guerrilla activity. I saw action in Korea first and then later we were stationed in the canal zone, as it was known then. There was a good bit of terrorist activity and I got plenty of experience in insurgency and counter insurgency warfare

"I see," said Pike, "and what are you in civilian life?"

"I'm a mechanical engineer Sir."

117

"I see. Well Mr Cross the Major tells me you are something of a strategist, and have given him some ideas on hitting the ordinance depot." Jake shrugged.

"Show me," said Pike. Now Jake had given this a lot of thought during the time Adam had been with the Colonel. Pike led them over to a chart table, he then selected a chart, it was a particular blown up detail of the ordinance depot, and surrounding terrain.

"Well Colonel like I say if I had a fishing vessel, or yacht, I don't see anything unusual about that, anchored as near to shore as practical. Then at a given time late at night or better still early morning, when all sane people are in bed, you lower over the side inflatable dinghy's, to carry say 40 men and their armaments, they beach and silently get as close to the depot as possible. Then from the North you launch a diversionary attack, this would draw their attention to that side which is the logical side to attack from. Then at a preset time the 40 men overrun the place, that Colonel is my strategy or the way I would engineer the strike.

"Also the Major tells me the NG keep their armaments there, so no doubt the first sign of trouble they would be contacted for assistance. Now according to the map there is only one way down to the depot from the main A5 highway, and that is this track," said Jake pointing to a particular area, "which is one and a half to two miles from the depot. Well I would mine the track, and by putting dynamite either side of the track at strategic points back towards the high way. How much and what distance would depend on how many men we would estimate they would send. This of course will be prepared before the diversionary attack is launched. Then when the lead vehicle hit the mine I would blow the rest and have say half a dozen men go in and finish off. Well Colonel that is the way I see it, but it will need planning, and of course the timing is critical."

"Why critical Jake?" asked Adam.

Pike was watching Jake with great interest.

"Well," said Jake, "let us assume you have a couple of mortars, then from the north side at 12 midnight we strike, such as myself with say 18 or 20 men attack with machine gun fire or whatever, then you Adam with 40 men who have been in position, waiting 4 minutes exactly, after the first diversionary salvo launches the main attack.

Now once you are on the depot, 12 minutes after the first diversionary salvo, I take 6 men leaving 12 men with mortars and machine guns to maintain the attack on the north side, and go to the ambush site.

The NG are 20 miles away to the North West, say it takes them 4 minutes to mobilise, that means they could be at the depot in 20 minutes. I leave after 12 minutes taking 3 to get to site that will give me 3 minutes to get ready. OK, the lead vehicle goes up, I then detonate the dynamite then my 6 men go in and finish off where needs be. I then get quickly back to the depot and help Adam with the spoils."

Colonel Pike was rubbing his chin in deep thought.

"Yes I like it, I do indeed like it, we have connections getting the boat should be simple enough, I've lived in Ligeria for the last 20 years Jake I know it better than my own home town, I will plan the strike along the lines you have outlined, and welcome to our happy band. They shook hands. "Fix Jake up with all the gear and clothing Adam with the rank of captain."

"Will do Sir it will be my pleasure." he shook hands with Jake, "welcome blood brother."

"Jake," Pike said, "As a mercenary under the command of General Adejumo, you will receive 1200 dollars a month, American dollars that is, if you give the Sergeant details of your bank account in UK we are paid via the National Bank of Ghana."

"I don't have a bank account in the UK colonel."

"Well, whatever you want to do or where ever you want to send it, give the details to the Sergeant and all will be arranged."

Jake gave his wife Jane's bank account number and bank address commenting casually it was his sister.

The details would be sent to the general in Kano headquarters, he would see to the arrangements, the next two weeks passed very quickly, Jake was walking quite normally, his hair was crew cut he still had the beard it was now grey. Whilst Jake was getting kitted out in the stores with Adam, who made the comment about the ambush he should take care, and not do as he did when he hit the Sandies, for the National Guard were a crack regiment and he should not take chances.

"I'm a cat Adam I have 9 lives."

"A cat you may be, but just a little care eh Jake?" these comments casual as they seemed at the time were to have a great significance on Jake's career as a mercenary.

The last two weeks Jake had lived in the clinic under a thorough course of physiotherapy, to rebuild and strengthen the muscles in his thigh and shoulder. He now had his own tent next to Adam.

Pike sent for Adam and Jake, "Well gentlemen all is arranged, the strike on the ordinance depot will take place next Sunday, at 2-0am, you Adam will take the land cruiser and three 3 ton trucks with 40 men, you will have one rocket launcher, and each man will have a Heckler and Koch automatic rifle, 10 magazines in his pouches and 4 hand grenades, you will leave Monday morning. You should arrive at the border with Benin in the early hours of Saturday morning. You cross the border and move direct south to this point," said Pike tapping the chart with his pointer, "Now Adam, this is the tricky bit, to reach the beach you have to cross the main highway, so you cross no more than 3 at a time, but I leave that to your own judgment. At 4-0am you will be picked up by 3 long boats which will beach whilst you load up, you will then be taken out to a trawler, you will then have in the region of 18 hours to prepare. The trawler will then sail to within 100 yards of the beach, here it will slow almost to a stop, you will have 10 inflatable dinghy's. Get into the sea and make for the beach, it goes without saying that you will all be blacked up. It will be a moonless night so you should be able to get to within 50 yards or so of the base. Dig in and wait, the first salvo will be at precisely 2am, exactly 6 minutes after this salvo you launch your attack.

"Captain, you will have 20 men with two mortars, two Bren guns and the same armaments as the Major's men. You will leave on Tuesday and will position yourselves and fire your first salvo at 2-0am precisely. It is important not to hit the main stores, because we don't want to damage our equipment," he said with a wry smile, "at

120

say 12 midnight you Captain will go to the ambush site and plant your one and only limpet mine. This area here I select as the ambush site," said Pike tapping the chart at the selected area, "then Captain you will place your dynamite, you will have Shan with you, he is an Asian electronics expert who will set up the dynamite, he will be dressed in regular army uniform. He and two others will set up a road block to keep civilian traffic off the mined track. They will not get involved in any action, they will go down with you Captain then return immediately after the ambush, bringing back the detonators. Captain you will arrive at 10-0pm which will give you plenty of time to set yourself up. I know this particular area that you want to deal with have you planned it?

"Yes Sir I know exactly what is required, after I have my men in position I take 8 men and go to lay the mine, it will be so laid that no matter which side of the track the vehicle is on it will go. Now Sir the Major tells me the NG will send at least 150 men, OK, that will require ten 3 ton trucks, therefore the convoy will reach back for at least 75 yards, so with the Asian technician and my 8 men we lay the dynamite, ten 5 pounder's at 10 yard intervals alternatively either side of the track.

They will be wired to two detonators both sides of the track 40 yards back into the bush, the dynamite is reaching back 100 yards that is to ensure the entire length of the convoy is covered. Having set up the ambush, I will be back in plenty of time for the diversionary attack. Then precisely 12 minutes after the first salvo I leave with 8 men leaving 12 to carry on with the attack, I will travel in the range cruiser, I should arrive in 3 minutes leaving me 3 or 4 minutes to spare, then as soon as the lead vehicles hits the mine, Shan and I detonate the dynamite. Then Sir me and my 8 men will tidy up, see Shan off back to base, then get back to the depot to assist the Major."

"You may need more than 8 men for an exercise like that," said Adam.

"No, believe me 8 men is all I will need," said Jake. "Then I will return and help you Major with the spoils, I don't see why you should have all the fun!"

"Well gentlemen that about covers it, any questions!"

"I have one Sir," said Jake. "It will be one thing sneaking down there, it will be a different story coming back."

"Good point Captain, but the NG will be preoccupied with their convoy loss, and the regular army will not want to get involved unless they are ordered to by the chiefs of staff and I know they will leave well alone. We have two small contingents in the South Eastern province, they will cover your rear end coming back, and that is a chance we take, plus the fact you will look like regular army anyway. And remember gentlemen we take no prisoners."

It was now Monday 22nd, Adam set off at first light for his rendezvous with the long boats and trawler. Jake set off on the Tuesday. They always gave themselves plenty of time to get to their particular rendezvous, because their policy was always stick to bush, never use the highways. Adam arrived at the rendezvous with time to spare, so they killed time in the bush before crossing the highway to the beach. As night fell they crossed over to the beach and within a few minutes the long boats were there, collected the men and rowed them to the trawler. On board, Adam got the men organised and made all the necessary preparations, then bedded down. They now had 18 hours before the strike.

Jake arrived to within 40 yards of the front of the depot. He made all arrangements, then went and laid the limpet mine and set up the dynamite bombs.

Jake then went back to the depot to wait, having left Shan with two other rebels manning the road block. In the meantime Adam and his 40 men were now rowing to the beach in the darkness which suited the situation, they pulled their dinghies onto the beach, they fanned out and started their approach up the beach towards the depot. They got to within 20 yards, then stopped. Adam had his gunner next to him as they waited, the gunner held the rocket launcher to his shoulder, aiming at the rear guard house, his two colleagues held the rockets.

Jake had set up his mortars, each one having a compliment of three gunners, at precisely 2-0am the first mortar fired, and scored a direct hit on the front guard house, then the mortar shells were falling like hail stones, this plus the constant bren gun fire were causing panic and devastation, Adam was watching the luminous dial on his watch, 6 minutes passed, he nodded now, the gunner fired the first rocket, which hit the guard house situated in the centre of the rear perimeter wall which was no more than 3 feet high. Then the 40 rebels lead by Adam advanced at the double firing their Heckler & Koch automatic from the hip.

They stormed the rear of the depot overwhelming the guards that hadn't perished.

Jake, in an open Range Rover, drove up and in through the front entrance of the depot, he and his eight men were stood up in the vehicle firing their Heckler & Koch's from the hip, Jake was followed by a second vehicle in a similar fashion. His party then dropped from their vehicle, the driver staying with the vehicle. Jake then ran towards a group of a dozen or so troops, firing as he ran gunning them down, he was about to enter the barrack block as a group of troops were coming out, he was too close to use his gun, so he started to butt, kick and punch with his free hand, his Heckler & Koch held in his left.

He made just enough room then started shooting. He killed them all, Jake was now in the block followed by his men, they were gunning down the troops as they were coming down the stairs, Jake removed one grenade from his pouch, hooked the ringed pin round his trigger finger, then snatched the grenade in a back handed movement extracting the pin and flinging it all in one movement onto the landing of the staircase, Jake then dropped into a crouch at the bottom of the staircase wall, the grenade exploded, bringing down the staircase and the troops with it. Jake was shouting orders to his men, and they were shouting warnings to him, referring to him as Captain Cat.

They all then ran out. The driver had turned the vehicle and was just approaching the block as Jake appeared and dived into the vehicle followed by his men, and they were off to the ambush site.

The noise of the battle at the depot could be heard at the ambush site, all was now set and ready. Shan was on one detonator and a rebel was on the other, on opposite sides of the track. Within minutes the NG came tearing down the highway, turned onto the track the lead vehicle carrying the commissioned ranks hit the mine. There was a tremendous explosion and the vehicle disintegrated, then the dynamite was detonated, with one hell of an explosion. Before the debris had finished falling, Jake was up and screaming, running to the nearest truck that hadn't been blown to pieces, he leaped onto the bonnet then onto the cab then up onto the tubular frame that held the canvas canopy, he would then empty magazine after magazine through the canvas, he then jumped down and headed for the next, he was shooting at anything that moved or seemed to move, he was a man possessed.

There were vehicles on their sides, some completely turned over, with NG men crawling or staggering out and Jake was in there amongst them gunning them to pieces. As his magazine emptied he would start to kick and to club, only when he got a minute would he reload. He was screaming cursing fighting and taking unbelievable chances. Then the petrol tanks started to explode, his men were shouting warnings but he didn't hear, the Sergeant named Lotti grabbed Jake pulling and turning, the tank exploded flooring them both.

Then Jake was on his feet in amongst it looking for action,

"Captain Cat Sir!" shouted Lotti from the deck, "Its over, can't you see Sir its finished." Jake stopped, he was in a daze trying to gather his faculties, from a man possessed to one in control.

Then he realised and looked at Lotti, he then went quickly to him helping him to his feet.

"There is nothing left Sir it is finished."

"I know Sergeant, I know, thank you." he then turned, screaming at his men. "Back to the depot now, move, come on Sergeant." he said in a quite normal voice, "lets go."

They ran to their vehicle, leaving Shan with his two men to gather any spoils and head back to base. They all got to their vehicle and headed back to the depot, the entire exercise had taken 18 minutes.

They arrived back at the depot, Jake was out and firing at anything above ground, he spotted Adam pinned down by a machine gun that was situated just below the single storey warehouse, Jake read the situation and ran to a maintenance ladder that was attached to the gable end.

"Cover me!" he screamed at his men. Putting his sub machine gun round his neck by the carrying sling, he was on the ladder going up, once on the roof he ran across then down the front of the building, taking hold of his gun ready to fire, then taking a quick look he jumped off feet first, firing as he fell, and landing feet first in amongst the five gunners.

Adam saw it all with disbelief.

"The bloody nut case!" he said to himself. There was shooting, shouting, screaming and cursing, then silence, coming from the machine gun post.

Adam ran across followed by his men, he looked down into the machine gun post, there was Jake sat amongst the dead bodies covered in blood and brains, he grinned up at Adam, saying "What kept you?" Adam reached in and grabbed Jake's outstretched hand, saying "You bloody nut case, you could have broke both your fucking legs, that is all of 10 feet!" he then yanked Jake out in a not too gentle manner, "That Captain, is asking for trouble."

"Details, details." replied Jake, "Well that's it Major, broken legs or no, the depot is ours." Adam then turned, shouting orders to his men to get into the warehouse, get every truck they could, and start loading up. They were soon loading the depot's own trucks with spoils, they had 8 modern sophisticated hand held type rocket launchers, with 100 rockets, 12 mortars with 250 motor shells, 50 limpet mines, 1,000 hand grenades 200 AK 47 automatics with 200 cases of ammunition, 100 colt 45 revolvers, with 100 cases of bullets.

Also they got 300 cartons of whisky, 200 Martell Brandy, 75 Gin and 700 cartons of tinned beer, they also took the refrigerated truck full of sides of beef, pork, bacon and sausages, cartons of tea and coffee, a small 600 gallon diesel tanker, and a petrol tanker.

"Not a bad haul eh Major?" said Jake.

It was now 7-0am and the convoy moved off, leaving what personnel were still alive, military and a few civilians, in total confusion after making them assist in loading the trucks. They had been travelling now for 19 hours, the convoy consisted of 9 three ton trucks 4 Range Rovers, two Land Rovers one refrigerated truck a diesel and a petrol tanker. Adam was leading in a Land Rover, Jake brought up the rear also in a Land Rover.

Adam halted the convoy, called Jake and the Sergeants together,

"We will take a 5 hour break, post the guard, one Sergeant and five men, then the Captain and myself will take the last two duties." The guard detail was posted prowling around the small clearing where they had made camp. The men built fires and cooked bacon which they ate with a can of beer, Jake sat with Adam as they ate their bacon and drank their beer, Adam then went talking to Sergeant Lotti and the men who fought with Jake. "He fights like a mad man! He doesn't care! He takes crazy chances!" How he lives they just couldn't say, "He is a devil! He never gets hurt it is unbelievable, he is defying death!"

"No," said Adam, "The Captain is a well trained British officer, that is how we won two world wars."

"Then we will win this one eh Major?"

"Yes we will win this one and that's a fact!" replied Adam.

Adam then went back to Jake.

"You know Jake you have made a name for yourself, the men say you fight like the devil."

"They are good men Adam, they fight well and do as they are told."

"They would be afraid not to Jake they say you are the devil himself."

"Why do you suppose they call me Captain Cat Adam?"

"I don't know but you did tell me you were a cat that had 9 lives, well I guess someone overheard and it has stuck, they are a superstitious lot you know, they believe in Voodoo and all that crap, and the Cat is a devil to be feared, they will follow you to the ends of the earth now Jake, at least you will always know that you will be able to trust your men. Get some sleep Jake, you've got 3 hours."

It took the convoy 8 days to reach base, it was now 9-0am on the 8th day they got down from their vehicles, Adam and Jake went straight into headquarters.

"Good morning gentlemen, it is good to see you and congratulations on your very successful outing."

"Thank you Colonel," said Adam. "We have the spoils outside." He quickly ran through the arms, etc. "That's it approximately anyway." Pike then called his Sergeant.

"Get a few helpers Sergeant and do an inventory of the supplies the Major brought back will you." The Sergeant came to attention. "Yes Sir." and left.

"Well gentlemen you are all across the papers, the NG claim they were ambushed by a contingent of 800 men backed by artillery."

"No, just twelve men, Sir. No artillery."

"Shall we sit down gentlemen?" going to Pikes desk Adam and Jake grabbed two chairs and sat down.

"Well gentlemen like I say you have certainly made the papers, how is this for head lines, Bakra News:- 'The Cat strikes in two places at the same time' who is this Captain Cat who can be in two places at the same time? The ordinance depot in Bakra was bombarded from the sea by battle cruisers, followed by the invasion by a battalion of infantry, at the same time the NG was ambushed by 800 trained commandos backed by artillery, both attacks led by the Cat who is a devil himself," it went on and on.

"How many men did we lose Major?" asked Pike.

"12 Sir," he said, "I don't think that is bad Sir, they must have lost 100 plus."

"One man is too many Adam, but it could have been worse, I appreciate that," said Pike.

"The only man I would expect to lose Sir is Jake, he is a bloody nut case, head first, feet first, no caution just in amongst it."

"I..." Jake was about to try and justify himself.

"Please gentlemen, this is not an inquest, the exercise has had a success rate beyond what I believed possible, you see the government will now have their chiefs of staff together, and undoubtedly they will believe that we are far better equipped then we really are, they will believe us to be a full scale military force backed to some degree by ships, and in fact it was 62 men two mortars and one rocket launcher, and who is this devil you have recruited called the Cat?"

"That is our secret weapon Sir," said Adam.

"Now hold on!" But Pike interrupted as Jake was once again about to start. Pike had a big grin on his face, and Adam was laughing. The next ten days were quiet, then Adam and Jake took Sergeant Lotti and 4 men to ambush a government armoured payroll truck, going from Florin to Kebba, with the payroll for a small dam project that was being built on the river Liger, where it flows into

Auna Lake. It was a simple exercise, but as Adam put it, it saves having a cash flow problem, half a million Guineas.

They had built corrugated iron and timber warehouses to store their new arms and equipment, and compounds to keep their newly acquired trucks.

The orderly sergeant went over to Jake. "The Colonel would like to see you Captain." Jake went across to head quarters, he noticed two rebels he hadn't seen before standing outside, they came to attention and salute as Jake approached, Jake nodded and tipped the bush hat he wore, he went inside the Colonel was sitting at his desk. Sat in front of it was a sergeant that Jake didn't know, as he approached the sergeant jumped to his feet and saluted knocking over his chair, Jake saluted Pike.

"As you were Sergeant," said Pike, he then corrected his chair and sat down again, for whatever reason the Sergeant looked very apprehensive afraid even.

"I would like you to meet Sergeant Creda, Captain, he has come form our mid west contingent, he is here with a request for your services." Jake looked at the Sergeant and offered his hand, the Sergeant was on his feet again.

"Shake hands with the Captain, Sergeant," said Pike. They shook hands, Major Hanslow wants to hit the ordinance depot in their area, he would like to know if he could borrow your services to lead the mission, Jake looked again at the Sergeant, who's eyes were popping wide open, he was obviously very unhappy in Jake's company.

Superstition can have a very unbalancing affect on some African tribes, this man as it turns out is Yorubar. To Jake all this superstition business was a pain in the arse.

"It is up to you Sir, you say go I will go."

"I would like you to Captain, if you can pull this off it would be good for the morale of the cause and devastating for the government."

"Then I will go Sir, and I'll pull it off, you can bet on it."

"I know you will Captain and that's a fact, and it will keep you in trim for the big one."

Jake Cross went and had an unbelievable demoralising effect on the Ligerian Government, and the armed forces, just as Pike had envisaged. It was to Jake a relatively simple exercise, but again the papers were full of it, 'The Cat strikes again', and all that crap, over the next 9 months Jake operated with several contingents of rebels throughout Ligeria, whoever requested his services, Pike would send him, and Jake was happy to go.

The cat was feared throughout the whole of Ligeria, Jake had arrived back at base, having satisfied all the contingents of rebel forces that had requested his services, the Cat had now become a Legend.

He went into headquarters.

"Captain how nice to see you." They shook hands.

"I see from the papers that you enjoyed yourself."

"Yes Sir it is all rather simple really, you hit where and when they least expect it, you can't miss, if they ever knew we were coming, then it would be a different story."

"Well Jake I have some serious work that I've been considering, after you have rested and cleaned up, I will discuss it with you and Adam." Just as Jake was about to leave Adam came in. "Hello Jake nice to see you I believe you have had a whale of a time."

"Something like that," he replied they shook hands.

"I sure have missed my drinking partner since you have been away, did you want me Colonel?" said Adam.

"Yes Adam I have for some time now been considering hitting the Kasunu air force base, they have 6 helicopter gun ships, and I want one, Jake you are the strategist what do you think?"

"Well Sir it covers a big area, it is going to need a lot of thought, if you don't mind Sir, I would like to take a shower and get something to eat, I think better on a full stomach, then I feel sure between the three of us we will come up with something."

"Of course Jake, I do apologise, you have had a long journey, we will resume after dinner." Adam and Jake left the office, when they were outside Adam said "Pike is crazy we would never pull of a caper like that, it would take at least 2,000 men and at the first sign of trouble they would scramble the gun ships, and we would be cut to pieces."

"Yes," said Jake, "They are devastating machines, that's why he wants one I guess."

"Lets have a quick drink Jake before you take a shower."

"OK," said Jake. "I can stand the smell if you can I guess I'm really high," he said pulling his shirt with finger and thumb from his chest. They sat in Adam's tent drinking malt whiskey. Jake was deep in thought.

"It could be done Adam from the inside."

"But how does one get an army on the inside?" he replied.

"It could be done from the inside over a period of a few weeks if necessary."

"How?"

"By mining the whole bloody area with radio controlled mine, explosive planted over the entire base, in stores that nobody ever enters, compounds that are hardly ever used, every where all over the fucking base we have bombs waiting to go off. We would need good men on the inside, technicians, then on the last minute we attach limpet mines to five of the six gun ships, then just prior to the attack we let the whole lot go with a bang."

"You are enjoying your bloody self just thinking about it aren't you?" laughed Adam.

"I'll see you at dinner Adam I must go for a shower." Jake went into his own tent, threw off his pack, stripped off wrapped a towel around his waist and went to the shower. He stood under the shower head, and turned on the tap, and let the water pelt him it was quite warm, with the sun being on the pipe work all day, he felt good just letting the water rid him of the grime one picks up travelling through the bush.

He finished his shower, wrapped the towel around him turned off the tap and went back to his tent, by the time he was back he was dry, even his hair which was kept cut in a crew cut by the camp barber, he still had his full set which was grey like his hair, it saved him shaving each morning.

He dressed in jungle green trousers a tee shirt and sandals, then went to the mess tent he sat down and shouted for the chef, he

131

came round from the back where he had a diesel cooking range, in a wooden shed, "I'm a little early for dinner chef I know that, but is there any coffee ready?"

"Yes Sir one moment." The chef then brought Jake a pot of coffee, he sat there with it, thinking about the air force base in Kasunu. It was one hell of a job to take on, but the idea behind it was to steal a gun ship not take the base, and that is feasible surely he told himself.

If the authorities knew, it would be in their own interest to give us one he thought, at this Jake chuckled, then as the thought sunk in he laughed out loud. Just as Adam and Pike walked in.

"What is the joke eh?" asked Adam, as they approached and sat down.

"I was just thinking about this strike the Colonel is planning to get us a gun ship," Pike smiled, and what is so funny about that Jake?"

"Well Sir, one way or another we are going to get a gun ship, and that's a fact."

"Correct," said Pike.

"Well Sir, it would be in the authorities own interest to give us one, it would sure save them a lot of pain." At that Adam roared with laughter.

"And you know Sir," said Adam, "The irony of it is Jake is right, and the authorities will know it," Pike chuckled to himself at the thought.

"Yes gentlemen, I will write to them tomorrow." That set Adam off again roaring with laughter.

The chef then served the evening meal, which was as usual stew. After the meal Pike got up to leave.

"Tomorrow morning gentlemen my office 7-0am, we plan our strategy for the Base strike. Good night."

"Buy you a drink Jake?" said Adam.

"I thought you'd never ask," replied Jake. They both went to Adam's tent, he got two glass tumblers, and a bottle of whisky from his refrigerator, filled the tumblers and gave one to Jake,

"Here's looking at you sunshine," he said, and they both started drinking.

The following morning Jake was in the office at 6-30am, the Sergeant had got him a pot of coffee, he was studying the detailed chart of the Kasunu base, and area, Pike came in.

"Good morning Captain I see you have made an early start, I like that."

"Yes Sir, now you have got me thinking about it, I'll have no peace with myself until it is done."

"Splendid," said Pike, "I like that attitude." At 7-0am Adam came in made his greetings and they got down to it. Jake spoke.

"I know this strike has been going on in your mind for some time now, and we don't have the men to take the base, but we can steal a gunship cause a lot of damage and embarrass the government. I've given it a lot of thought, having studied the charts and maps of the area, we can do the job with the men we have, but it will have to be an inside job, take this building here,"

Jake pointed to a small building at the extreme right hand corner of the base, a little further down than the main hanger, it was close to the back perimeter fence, which backed on to the desert and ran parallel to the Kasunu airport main runway.

"This is the transformer house, I could load that up with limpet mines, the ones we got from the depot caper, but having done that we need to get them planted. Colonel have we any people on the base?"

"Yes we have four that I can trust," said Pike, "All of them dedicated to our cause, they are a Gloria Vora, she is chief admin, Gerald Shanti these people are both Asian, Gerald was a barrister before he defended the wrong person, now he is a maintenance manager, and Joshua and Gerimia Moto brothers both technical store men."

"Excellent," said Jake, "Then they can retrieve the mines from the transformer house, and plant them. I've been discussing various aspects of explosives with Shan, and he tells me that he could make the limpet mines radio controlled. Now to do most damage and allow us to steal a gun ship, we must bring down this hangar roof, and this main barrack block we must cause as much damage to as possible, it is 4 storeys, now we couldn't destroy it, we couldn't possibly plant enough mines to do that, so we do enough damage so that when the men come pouring out of it, and they will be in the hundreds, we will be on our merry way."

All aspects of these particular buildings were discussed at length, then they broke for lunch, after lunch they carried on with the strike plans. Jake asked for and was given a box of matches, which he emptied in front of himself, he then placed matches in pairs across the rear of base inside the perimeter fence, each pair about 10 yards apart, he then put a continuous line of matches right across the rear of the base forward of the pairs, then again using matches he put barriers across the road ways outside the front main entrance of the base.

Jake then went on to explain, "These are detour barriers to keep the front of the base clear, they will be manned by police our own of course, but the uniforms must be authentic."

"No problem," said Pike.

"Oh yes, said Jake, placing two paper clips at either corner of the rear perimeter fence, and the empty match box at the centre well to the rear of it.

"We may as well have a little propaganda." It was now well into evening the Sergeant brought sandwiches and coffee, Jake then went on.

"Now we need at least 3 Mammy wagons." (Mammy wagon is a slang expression for bus.) They are termed such because there are no regulations governing their use, when a bus is full people hang on, from anywhere and anyhow they can, from open windows, they even lie on top, the entire bus is enveloped by bodies.

"OK our men will be dressed in peasants clothes hanging all over the Mammy wagons, they will come in from the North of Kasunu airport, they arrive hanging all over the bus with their weapons inside, they drive up to the barrier and are directed by our own police to this street, and then into this back entry, where they get off the bus discard their peasant dress retrieve their weapons, and wait for the signal.

The Mammy wagons will then be driven off and abandoned at

least 10 miles away. Now let us for arguments sake say the strike is for 10-0pm I dispose of the back perimeter guards with crossbow, or some other silent means, "Adam and Pike were hanging on to every word.

"At 9-45pm having disposed of the guard I will cut the rear perimeter fence and drive onto the base dressed as a flight lieutenant in my jeep, that has been painted exactly as one of theirs, I drive up and stick a limpet mine on each of the five gun ships, leaving just one the one we are going to steal."

"That's madness!" said Adam,

"Why?" said Jake, "A flight lieutenant driving a base jeep on the base, nobody will take a blind bit of notice, and that is a chance I take. All mines are radio active so in the unlikely even I am caught I shall have left instructions for all the mines to be blown anyway. To get back to my strategy, when all the mines are correctly placed on the five gun ships, I drive back to the rear perimeter, then at 10-0pm precisely, I detonate the mines, and bang! The whole bloody place goes up. Now Adam, Colonel, the frontal assault is all yours, I have neither the knowledge or experience to tackle it. But timing is critical we are talking of seconds, it will be a matter of blasting your way up to the one remaining gun ship, getting the Colonel in then getting the hell out of it. At the moment the blast noise has died I will start the generator and start the stereo gear to spout the propaganda, with a little theatrical stuff, this here," said Jake pointing to the single line of matches.

"Is polystyrene soaked in petrol these," pointing to the pairs of matches, "will be my rebels in pairs each will be soaked in water with gloves face masks and goggles. The stereo starts blasting Wagners 'Ride of the Valkyries', followed by the taped voice which will be weird, spouting the devil is amongst you, first the Sandies, then your ordinance depot, now your base I spew out my demons, to exterminate you all. I then fire the polystyrene with the flame thrower then the rebels with their AK 47 autos wrapped in asbestos blanket jump through the flames one at a time in line firing their autos on repetition, this part of the exercise will distract and confuse, and possibly frighten anybody who may be in a position to act. I then

135

follow my men through, we make for the vehicle compound, take 6 quad vehicles and race for the main entrance, picking up our foot soldiers and getting the hell out of it.

On our way out of the city we blast petrol stations as we pass them, starting explosions and fires, to keep everybody's mind off chasing us. It is timing we need to be in and out in well under an hour to be successful, I estimate to be successful 40 minutes maximum."

"That's my strategy as I see it, it now needs detailed planning, that's it Colonel."

"Well Jake I like it."

"Good because I was up half the night figuring it out." Adam then said.

"What about the men jumping through the flames they will be burnt to a chip!"

"No, like I say Major they will be totally covered, and wet through, the flame at best will be 2 inches deep, when the men jump and hit the flame, they will be travelling in excess of 20 miles an hour, they won't be in the flames for one tenth of a second, not even long enough to get dry.

Well Colonel if that is acceptable to you could you arrange a meeting with your people on the base. The whole idea behind this exercise is to give yourself and the Major time to get you to the gun ship, which must be all of 300 yards from the front main entrance, so detailed discussions with your people on base Colonel are vital, one slip and all will be lost."

"Captain the strategy is good, the Major and I will plan it along those lines, thank you gentlemen we will call it a day.

"Come on Jake I will buy you a drink."

They went over to Adam's tent, he got out the two familiar tumblers, then the bottle of malt whisky filled both tumblers handed one to Jake then he raised his glass saying, "Here's looking at you sunshine," they both then started drinking. Jake sat down leaned back in his chair just looking in to space and drinking, as their tumblers emptied Adam would top them up, time passed they were now starting on their 3rd bottle, Jake was thinking of his Janie and their children, they would have the £30,000 insurance money, plus the 1200 Dollars a month that would go in Janie's account, she wouldn't know where from or why, but that didn't matter as long as she got it that was what mattered.

He tried to dismiss the thoughts of Jane, for he could never go back to her, not now his hands had shed too much blood for him ever to be able to hold her or their children again, Joe Tully was dead, but the bastards who killed him would pay, and were paying. He had paid, everything in life that mattered was now lost to him, so therefore he didn't want anything, only to make the bastards responsible for the whole goddamn thing pay.

He thought of the atrocities he had committed since the whole business started, he Joe Tully the harmless Mr average, was now known and feared as the Cat, he had, had more than his nine lives, but time must run out he hoped.

The cat, he had only ever been a pussy cat, at that he laughed! All his life a pussy cat, at these thoughts he laughed out loud he laughed and laughed.

"Share the joke Jake, you haven't spoke a word all night." Jake controlled himself just enough to tell Adam.

"I never was much of a ladies man Adam, and once a woman called me a pussy cat, he then pointed to himself, me! A pussy cat," Adam saw the funny side of it and roared with laughter, starting Jake off again, they were both now helpless with laughter.

It was 10-30pm and bellows of laughter was coming from Adam's tent, a few of the rebels were having a quiet drink in the open in their area, they had a table outside and on it they had lit candles in bottles, they were sat round thinking of their wives and families and talking, they also missed and worried about their loved ones. They looked across at Adam's tent with pensive looks on their faces, they all had the apprehensive feeling towards the Cat as they knew Jake to be, as long as he was with them they would be winners, but the devil is the devil and in their hearts they feared him and believed they would be better off without him, no good could come of associating with the devil.

Adam and Jake collapsed in fits of laughter, they were both

very drunk. At 6-30am next morning Jake awoke, he was on the camp bed, there was one such bed in each of their tents for these such occasions, which were regular. He was fully dressed, he swung his legs to the floor and sat up, elbows on knees head in hands, Adam had awoke earlier, he was lying on his bed fully dressed, he said.

"How do you feel Jake?"

"Never better," he replied, "My head and my back are in agony, but me I'm fine." Jake then got up his hands into the small of his back then arched himself.

"This back of mine is broken." he said.

"I'll take a shower," he then went over to the shower, Adam joined him, they both walked under a shower and turned on the tap, and let the cool water pelt down on them. It felt great, they were both fully clothed, Jake then started to shed his clothes, the medic came in he had been watching for them since

6-0am, he handed them both a tablet of soap, and they started to lather up, then Jake rinsed himself off and walked out of the shower and turned it off, he took the towel the medic handed him, wrapped it around his waist and walked out leaving Adam in the shower, it was now a beautiful morning.

It was 1-0pm when Jake walked into the mess tent, Adam had eaten and was now on his third pot of coffee. Jake sat down.

"Whats for eats?" he asked.

"Stew," replied Adam, at that the medic came over and set down a bowl of stew in front of Jake. In addition to assisting Doc, which is what he'd been trained to do, he also acted as valet to all 4 of them.

"When will Doc be back?" asked Jake.

"Don't know," said Adam.

"He goes into Kasunu for the supplies which he buys little by little at each pharmacy, and then he stays there a few days, sometimes he likes to do a tour of the brothels."

"Lucky for some," said Jake.

"If it is a woman you want Jake that is no problem, I can get you a clean one in the village."

"No thanks Adam it is my back that needs attention not my

prick."

"Its all these late nights," said Adam.

"Your right," said Jake."

After lunch Jake went to base workshops and spoke to Shan the Asian electronics engineer, or he was until he turned thief, and made a good thing out of stealing software, plus the odd piece of hardware, but the company a construction company in Kasunu tumbled to him and he had been running ever since, until he joined up with the rebels. Jake explained what he wanted.

"Similar to what we have talked about, only this time it is for real, I want to be able to detonate the limpet mines by radio control."

"No problem if I can get the right materials," said Shan, he needed a transmitter which they had, and some toy radio operated airplanes, that you can buy in any model shop and some department stores."

"Make a list of all you require I will see that you get it." He then went back to his tent, as he arrived the orderly sergeant was arriving.

"The Colonel wants you ,Sir." Jake then followed the sergeant to headquarters.

"Captain I've arranged a meeting with our people on the base for two weeks on Sunday, it can't be done any earlier I'm afraid."

"That's OK Sir it gives us plenty of time to plan and prepare."

"I will send my sergeant into Kasunu to get you some civilian clothes you are about the same size."

"Fine," said Jake. The next day was Sunday the Sergeant left for Kasunu to get kitted out with civilian clothes. The following Saturday the Sergeant returned, he had for Jake a light weight pale blue single breasted suit, 4 white shirts, brown shoes size 8, socks, underwear and a silver grey tie.

He handed the clothes over to Jake who removed the plastic covers.

"Very nice Sergeant you have good taste," said Jake.

Wednesday, Pike and Jake set off for Kasunu their good clothes neatly packed in the back of the Range Rover, Jake wore an old pair of denim trousers a tee shirt and sandals, Pike wore an old safari suit. They arrived at the Queens hotel Sunday morning at 1-0am they checked in, their reservations had been booked previously. They were both booked on the third floor.

"See you at breakfast say 9-0am," said Pike.

"9-0am, Sir that's fine, good night." The room Jake had was a double room, immediately opposite the door as you walked in was a set of drawers and a wardrobe, at the side of the drawers was an easy chair a writing desk and straight back chair, immediately left of the door was a double bed, and on the adjacent wall was a door leading to the bathroom.

The following morning Jake met Pike in the breakfast room,

"Sleep well?" asked Pike.

"That was the best night I've had in over a year, Sir, it was fantastic and civilised," said Jake, Pike smiled. They ordered break- fast, of bacon eggs mushrooms, the lot, with gallons of black coffee. They both ate and enjoyed their meal. Jake was dressed in white open necked shirt with the slacks from his suit, and shoes, Pike was dressed in a blue safari suit. Both then left the breakfast room, walked through the lounge and out to the back to the swimming pool, which was a full size of Olympic standard, there were tables chairs lie lows and deck chairs around the pool.

"It is all very nice and pleasant," said Jake, "We should do this more often."

"Wishful thinking," said Pike. They walked round the pool to the far corner near to the deep end, they sat at a table on straight back chairs, Pike called over the steward.

"Would you like something?"

"A nice cold beer would be very nice, Sir," replied Jake.

"I think under the circumstances Jake it would be more appropriate if you refer to me informally, my name is Clive."

"I see yes of course, well Clive like I say a beer please, I may as well enjoy my holiday." Pike ordered.

It was now 10-30am, "We will meet 4 people today, two should be arriving at any time." Just then Jake saw a very attractive tall Asian woman, with a short fat powerfully built individual who was also Asian, they stood just outside the large glass double doors that open out from the hotel. The couple had a brief look round then moved off, they came round to Pike.

"Hello my dear," said Pike rising, Jake also stood. Jake this is Gloria and this is Gerald, they all shook hands. Pike called the steward over.

"What will you have to drink?"

"A lemon and lime please," said Gloria, and Gerald ordered a beer.

Jake noticed a Ligerian in the shallow end of the pool with his two children, he was teaching them how to swim, they were wearing inflated arm bands and were laughing and shouting having a great time, a Ligerian woman sat at a table watching and laughing, obviously their mother, a lovely family Jake thought. "Are you with us Jake?" said Pike.

"Oh! I do beg your pardon, I was miles away just then."

"Well," said Pike. "We can talk tell Gerald what it is you want," Jake then spoke.

"Is there any way you can get explosives on the base?"

"No way" said Gerald."

"OK," said Jake, "I will get them on, could you move them about once they are on?"

"Yes that would be no problem I'll put them in the commandants office if you want?" Jake smiled he liked that kind of attitude.

"That won't be necessary," said Jake smiling.

"At the extreme right hand rear of the base, there is your transformer house yes?"

"That is correct," said Gerald.

"Do you have the keys?"

"Yes I have all the keys for all the locks on the base in my key cabinet in my office."

"Good," said Jake, "I want a copy."

"Yes that is no problem," said Gerald.

"OK Gerald today is November the 11th this is the way we do it. On November 21st at 11-0pm I will drive down the main runway apron of Kasunu airport, and at precisely that time 11-0pm I want the rear perimeter lights to blow a fuse, can that be arranged?"

"No problem," said Gerald.

"And I could do with them off for at least 20 minutes."

"I can arrange that," said Gerald," "You see rats will have nibbled through the main cable, or should I say that is how it will appear, it will take at least 40 minutes to repair, it has happened before."

"Well that's great," said Jake. "Whilst on the apron I will be 1 and a half miles from the control tower, if they see me they will think I am runway lights maintenance, but I doubt they will see me anyway. I will park up behind the hanger get through the barbed wire, and then into the transformer house, where I will store the mines, would they be likely to be discovered Gerald."

"No maintenance in the transformer house is done on the first of the month every month, and that is only a matter of vacuum cleaning, I know my engineers give me the technical details I write the schedules and programmes."

"Good," said Jake, "What is required for us to bring this caper off, is for starters, we must bring down the roof of the main hanger, the admin block, and do as much damage to the main 4 storey barrack block as possible. The idea behind the exercise is to steal a gun ship and embarrass the government. Now if we can explode what I've just outlined we can do it.

As maintenance manager you will have access to all these areas and will be able to plant the mines, yes?"

"Yes," said Gerald, "That will be no problem. How big are the mines?"

"Equivalent to 25lbs high explosives, they are 10 inches in diameter and 3 inches deep and very sensitive."

"I can do that," said Gerald "I will need two for the hanger roof blast the two main centre columns, they go with their cross members, and the whole roof will come down, I will need one for the admin block, now the main barrack block, well let me put it this way," said Gerald lapsing into deep thought. "Terraced onto the barrack block is the armoury fuel stores, and the boiler house, and the boilers are natural gas, I will plant two mines between that lot in there, and that will do a lot of damage, and two in the main barrack

142

block, as I say a lot of damage but I doubt we will demolish it, the armoury and fuel stores will go though."

"No I realise we could not demolish the entire barrack block," said Jake, "What I need is a lot of confusion, because when the men come to spew out they will be in the hundreds."

"Yes of course," said Gerald, "I know you have a meeting with the Moto brothers speak to them about the fuel stores armoury and boiler house. A mine there would cause a tremendous fire, and they are better qualified to deal with that area, they know it so well."

"We have a meeting with them at 1-0pm, how long do you need to plant the mines."

"Well," said Gerald, "I assume it will be a night strike."

"Correct," said Jake, "12 midnight November 23rd."

"The main hangar and admin block we plant after working hours Friday 22nd, the fuel store and armoury can be planted at the same time, or earlier in the day, I don't see any difficulty there, I'll leave that to the brothers, but I can assure you they will be planted," said Gerald.

Gloria then spoke, "I will plant the mine in the admin block, my office is on the ground floor, and the main column is right in the centre, we finish at 5-0pm then the cleaners come in until 7-0pm, I know, I do their time sheets."

"Very well," said Pike. Now once you have planted the mines, on Saturday morning you leave the base and you can never return, neither you nor the brothers, you will have to prepare for a long hike through the bush, do you have use of a vehicle that you can take off the base."

"Yes," said Gerald, "the one I used to come here in, it isn't a four wheel drive though."

"That's OK, all four of you leave the base on the Saturday morning, you will have to make these particular arrangements with the brothers, once off the base you drive South on the A125 until you reach the native village of Womba they are friendly towards us so you can freshen up there if you wish, but don't tell them what you are about, safety first you understand, we have passed through the village many times as a rebel force and always been welcome as we have never seen them short of anything.

From there you go North for 30 kilometres, there you will arrive at a water hole it is where the river Kasunu forks and starts to peter out. That is where you will be collected, I would point out that you will have been observed for some time to be sure that you have not been followed. Now I need not tell you to travel light, you will need a good compass, South on the A125 then West then North for 30 kilometres, any personal belongings that you wish to take you will have packed and delivered to me by 8-0am tomorrow morning, but please no truck loads."

"Gerald," said Jake, "these mines are sensitive so you will need to exercise care, don't stack them on top of each other, that is to say be reasonable, you could drop one and be OK and then again you could just lean on one and bang."

"Well that's it," said Jake. "I think we have covered everything, any questions?"

"No, all is understood," said Gloria.

"I'll have the key ready for your and delivered with our gear by 8-0am tomorrow morning," said Gerald.

Jake then said, "Can we just recap before we say goodbye."

Gloria and Gerald then went through their parts like reciting a poem. "You'll do," said Jake.

The visitors then got up to leave, and they all shook hands.

"They seem a good couple," said Jake after they had left.

"Yes they are," said Pike. "She worked for the international red cross you know, she lost her parents and a brother at the hands of the Mausa, Gerald lost a daughter, they are in-laws, Geralds daughter was married to Gloria's brother, all very tragic. It was the demise of President Elido that brought things to a head.

A lot of very influential people could see the situation and what could develop, so they put to one side in Ghana, one million Dollars and it is that which is financing us now, plus of course what we plunder. When I say died at the hands of the Mausa, what I mean is they were outspoken critics of the Sandies, and the NSP backed of course by the National Guard, who are all very powerful. You know Jake the first and foremost qualification to be a National Guardsman is to be Mausa, not all Mausa's go along with this philosophy though Jake, Elido was Mausa, and our leader now General Adejumo is Mausa."

"It takes all sorts," said Jake.

The time was now 12-0 noon. "Shall we go?" said Pike. "Do you fancy lunch?" he asked.

"A sandwich and a beer will do me," said Jake. They went into the bar and ordered two steak sandwiches and two beers. At 12-50pm they went to Pikes room. At 12-55pm two Ligerians walked into the hotel, they went to the gift shop and bought an English newspaper, then they walked over to the restaurant and read the menu that was on display outside the entrance. Sunday morning is always a busy morning, there were lots of people about buying papers and visiting the restaurant. The two men then strolled over to the lift and pressed the call button, the lift came and they stepped inside and pressed for floor 3. The lift stopped at the floor, the two men walked out and went to room 315, knocked and the door opened they stepped inside, Pike closed the door.

"Good afternoon gentlemen," said Pike, he then made the introductions, "Jake this is Joshua, and Gerimia, they shook hands." They didn't look much like a Joshua or Gerimia to Jake, they were both very large and very black, and from what he had seen of these people (and judging by his labour force with Akeja Construction) they seem to live on peanuts and Bananas, yet they sure looked powerful.

"Hello," said Gerry, in perfect English without accent, another surprise for Jake. They had lost their father and brother in a similar manner to Gloria. They were both technical store men at the base, Jake outlined his strategy to the two of them, Gerry had access to the fuel store, and Josh to the armoury. One mine in the armoury one in the fuel store and one in the boiler house, it was up to the brothers to select the best possible place. Jake had them go over it again and again.

Pike liked this, if only he would fight the same way he thought, it would sure save Adam a lot of worry.

"Well that is it gentlemen," said Jake, the two men then shook hands and left. "Well that is that," said Jake, "as soon as we have the gear off Gerald we will start back, we will be back at the latest Thursday 14th, that will give us 8 days to prepare for the 23rd."

"Can you be ready for then Jake?" asked Pike.

"Yes, Sir I'll be ready, Shan and I have put a lot of work in on the limpet mines, they are ready, and he assures me the five magnetic mines for the gun ships will be ready by the time we get back."

The following morning, a relatively small wooden crate arrived for them at the hotel, it came by special courier along with a small package. Pike signed for them, and gave the small package to Jake, who opened it, there were two keys, a small flat cabinet type key, and a larger door type key, "That is interesting," said Jake as he put the keys in his pocket.

Pike had the crate put in the Land Rover, he settled the account and they left.

They had an uneventful journey back to base, Jake now had the 8 days to make his final arrangements. The radio activated mines had been made up. They consisted of dynamite packed in small peanut tins and when tested they worked perfectly. Shan had taken Jake out into the bush, buried a mine, then walking 200 yards away, set the frequency dial gave the transmitter to Jake saying, "When you ready flick the dial to '0'," then watching the mound of earth Jake flicked the dial as instructed, the mine went off with one hell of a bang.

"You have done a good job there Shan."

"Thank you, Sir I aim to please," he said with a satisfied smile. Jake called a meeting with Pike and Adam.

"Well Jake what is it?"

"We now have 6 days to deadline, Sir."

"Correct," said Pike.

"Could we have Sergeant Lotti here, Sir?" asked Jake.

"Of course, Sergeant go bring Sergeant Lotti," the Sergeant left immediately, he returned in a few minutes with Lotti, who came to attention and saluted, "You sent for me, Sir?"

"At ease Sergeant." Jake then carried on.

"Well Sir I would like to leave at first light tomorrow, we will camp 3 miles out from the back perimeter. "He then went over to the chart table and pointing to a particular area, "This is where I shall camp by this water hole, you see Sir I want these mines in the transformer house by 11-00pm on the 21st, that will give Gerald more than 24 hours to plant the mines, with safety, before they leave the base. Gerald seems to me a very shrewd character, I know he will keep his eye on the transformer house for the mines.

I would like to leave at first light with two men, and Sergeant Lotti following the following day with my other 16 men to this reference, record this reference Sergeant."

"Recorded Sir I know the area well."

"I want you there by 10-0pm Friday 22nd there will be a lot of work to do before the strike, and I want the men rested and fresh."

"No problem Sir we are always fresh when we go into action," said Sergeant Lotti.

"I will take the equipment Sir I'm having it prepared now, one small generator two 500 watt speakers, and one amplifier and one tape deck, 50 yards of polystyrene strip, and a total of 80 gallons of petrol. The mines will be detonated at 12 midnight precisely, the timing is critical Sir, I expect the whole exercise to be over without loss in 40 minutes.

The frontal assault Major is the difficult bit, but I know all will go well, Major precisely midnight."

"Don't worry Jake, all will go as planned," said Adam with a smile.

Jake left at first light with two men, he had all the equipment in the Land Rover, they also took the jeep and a flight lieutenant's uniform, their journey was uneventful, they arrived 4-0pm Friday, Jake soon got everything organised the generator the cable all was ready. He then got into the jeep with the driver, they had with them the mines, and the jack that he had constructed in the base workshops. It was similar to the jack used on the Elido hit. The night was dark and it was raining, the rains were early this year, they drove without lights onto the runway apron of Kasunu airport and began to coast gently towards the hangar, it was now 10-50pm Jake told the driver to stop, then using his infra red binoculars courtesy of the

147

ordinance depot, he watched the guard approaching the centre of the rear perimeter fence, where he would meet with a colleague coming the other way.

It would be just great thought Jake, if the lights could go out now. At that precise moment they went 11-0pm precisely.

"Good man Gerald," Jake said to himself. "Now," said Jake to the driver, who moved off at speed then cut his engine, and let the jeep coast up and past the hangar, they stopped and got out of the jeep, they then jacked open the scrolls of barbed wire, Jake then threw the rubber mat out of the jeep across the bottom scroll, and got through, the driver then passed him two of the mines, Jake ran across to the tranny house put the mines on the floor, he then took out of his pocket, the larger of the two keys Gerald had given him. He opened the door, and stepped inside pulling the door to behind him, using his small torch he looked round there were the 4 transformers, and on the back wall was a cabinet, Jake then tried the second key, which opened it, and the two bottom shelves were empty, Jake smiled and said to himself. "Gerald you are a belter."

He went back to the door got the two mines and placed them in the cabinet, he completed the task in 4 trips, he then locked the cabinet. He moved to the main door, it opened out towards the perimeter fence, Jake then peered out through the small opening, the guard was just about to go out of sight passed the tranny house, he waited 5 minutes then went outside closed and locked the door, took out his binoculars and looked round the tranny house wall, the guard was well on his way head down against the rain, towards the centre of the perimeter fence. Jake then ran back towards the wire, signalled the driver who was there in a matter of seconds, and was jacking like mad opening the scrolls of wire, he then threw the rubber mat across the bottom scroll and Jake was through. They quickly removed the jack and rubber mat, ran to the jeep and threw them in the back, they pushed the jeep down the whole length of the hangar. By now the storm was horrendous with loud and consistent claps of thunder, they jumped into the jeep, started it and drove at speed, until they reached the end of the hangar, then the driver cut the engine and let the jeep coast up the run-way apron, there was no chance that anyone could have heard or seen them.

But Jake was always meticulous with the preparation of all his missions, it was only in battle that he threw caution to the winds, the hangar would absorb any engine noise particularly with the weather as it was. They turned through 90 degrees, Jake told the driver to stop, he took out his binoculars and looked back the guard was just starting his return towards the tranny house, head down plodding on the best he could against the weather.

Jake was all smiles it couldn't have gone better, just then the lights came back on at the base. They drove into the bush and went back to their camp, the other rebel had made sleeping arrangements in the back of the Range Rover. The whole exercise had taken fifty-five minutes, Jake stripped off wrapped himself in a blanket, and bedded down for a few hours sleep.

At this time Adam and Pike were arriving at their particular rendezvous, North West of the city Kasunu two miles into the bush, it was now 1-0am Adam got everybody bedded down, organised a guard detail with instructions to call him at 3-30am. Adam was duly called as instructed, he freshened up then he and three men left camp, they drove South East into Kasunu at 4-30am, Adam and his three men went into a bus depot such as it was, it looked more like a derelict cow shed, it consisted of one shelter which was in fact just a corrugated iron canopy supported by six 8 feet high 3 inch diameter steel poles, it housed 6 buses or Mammy wagons, there was a shed with a watch man who was asleep with an empty bottle on the table. Adam selected what he considered the best two vehicles of the six, they climbed in and one man went back to the Range Rover with instructions to follow. They shorted out the ignition started up and drove out of the depot, without disturbing the sleeping watch man. They drove for 30 minutes then turned into the bush.

They stopped at a convenient place, all got into the Range Rover and drove into their camp, where Pike and the other rebels were waiting.

The local police would be informed of the missing buses, but they would spend their time interrogating the staff, for they would be convinced that they would have sold them.

149

November 23rd 2-30pm a civil engineer along with several workmen, arrived outside the Kasunu air force base, and set themselves up with a theodolite, operated by the civil engineer, who was in fact a rebel in civilian clothes, all were very authentic, even the language as the rebel in civilian life was a civil engineer. The workmen then put up barriers, as planned to divert traffic around the front of the base. Then a police commissioner arrived, along with a Major in the military police and 6 constables.

The police commissioner was Pike, and the military police major was his sergeant, by 6-0pm all traffic was being successfully diverted.

Adam back at the bush rendezvous got all the rebels organised in the Mammy wagons with armaments and weapons, they all got dressed up in the peasant dress over their jungle greens. Adam, then driving the lead Mammy wagon, moved off for base. At 11-30pm they arrived at the base with the rebels hanging all over the bus, it was all just typical, much to the amusement of Pike. The constables then directed them into a side street, then from there into a back entry, they stopped got off and out of the bus, tore off their peasant dress got their arms and assembled ready. The Mammy wagons were then driven off to be abandoned at least 10 miles away, the drivers being given expenses for two days, they were to go to a particular bush bar where they would be collected at a particular date and time. Adam was then joined by Pike who threw off his uniform as did his sergeant. At 11-40pm Jake who had taken care of the rear guard by crossbow, cut the perimeter wire and drove through in his jeep dressed as a flight lieutenant. He drove boldly up to the first gun ship got out of the jeep and stuck the mine to the under side of its belly, he then got back in the jeep and drove to the next one, and so on, until he had mined 5 of the 6 gun ships.

In the meantime with the rear guard being disposed of, the rebels were laying the polystyrene strip and soaking it with petrol, Jake always adhering to the 20 mile an hour speed limit, casually drove back to the rear perimeter fence. Shan was standing by with the stereo gear, it was now 11-58pm Adam is approaching slowly, towards the front of the base, then the front guard looked at Adam he was just a little bewildered, 12-midnight precisely Jake threw the dial on the transmitter just at that time Adam stood up, levels and aimed the rocket launcher, and bang! There was one hell of an explosion, and the entire base seemed to be going up, the main hangar was down the admin block was down, and a tremendous fire was raging from the armoury fuel store and boiler house.

The whole base was chaos, Adam screamed at his driver as the rocket took the front main entrance and guard house into oblivion, "Go! Move! Move!" His driver stood on the accelerator and was in the front entrance before the debris had finished falling, he was followed by two 3 toners with the canvas canopy removed, the men were firing from the moving vehicle at anything that moved.

Jake then grabbed his flame thrower and fired the polystyrene, which threw a wall of flame 8 feet high illuminating the base. Shan then started the stereo gear and switched on Wagners' classic 'Ride of the Valkyries', which came blasting forth, it could be heard right across the base, in fact it could be heard all over town. Then it stopped, and a peculiar voice with a deep weird accent, came on.

"The devil is with you, first the Sandies, then your ordinance depot, now your base, I spew out my demons to exterminate you all."

At that Jake's rebels started leaping through the flames, firing their AK automatics on repetition, Adam and Pike were tearing across the base, in the jeep, making for the one remaining gun ship they all stood firing their automatics from the hip. Adam smiled when he heard the stereo.

He shouted to Pike. "You have got to hand it to Jake Sir, he is a bloody nut case, but he tries." In the meantime Jake followed his men through the flames in his jeep, just covering his eyes with his forearm as he went through at speed.

He drove straight up to the vehicle compound, where his men were to make for, he leaped out of his jeep and ran towards the vehicle compound guard, he was gunning them down with his A.K. automatic, some men just ran away, some were too confused to know what to do, and they ended up dead, the whole thing was unbelievable and mesmerising, base personnel were in total confusion, nothing in their wildest imagination could have envisaged such as this.

Adam's jeep screeched to a halt at the one remaining gun ship. Pike was out of the jeep, and into the ship in a flash, then the rotors caught and he moved off, Adam's driver was then off like a shot heading for the front main entrance. Jake and his men were in the 6 wheel drive quad vehicles, six in total, heading for the front main entrance, to pick up the foot soldiers who had left their 3 toners to do more effective work, Jake was in the back of a quad vehicle screaming orders to the men to jump aboard the vehicles, and they were, all was going as planned, the men were leaving the fighting and jumping in the vehicles, Jake could see Adam coming fast.

The base personnel were all frightened and totally confused, this was a nightmare beyond all imagination, but confusion was all it needed. Then Adam's jeep got the front tyre shot out, it went into a somersault, throwing Adam his driver and gunner out, Jake saw this and immediately dropped out of his quad, and ran towards Adam who was in a daze on hands and knees, there were 6 base troops running towards him and taking aim, when there was this hideous bloody screaming coming from Adam's rear, when Jake appeared jumping over him and running square on to the troops, firing from the hip, this just put them off their aim momentarily, but it was enough Jake got the lot, then he turned grabbed Adam under the arm pit yanked him to his feet, then assisted by another rebel between them they threw him into the back of the last quad.

Adams driver was shot just as he made for the quad his head was blown apart.

Then they were out and on their way, in the meantime Pike was firing rockets at the main barrack block, impeding the troop movement. The six quad vehicles were now heading west on the main highway, and as instructed as the last quad passed a petrol station, Sergeant Lotti fired a rocket at the base of a petrol pump, and the whole place exploded in flames, it was the same with the next 4 petrol stations.

The convoy then headed North and turned into the bush. Jake was sat on the floor of the last vehicle next to Adam, they were both now beginning to relax. "I guess I owe you Jake," said Adam, Jake looked at Adam smiling. "Now we are even!" said Jake and they shook hands.

"You are a bloody nut case Jake but thank Christ you're on my side," said Adam.

"Always was, Adam, always was." he replied.

Gloria, Gerald and the Moto brothers were now hiking through the bush towards Womba, Gerald looked back it was now 1-0am Sunday 24th. He could see the reflection in the sky, of the horrendous fires at the base, well it would appear they pulled if off, whatever Colonel Pike goes for he gets, the NSP and the National Guard have got a formidable opponent, in Colonel Pike.

At the first fuel stop Shan was waiting he had gathered up all the stereo gear, and the generator immediately the propaganda ceased, he then loaded the Range Rover, and got the hell out of there.

The men lit fires and were making tea to go with their rations. Adam asked Jake "How did you create that weird voice on the tape?"

"Simple," he said, "first I recorded the little speech in 3 different keys, then Shan did the same, then we recorded the whole lot on one tape synthesised, and there you have it the result I thought was great, it was the best part of the whole
exercise."

"You are a weird fucker as well Jake!" said Adam laughing.

"Well you know Adam you have got to stay humorous, or you would go up the wall."

It was now Sunday the 24th at the next fuel stop Pike was waiting, he was all smiles.

"Well gentlemen that was a very successful exercise, it took exactly 37 minutes, I'm going back now to check on Gloria and party they should be within a days walk of the rendezvous."

"Is that wise Sir?" asked Adam "They may send up spotter planes."

"How?" replied Pike, "What they had on base were destroyed when the hangar went, to bring planes up from Bakra, will take a couple of days, because they have no facilities left, not at this time anyway. The military will make a half hearted gesture, and that will be a ground search, I'll see you back at base."

Pike with his two gunners then lifted off, Adam called Sergeant Lotti over.

"Sergeant get the men bedded down, me and the Captain will take first watch, we will be relieved in 2 hours, we move in 5 hours, got that Sergeant?"

"Yes Sir as you say."

The convoy of quad vehicles arrived back at base Wednesday 27th, a further camouflage area had been made to house the gun ship. On arrival Adam and Jake went right over to headquarters Pike was there all smiles when they walked in.

"Congratulations again gentlemen, that was a first class job well done. How many men did we lose Major?"

"One Sir, my driver, he was a good man Sir he will be missed, but it was more by accident that battle. You see my jeep blew a front tyre, it somersaulted Jake got me back in a quad, but my driver took one in the head just as he reached the vehicle. The only man I would expect to lose Sir on this kind of exercise is Jake, he is there again, head down screaming and tearing at the fuckers, square on."

"Now Adam," said Jake "I fight my fight my way, you fight yours!"

"Gentlemen gentlemen please," interrupted Pike "This is not an inquest, we lose one man they lose 34 the papers are full of it."

He handed them both Mondays papers, Jake looked at the headlines, 'The Cat strikes again'. He folded the paper up threw it on the table, and said, "Excuse me Sir I would like to get a couple of hours sleep, that is if you have nothing for me just now."

"Yes go ahead Captain see you at dinner," said Pike, Jake saluted and then left, leaving Adam reading the papers.

Jake took a shower then got into bed, he slept. He awoke at 5-30pm and had another quick shower, then went to the mess tent, it was now 6-0pm, everybody was there, including Gloria, Gerald and the brothers. He made his greetings and sat down next to Adam. The steward came with a steak, a bowl of salad, and a beer, and put them down in front of him.

"My my!" he said, "are we celebrating!"

154

"Why not said Pike we celebrate a job well done." Jake shrugged and started to eat. After the meal during the small talk.

Jake said, "Buy you a drink Adam?"

"Why not." he replied. "Will you join us?" said Adam to the rest of the mess tent. "This is on me," said Pike, "Shall we go?"

All got up and went to Pikes tent, it was big with plenty of exquisite furniture, "Take a seat please," said Pike. They all sat down, Jake and Adam sat on two basket weave chairs with an occasional table in front of them, Gloria and Gerald sat on a hide settee, along with Joshua, Gerry sat on a straight back chair. Pike got 7 crystal glasses out of his cocktail cabinet, Jake looked around at the splendour, looked at Adam and raised his eyebrows. Adam smiled.

Pike poured the whisky good doubles, "Gerald, what will you have to drink? I know you never drink whisky."

"A gin and tonic would be nice, if that is possible?" said Gerald "Yes of course, courtesy of the ordinance depot, eh Adam?" replied Pike. "That's it Sir." he replied.

"I would prefer one of those if I may please," said Gloria.

"Forgive me my dear, I am forgetting my manners, I should have asked." Pike then got another tall cocktail glass to mix the drink.

Jake thought to himself "Pike is a cool one, very suave, but deadly, a real killer he would hate to be up against him, the Sandies were just small fry by comparison, the British army officer is a deadly creature to be sure. Pike then passed the drinks round, Jake took his then looked at Adam.

"A toast ladies and gentlemen, to the future," they all raised their glasses in acknowledgement.

Adam's and Jake's drink went in one, Pike read the situation, filled their glasses to the brim, then put the bottle of malt whisky on the table in front of them.

Pike then went on, "Our guests will be with us for some time it would appear, however whilst we were away I had arrangements made to accommodate Gloria, there is now another toilet at the rear of the clinic with a bolt on the door, Doc has partitioned off one of the showers to enable her a little privacy.

"We could make arrangements for them, in the city of Bakra," said Adam.

"I would like to stay, I am a trained nurse I could help Doc." Jake then spoke, "Where is Doc?"

"In Kasunu assessing the outcome, as well as getting supplies." replied Pike.

"Isn't that a bit risky?" asked Jake.

"We have a lot of friends in Kasunu Jake, more friends than enemies, you see these National Socialist Party have been active for some years now, and the people as a whole are opposed to them, they are all Mausa which is the biggest tribe in Ligeria, and they want to dominate the country as a whole, and bring about a situation such as in the past, where tribalism was a way of life. Well in a modern society there is no room for that attitude, in a society of equality." Jake just shrugged.

"I think I will retire if you don't mind Sir." Jake didn't like this kind of talk, it wasn't his problem, he just wanted old man Sandies, and with a bit of luck Lentoy and Buhari as a bonus, and Denning.

"Thank you for the drink Sir."

"My pleasure Jake," said Pike.

"I will retire also if you don't mind Colonel," said Gerald who stood, the brothers also got to their feet and walked over to Adam and Jake, shook hands the elder one then said, "We would like to thank you both our friends, most sincerely you and men like you are Ligeria's only hope."

"Not forgetting yourself your brother, and men like you," said Adam. The Ligerian smiled then left.

As Jake was leaving Pike said.

"Here is last Sundays Express if you fancy a read Jake." He took the paper.

Jake then walked to his tent. Adam caught him up, and said, "How about a drink Jake?"

"Sure, why not?" he said

"It is about time you and I got down to some serious drinking," said Adam. Jake got the tumblers and the whisky, then they both drank themselves into oblivion.

Next morning Jake awoke 6-0am his head and back were aching something cruel, he grabbed a towel, toothbrush and soap, and went over to the showers block, had a wash and brush up, then went back to his tent, there was a pot of coffee waiting for him. That medic sure looks after me, he thought, as he opened the paper. He liked to keep up with events in the U.K. but sometimes he wondered why, he didn't think he would ever see the place again. It was now December 2nd Monday the duty sergeant came over to Jake's tent, "The colonel would like to see you Captain."

"Thank you Sergeant I will be right there," Jake went to headquarters, he walked up to Pikes desk and saluted. "You sent for me Sir." Pike got up walking over to the chart table. "Yes Captain I have a job for you, General Adejumo has been in touch, there is a computer consignment arrived in Kasunu it has been air freighted out from U.K. It has had some peculiar modifications done, at the C.T.L. agents in Kasunu, it is to be transported by road, to Auna, that is the dam project you and the major hit their pay roll truck some time ago, well he wants it, the computer that is. It will be transported in 3 three ton trucks, there are voltage stabilisers the lot. The trucks will have a National Guard escort, that is because of the pay roll job you did. They won't take any chances with the computer."

"Well Sir I'm afraid they are going to lose it, escort or no escort," said Jake.

"The guard captain will be front and rear, a Range Rover with mounted machine gun will lead, and it will be similar at the rear. Jake the General is very thorough, so please note these details, the convoy will depart Thursday 10-0am December 5th, it will take the A125 to Kontogria approx 7 hours, then on the A1 to Abeto another 2 hours, from there it takes this track to Salka about 40 kilometres, say one hour, then using the same track on to Auna, it will take the convoy 9 or 10 hours to be in an area where am ambush would be practical, I'll leave the details to you Captain," Jake started a detailed study of the map.

"What range do our walkie talkies have Colonel?"

"One mile possibly a little further in open terrain."

"One mile will be fine Sir, I will leave one man a mile down from Ibeto, he can observe the convoy and let me know when they are leaving the Ibeto area, that will give me two minutes to make my final preparation. I'll carry out the ambush here Sir," said Jake, pointing to a particular area on the chart.

"A good choice that Captain, how many men will you require?" asked Pike.

"Just enough to drive the trucks back Sir say 3," at that Pike smiled.

"They will have a guard of 10 experienced men Captain I would take more I think."

"You are the Colonel you tell me Sir, I need only one mine, I know I could do the job alone Sir but I couldn't drive 3 trucks back."

Pike was smiling he liked the attitude, foolish though it may be, it was attitude that mattered in the kind of situation that they were in.

"Take 8 men Captain and Sergeant Lotti."

"I will take the men that worked with me on the last ambush then Sir."

"Very well Captain, Sergeant go bring Sergeant Lotti will you." Lotti came and Jake gave him his instructions, and what provisions to draw, he would draw the mine and walkie talkies.

"Be ready to move at 1-0pm Sergeant."

It was an uneventful journey, the arrived at their chosen site 6-0am Thursday, he sent one man back to Ibeto in the Range Rover, with instructions to stay hidden this side of Ibeto and observe and report the convoys movements, and anything that might be relevant.

He then prepared the track by cutting a shallow trench across it then laying the mine in the centre, and piling small mounds of earth each side of it. Then by laying the light weight plank of wood that he had brought with him across the mounds of earth, the plank coming to rest just above the top of the mine. Now which ever side of the track the convoy passed on the mine would detonate. He then removed the plank and mine, in case civilian traffic used the track before the convoy, they waited.

The observation rebel then came on.

"The military convoy is passing now Sir, no civilian traffic just the convoy." Jake and his men then got the mine and the plank in position, then they spread lose bracken about, to give the track a normal appearance. Four men were positioned either side of the track, about 30 feet apart, Jake with Sergeant Lotti and three men were on the near side, the convoy then came into site, the trucks were about 30 feet apart, the leading Range Rover hit the plank the explosion was deafening, the vehicle just disintegrated, the plan was simple as the trucks came to rest, the rebels would move out on both sides of the track aiming their AK autos, the drivers being civilian weren't expected to be armed to fight. This would then allow Jake to concentrate on taking out the rear guard. Before the debris had finished falling, Jake was up screaming and running at the rear guard, now the rear machine gunner swung his gun round directly at Jake, but he ran on, the three toners were now buffeting into each others rear end, it wasn't a crash pile up, these drivers were good. The rear Range Rover just buffeted into the truck in front of it, and it was enough, the machine gunner was lurched forward over the machine gun, Jake jumped putting his left foot on the bumper of the truck in front of them then leaped up onto the bonnet of the Range Rover, spraying bullets into the disorientated Guards, Jake just stood there flat footed spraying bullets into the already dead guards, magazine after magazine, at the same time screaming and cursing all kinds of foul odes, Sergeant Lotti just stood there mesmerised, Jake's 3rd magazine was now empty, he stopped, then jumped down from the vehicle, and just stood there for several seconds collecting himself. Lotti was stood about 2 yards away watching, he didn't move or speak he just watched Jake, who then seemed to snap out of it.

He turned.

"Right Sergeant get the drivers and our men to the offside rear now Sergeant."

"Yes Sir Captain Cat Sir." The Sergeant lost no time shouting the orders all drivers and the relief drivers, 6 men altogether were lined up at the rear, the six men were all terrified.

"What do we do with them Captain Cat Sir," asked Sergeant Lotti.

"Tell them to clear the bodies out of the Range Rover."

"Right Sir, you heard the Captain move the bodies now."

The six men rushed to the vehicle and started to fling the bodies out into the bush, Lotti and two rebels removed the machine gun and small arms. Then they stood looking at Jake with apprehension, for he was splattered with blood and brains, he was an awesome sight.

"Now you six men you get into that vehicle, and go home, you understand straight home you call no one you call nowhere, if you disobey me I will know, and I will see to it that you join those guards do you understand?"

"Yes Sir we do nothing we go straight home yes Sir."

"Right then move it." The men were off like a shot, they jumped into the vehicle reversed it then swung it round and were off.

"Right Sergeant lets go." The rebels then got into the trucks, Jake and Lotti drove back in their Range Rover, the convoy moved off. Sergeant Lotti driving the lead vehicle, with Jake sat passenger.

"We will have to stick to bush country Sergeant, just to be on the safe side, they won't know which contingent did the job, so if we stick to bush all the way back we shouldn't have any problems."

"It will take maybe 5 days going back then Sir."

"That's OK Sergeant we are in no hurry, I think we will hunt a little bush rat on the way, how's that grab you fresh meat for dinner and all that."

"That will be great Sir, it sure will please the men."

It was Tuesday morning when they arrived back at base, Jake and Lotti went straight to headquarters, they walked up to Pikes desk and saluted.

"Hello Captain, Sergeant, we expected you back Sunday, Monday at the latest."

"Well Sir we kept to bush country all the way, to be on the safe side, and to be honest Sir I didn't think there was any rush, so we relaxed a little on the way back."

"Oh that's OK Captain, its just that that the Major has got to worrying these days, he thought you had maybe taken one chance too many."

"No Sir, it was all very simple really, like taking butties from a baby, wasn't it Sergeant?" At that Adam came in.

"Nice to see you Captain, you had the Colonel worried."

"Well Sir all is intact with a few extra arms thrown in, I'd like to take a shower now Sir if I may, I'm rather high, then I'll go through the detail later."

"Yes of course Captain we will discuss it later," Jake left.

"Well," said Adam.

"Was it as simple as the Captain makes out Sergeant?"

"Well Sir I know, we all know, that is Sir you the Colonel and me, that this business of Captain Cat being the devil an all, is nonsense, but Sir I tell you I see with my own eyes, we mine the front vehicle, and before the debris has finished falling, the Captain is up and running, straight at the rear guard. The gunner Sir I see him turn the gun right at the Captain, still he run on at him screaming, next thing I know the Captain is stood on the bonnet of the vehicle spraying them all with bullets they stand no chance Sir, he just spray them. He change a magazine quicker than you can blink an eye, then there is silence like you wouldn't believe. Even the beasts and the vermin are silent. He then drop down from the vehicle, and I'm as close to the Captain as I am to you Sir, it isn't the Captain, no Sir it is not the Captain, the face is all twisted weird. I, I can't explain it Sir, but it isn't the Captain I see plenty war, I'm Ibo I was with Cheif Elido and Montgomery in the Africa campaign, I fought with you Sir in our own civil war, you know me Colonel, you never see me afraid."

"That's true Sergeant your courage and fighting ability have never been in doubt," said Pike.

"Yes Sir well I'm telling you Sir I was sure scared, not of the fight no Sir," Lotti just shook his head, "I can't explain it, then he turn and he speak to me, and he is the Captain again, yes Sir first one thing then another."

"Right Sergeant stand the men down, you are excused duties for the next 24 hours all of you. You've earned it."

"Thank you Sir, he came to attention saluted turned and left.

Adam turned to Pike.

"Well Colonel what do you make of that?"

161

"After that kind of operation Adam, you would all be tense and absorbed in concentration, then when you have gathered yourself you relax, and the face muscles relax and your looks definitely change, and when you are Negroid the white mans features move and change more rapidly, and are not so easily understood, you can look pretty mean and weird during battle Adam."

"Yes I guess your right Colonel, but you know it is, as if Jake is inviting a bullet, he takes some figuring out, what about the spoils Sir?"

"Have the trucks painted that dark green colour, with 'Pikes Haulage' painted across the doors. The Moto brothers will take them up to the General in Kano, all in green boiler suits with 'Pikes Haulage' across the back. They will move out as machine tools, I have all the paper work, it will be authentic."

"Right Sir." Adam saluted and left. Jake went across to the showers and let the water beat down on him shifting his weariness.

He then went back to his tent, and there was a pot of coffee waiting for him, next to a copy of the Bakra Sunday times. He sat down poured the coffee and opened the paper, on page two there was a photo of Colonel Mires the now acting President, with old man Sandies and some other character a U.K. chairman from ECC they had just signed an agreement to allow ECC to open a mining project in the Olantika mountains, on the border with Cameroon.

It went on to say that the British government, would ensure Ligeria every help and cooperation, in bringing about a speedy end to their domestic conflict. It went on to say that the now retired British ambassador to Ligeria, Simon Denning had been instrumental in securing this agreement. A celebration dinner was to be held at the National Guard Headquarters on Saturday January 25th, to launch the election campaign of the NSP the elections would be held on Thursday March the 6th.

Jake sat there brooding over this for some time, Denning had been instrumental in the assassination of Chief Elido, and of providing the finance for Sandies NSP campaign, all of a sudden he drops out of the picture. Why?

The object of the whole exercise it would appear was to get

these mining rights for ECC which Elido was against, for whatever his reasons. Could it be that the British government was behind it all, or was it the ECC? Why had Denning retired had he got the wind up after the young Sandies got their lot. Why? Why? Why?

If he got rid of the NSP leaders there would be no party, and that was the sole object of his being now anyway. Then maybe the Elido supporters would have some chance, he owed Elido that much, and if he was successful, that would be an end to the mining project of the ECC That was the answer at least without the mining rights going to ECC the whole exercise and money they have spent, would have all been for nothing.

Jake stood up and started pacing the floor, then he went back to reading his paper, he read on, a Geologist had set up camp with the mining engineers at the base of the Olantika mountains, with all the latest and most sophisticated mining and processing equipment, and computers worth 9 million pounds Sterling. This project would make employment for at least 200 Ligerians. "No it won't," thought Jake.

"No it won't".

What was it Jake wanted revenge, justice, or was he trying to make amends for the terrible wrong that he had done. He didn't know, and he didn't care.

"Fuck the lot of them!" he thought. But they would pay, he had paid with the destruction of Joe Tully.

Them bastards would pay every last one of them, and that was a fact he would see to it.

At lunch time over beef stew, everybody was there, Gloria, Gerald the brothers Pike and Adam, Jake was sat on the end of the table next to Adam who was sat opposite Pike, Jake was just playing with his stew, deep in thought. Then he spoke.

"Could I have word with you Colonel, when you have time, you and Adam that is?"

"Go ahead Jake," said Adam, "shoot", this easy going attitude rattled Jake, who was in a very serious mood.

"It is just for yourself and the Colonel, not the whole fucking mess tent." snapped Jake.

"Steady Captain," said Pike, "lets not get offensive."

"I'm sorry Sir," said Jake "I." He paused as though lost for words, a hush descended on the mess tent.

"Excuse me," he said, then got up and made to leave.

"Captain Cross!" snapped the Colonel.

"Sit down and finish your meal," then the Colonel was his old deliberate self, as he said, "Then Jake later we will have a little informal talk, say 6-30pm at headquarters." Pike looked at Adam, then at Jake. What is it Pike thought that drives Jake the way it does, makes him fight the way he fights, sooner or later he must go over the top, totally insane or dead.

"I'm rather busy just now Jake," said Pike. "Arranging the computer for dispatch." Jake was sitting down playing with his stew again, but silent, Gloria looked across at Jake. That is one troubled man she thought, since she had been living on the base, she had heard all about Jake's exploits, and how the men considered him to be the devil, how they would follow him through fire if needs be, however, they all had this uncanny fear of him.

At 6-20 Adam walked into headquarters, went over to Pike and saluted. "I thought I would get here early, so as not to miss anything. What do you suppose Jake has on his mind?"

"I have no idea Adam, we will soon find out he's here now."

The door opened and in walked Jake, walked up to Pike's desk saluted.

"At ease Jake. What is on your mind?" asked the Colonel.

"I want to hit the National Guard."

"You what!" exclaimed Adam.

"I want to hit the National Guard Headquarters." repeated Jake. Adam looked at Pike, with a look of utter disbelief on his face.

"Why that particular target Jake?" asked Pike, with a calm inquiring voice,

"Why, because the whole situation is held together by a minority of the Ligerian armed forces, the National Guard, who took power when Elido was killed, Sandies of the N.G. who is in power now Mires of the N.G. and who are they holding power for Sandies and the NSP who are financed by the British, and why, because of

Uranium in the Olantika mountains, that Elido for whatever his reasons, was totally against allowing anyone to mine."

"I see," said Pike.

Adam said, "But it is right in the middle of Bakra, it is fucking impossible to get there, and it is fucking nigh impregnable, it is madness," said Adam waving his arms about.

"Its fucking madness." he repeated lowering his voice and putting his face right up close to Jake's. Jake didn't speak or move, he just held Adam's gaze, eye ball to eye ball.

"I see," said Pike. "I assume you have a plan."

"No Sir not at this time, but I will put something together for your approval, it will need a lot of thought." Then he came to attention saluted.

"Permission to leave Sir."

"Granted," said Pike.

Jake said, "Buy you a drink Adam?" As he was making for the door, Adam looked at Pike with a look that said what do I do, Pike returned the look and nodded at the door, Adam understood and followed Jake out.

Jake went to his tent got two tumblers, filled them with whisky handed one to Adam, Jake raised his glass.

"How are supplies lasting Adam."

"We have a few cartons left yet." Adam replied.

"I managed to break into a couple of breweries, during a couple of my smaller outings." Jake replied.

"Good I don't know what we would do without our little nip."

Little nip Adam thought looking at his tumbler full of whisky. He smiled raised his glass, saying, "Here's looking at you, you bloody nut case."

They both burst out laughing and took big drinks on their whisky.

Jake had been working with Doc improving the clinic, Gloria had also been putting in a good days work, they had constructed an emergency treatment room, similar to an out patients, an operating theatre separate from the 6 bed ward.

165

"What is a doctor doing with a wild bunch of mercenaries anyway?" asked Jake.

"Its a long story Jake," replied Doc.

"Enough said then," replied Jake, for he knew that all people that lived the way they did, must have a skeleton in a closet somewhere, problems only they could live with, just like himself.

"I think we have earned a drink Doc," said Jake.

"Good thinking," he replied and went to his medical cabinet got 3 glasses and a bottle of whisky.

"Not for me," said Gloria, Jake took his drink and downed it in one. "It would appear there are two things that you do well," said Gloria looking at Jake.

"And they are?" he said.

"Drink and fight." she replied and walked out, Jake looked at Doc with an amazed look on his face, "What did I do," Doc just raised his eyebrows and topped up Jake's glass, and his own. After Jake made towards to headquarters, went up to Pikes desk saluted.

"Have you give my suggestion of hitting the N.G. any thought Sir?"

"I have and I'll say this, you have a point regarding the fact that it is the N.G. that are controlling the situation in Ligeria at this time. And it would be a tremendous boost, in fact it could well end the conflict, because it is felt that the regular army is sympathetic to General Adejumo. However, be that as it may." Pike then got up and walked over to the chart table, "Call Major Campbell Sergeant will you."

Pike then took out a map of Akeja spread it out, it showed the N.G. headquarters in detail, and the surrounding area, Pike had a map or chart of every city, and military installation on his chart table.

"As you can see the Akeja area covers about 3 square miles and is surrounded by bushlands, there are few scattered villages then it is dense bush."

"I know, I've made the trip," said Jake.

"I see, of course! After you hit the Sandies, OK then our escape would not be as problematic as first thought."

"What do you mean escape, Sir, if we hit the N.G. we hit period, there will be nobody to escape from, we devastate them, we go for broke Colonel, shit or bust. The regular army are 22 miles the other side of Bakra, they would be in no hurry to assist the N.G. We could probably recruit half of them to join us. Pike looked up and Jake looked round, Adam was stood in the door way. "Did you hear that Major?" asked Pike.

"Yes Sir, Jake has a point about the regular army, they wouldn't want to get involved, unless we start on them."

"But we did start on them when we hit the ordinance depot."

"Yes," said Pike, "but you see the N.G. commandeered the depot from the regular army, the weapons we got were the N.G.s weapons."

"Yes and that is another thing," said Jake. "Does it not strike you as odd, that they were A.K. 47 automatics, which are Russian made, so the N.G. must have Eastern European connections."

"There are arms dealers everywhere Jake," said Pike, "dealing with anybody if the price is right."

"But," said Adam, "we don't have the men or equipment to attempt such an attack on the N.G." Jake wasn't listening he was studying the map of Akeja, "I have an idea maybe we can work something out."

Adam came across, and all three leaned over the map, "How many rebels in this area?" asked Jake, pointing to a particular area West of them about 200 miles. "Maybe twenty they are for aggravation purposes only, nothing special."

"What about this area South of Kano."

"Ah now, that is different, that is the Generals area, there maybe 200 men there, and the General has the run of Kano anyway."

"What about this area North of Akeja?"

"That is just open bushland," said Pike.

"Would it hide 200 men?" asked Jake.

"Yes" replied Pike. "What are you thinking?"

"We could fly men in from Kano, how many flights are there in a day."

"Two flights each day, one in the morning and one in the

167

afternoon, the morning flight arrives 12 noon, the afternoon flight arrives 8-0pm," said Pike.

"OK, well we bring in 20 men on each flight, all as separate individuals, then when they arrive they take taxis, 4 men to each taxi, and go to these respective bush bars, then say at 2-30pm they are collected by one of our people, and taken to this rendezvous by truck. Then after the noon flight, it will be similar they wait in the bush bars, they have a drink and are discretely collected at some particular time, and so forth and so on.

Then gentlemen in three days we have 120 men, plus our own 60, 180 men we use this particular rendezvous. Jake indicating the particular area on the map. Then we bring them from the rendezvous in Mammy wagons, as we did when we hit the base.

"We have done that once we would never get away with it a second time."

"Why not?" asked Jake, "You have never seen any report or newspaper article saying anything about using Mammy wagons. They haven't got a clue as to how we did it."

"That is true," said Pike, "They never did figure it out,"

"Or alternatively we come in late at night and commandeer the surrounding property."

"That is an impossible task," said Adam, "We would need at least 2,000 men to even dent the N.G. You couldn't hole up 2,000 men in commandeered property, it is ludicrous we could get as far as the rendezvous here, he said pointing to the map, and that is 7 or 8 miles from the N.G. and the strike would have to come from a situation similar to the base strike."

"What are these buildings here Colonel?"

"That is the Cafprint Textile Mills warehouses."

"OK said Jake we commandeer that lot on Saturday 25th of January. We then move in all the men in civilian 3 toners, all men and equipment, a truck pulling up at a warehouse and unloading is normal enough, what employees are there will be night shift, we just lock them up no harm will come to them, they would not be missed.

From the looks of this plan the warehouses have flat roofs, so we bombard with mortars from the roof tops a constant bombardment on all buildings, we drive up blow the front away with rockets. The entire headquarters is just a horse shoe shape set of buildings around a square, with a warehouse and vehicle compound at the back."

"Why Saturday 25th of January? That is 7 weeks from now." asked Adam.

"Because that is when the N.G. are playing host to the NSP and throwing a dinner dance to celebrate the start of their election campaign, half the N.G. will be pissed and we get them all in one throw.

Old man Sandies and the NSP hierarchy, the lot, for they are the cause of all the bloody trouble in the first place."

"Jake you are bloody obsessed with the NSP and the Sandies," said Adam.

"O.K. gentlemen please," interrupted Pike.

"I'll get them bastards, with you or without you, I'll go it alone if needs be, but them bastards will never see the dawn on Sunday morning, one way or another, they go down on Saturday the 25th, and that's a fact Adam," said Jake.

"Gentlemen please we now have some form of strategy, I like the idea of using the warehouse roofs, a continuous bombardment could well do it. I will need to give this a great deal of thought, and formulate a plan. We will leave it there I think gentlemen."

"Colonel I have a request."

"What is it Jake."

"Well Sir the British have set up a camp at the foot of the Olantika mountains, it is the ECC actually, they have got the mining concession for a particular mining project, they have mining equipment on the camp worth nine million pounds Sterling, I want to destroy it, the lot."

"Why, we have no quarrel with the British," said Pike.

"I won't hurt anyone Sir, but you see the ECC provided the money to finance the NSP" at that Adam raised his eyebrows and looked at the ceiling, Jake went on, "I want to make their little enterprise unprofitable."

"Do we have a contingent in that area."

169

"Yes, we do as it happens."

"Well perhaps they might assist."

"But Captain that is 800 miles away."

"Well Sir I have the time."

Adam then broke in, "Jake, forget the NSP, relax, if you go after that camp you would slaughter the bloody lot of them and you know it."

"No, I do not want to harm anybody, the whole situation arose because the NSP got financial aid from the ECC"

"How do you know that Jake?" asked Pike. That caught Jake for a moment, "I just know, that's all, just give me a couple of weeks and lend me a truck, that's all I ask." Pike studied Jake for a while, he never asked for anything, he carried out his orders to the letter, he worked hard, took risks.

"OK Jake I'll contact the contingent to assist you, if they are prepared to do so, then I agree, but you do not go it alone, and you hurt no one, agreed?"

"Yes Sir agreed."

"Come we will try to contact them," said Pike, and made for the door, they went to the radio shack, Pike spoke to the radio operator, "Get me Baker corporal, I want to speak to Major Horn," the corporal then flicked over the frequency dial, and spoke into the mike, "Able calling Baker, Able calling Baker how do you hear me over?" the reply came back, "Baker calling, loud and clear over." he handed the mike to Pike, "This is Able number one, I wish to speak to Baker number one over."

"One moment please over," came the reply."

"They have gone to get him," said Pike a few moments passed, then, "This is Baker number one over."

"Hello Mike this is Clive, I would like to send a colleague over to pay you a visit, he has a proposition to put to you, would you be in a position to assist him, he is no trouble and he eats Kitty Cat over." the reply came.

"My pleasure Clive we would be honoured to assist in any way we are able over." Pike was all smiles, Jake was a little bewildered, and this amused Adam, Pike carried on, "are you still at the same coordinates over?"

"Yes over."

"He will leave sun down today, should arrive day after tomorrow over."

"Will comply out." Pike then gave the mike back to the corporal, "What is all this Kitty Cat business," asked Jake.

"Well Captain whether you like it or not, you are quite a celebrity, all contingents have been on to me at some time or other, about the Cat, as you know you have operated with most of them, when you were on loan, so to speak."

"Yes I see and the Kitty Cat is to let them know who they are getting."

"Yes you see Jake in these circumstances when we are calling in general terms, when not in action, we use general code like first names, anyone able to pick us up, could never be sure who we were it is just a precaution."

"You are sending my by chopper then Colonel, to be there in such a short time, it would have to be."

"Yes Jake but you only travel by night, again just a precaution, there is no radar between us, but I believe in safety first, so you can only travel after dark, 800 miles will take maybe 10 hours."

Jake set off at sundown with the Ligerian pilot and arrived at 6-0am Thursday. They came down 10 miles East of the base, at the coordinates given to them in the air. They were met by 8 rebels who checked their credentials, the rebels then got in touch with their base, who gave them the all clear to proceed. When Joe arrived at the base he was met by Major Horn, a tall slim character of about 40 years, "Well Captain, it is a pleasure to meet you. I must say I expected a much bigger man."

"Why?" asked Jake, "I consider my size to be convenient, I can drive a mini in comfort."

Horn laughed, "Well I do say you have got yourself quite a reputation."

"By pure accident I can assure you, I've had a lot of luck on my outings," said Jake.

"Ambushing a convoy of National Guard, and killing 75 of the bastards, I don't call that luck, and that being incidental to the actual hit, the ordinance depot."

"I have a good team," said Jake.

They went into Horns tent, he had a refrigerator powered by a small diesel generator.

"Beer?" said Horn.

"That would be nice," said Jake.

"How's Adam?" asked Horn.

"Fine." answered Jake.

"Adam and I go back a few years, we fought together in the Congo, we had three years there and the money was good. We are a bit thin on the ground here, it isn't like a full scale civil war, this is money for old rope so to speak. How long have you been in the business?"

"I'm not in the business, I got caught up in it by accident, you could say," replied Jake.

"Well what is this caper you have in mind for me and my lot,

I'm a small band, 28 men including me."

"No doubt you have read about the mining project in the Olantika mountains," said Jake.

"Yes, that's about 70 miles North of us, well North East actually, we have been up there and had a look round, there is a small camp at the base of the mountain with several warehouses, it's nothing special, they use their own security guard at night, they are only retired policemen and old army hasbeens. What exactly do you have in mind?

"I am going to destroy the lot, equipment that is, I want nobody harmed."

"Can I ask why?"

"Well," said Jake, "This project is the ECC project, they are financing the NSP which is run by the Sandies family."

"Yes, acting President Major Steven Sandies got himself knocked off and his sister, they got it together, some guy eh, the man who did it, bald head and beard, gunned them and seven of their guards down, National Guard at that, some character, eh Jake?"

"Anyway," carried on Jake, "Old man Sandies has agreed to give ECC the mining concession for the right kind of finance, it was that finance that paid for the Elido hit, so I want to make the whole thing uneconomical for them. There is something in the order of nine million pounds worth of gear at the camp." Horn raised his eyebrows. "As much as that? I guess that must be the big laboratory they have there, it looks more like a bloody refinery of some kind, they also have a helicopter, I could do with that."

"Do you have a pilot?"

"Yes, me. I flew in the Royal Navy, the experience came in very useful in the Congo.

"Then the helicopter is yours," said Jake.

"What I would like to do is reconnoitre the area then plan and execute. I intend to destroy it, the whole lot, without harming anyone of course," said Jake.

"Well its your caper Captain, I will assist you anyway I can, it takes maybe 6 or 7 hours by Range Rover to get there, it is rough country."

"O.K. if we can take a small party say 4 men for a couple of days and size up the situation."

"That's fine Captain, I will join you of course, I'll leave Sergeant Odel in charge here, if we leave at 12 noon we would arrive there by 7-0pm tonight, that way we approach the area after dark, nobody will be about, if we arrive in daylight we could bump into some bloody idiot catching butterflies, you would be surprised at what some of them bloody morons get up to. The nearest village is 22 miles East of them. They are friendly towards us and we see them right, they go short of nothing where we can help, and I found in the situation such as we are in, it pays to be that way."

The base camp of Major Horn was in a small clearing, close to a water hole, which they relied on for all their water, they didn't have a bore hole with submersible pump.

The Range Rover with two men, and a second with four men set off at 12 noon, they had supplies for 3 days, and enough petrol in gerry cans for the round trip. They made camp in a very rocky area, about half a mile from target.

"We will get no intruders up there," said Horn.

"There are no butterflies up here I take it," said Jake, and they both laughed. They had camped on a small rise at the base of the mountain range, it rose out of dense bush, and was rather barren. They were about 60 feet up and sheltered by huge boulders, "I suggest we bed down now and go on reconnaissance at day break," said Horn, "there are 8 white men I assume to be British."

"They are," said Jake.

"And 8 black men I assume to be Ligerian."

"They will be I guess." They made camp sleeping in the open, they had a small propane primus stove for making tea, coffee and fry ups. They retired leaving one man on guard, at daybreak Jake and Mike set off on foot, they dropped down into the bush, moving quickly through medium dense bush and approached the camp, they then went up onto the start of the mountain rise, they were about 40 feet up then, moving parallel with the camp, they stopped and looking down with their binoculars they made their observations, they had a perfect view.

There was no perimeter wire, everything was in an open cluster, about 100 yards out from the mountain range, there were two large warehouses, at 90 degrees to these was the lab, or refinery as Mike put it. Opposite the warehouses were the eight portakabins, which were the accommodation units, there was a distance of 50 yards between these and the warehouses, at the back of the cabins were the ablutions and the toilets.

At this time they were just sinking their own water hole, at the centre of this arrangement of buildings, there were two earth moving caterpillar drive vehicles, a three ton truck, two Range Rovers, a jeep, a Jumbo Crane and a helicopter. There was one Ligerian on guard just the one all night, the he was off all day, he had a small stove with a kettle constantly on to keep him supplied with tea or coffee. Jake and Mike studied the area for some time, Jake lowered his binoculars.

"I reckon one of the warehouses will have all their dynamite."

"The one nearest us," said Mike. "We have been all through this when they first arrived here, we watched them set up shop and raided their ration store a time or two.

The lab has the sleeping quarters of boss man, or chemist or whoever, they will be rising any time now, then you can see who sleeps where." It was no 6-0am first one cabin door opened, out walked a couple of guys with towels they walked round the back to the ablutions, then the side door of the lab opened, and a large elderly man appeared also carrying a towel.

Jake and Mike studied the activity.

"OK" said Jake, "The extreme left hand cabin is the mess hall, they obviously all eat there." After they all had breakfast, the mess hall door opened and they all came out, the large elderly man went back to the lab, with two Ligerians. Two white men and two Ligerians went to the bore hole they were drilling, two Ligerians and one white man went into the cabin next to the mess hall.

"The cabin next to the mess hall must be the office," said Jake. "Looks that way," said Mike. The four remaining white men went to the earth moving vehicles, and drove to about 50 yards from where Jake and Mike were, and started to level the face of the mountain.

"Right," said Jake, "In the lab is where all the expensive equipment must be, computers and all the analysing gear, and who knows what else these scientists need for this kind of venture. So we plant 3 charges of 100lbs along the length of the lab, one under each warehouse, and one under the vehicles, I reckon we can take the lot out without touching the living quarters."

"With 600lbs of explosives you will shift the whole fucking province," said Mike.

"Details, details!" said Jake laughing. "OK Mike I leave all the technical aspects of the explosives to you."

"Three 5lbs will shift the lab, and one under each warehouse, and the same with earth moving vehicles. 30lbs will do the job with safety."

"The one diesel generator at the rear of the lab, which is going continuously, I guess that must be for the computers," said Jake "They must have voltage stabilisers, the lot inside the lab, well the generator noise is on our side, lets go." He said.

They moved back along the mountain ridge, then down into the bush, then they returned to Mike's base camp to plan the caper.

"We will have to remove all the dynamite from the warehouse before we blow it," said Mike.

"I see," said Jake, "Or it could endanger the portakabins."

"Well I reckon if we don't the whole area will go up."

"OK" said Jake "I get your point. Either we empty all the explosives or we don't blow the warehouse."

"Well, said Mike, "Blowing one warehouse could start a reaction that would blow the other anyway."

"What you're saying is we don't have a choice," said Jake, "Let us consider the alternative, we could round up all the personnel, take them under guard into the bush, then blow the whole bloody lot, no problem, the snag with that is, if somebody played the have a go hero bit, it could get messy, and I can't risk that. So we empty all the dynamite, let us hope it doesn't take all night."

"I don't think they keep all that much anyway," said Mike.

The following day Jake, Mike with 8 rebels moved out in two

Range Rovers and a 1 ton truck, they arrived at the site at 11-0pm, they made camp as before, then Jake, Mike with 6 of the rebels made their way to the observation post, it was as before with just the one old guy on guard duty. All was quiet but there was some light showing in one of the cabin windows.

"We wait until all is in darkness," said Jake.

At 12 midnight all lights were out, they went back down into the bush, Jake then from the bush ran quietly to the end warehouse, then he peered round it at the guard who had his back to him, Jake then crept up on the guard very quietly and placed the spout of his AK 47 behind the mans ear, and spoke very gently, "Don't make a sound and you don't get hurt." The man froze, he was an old man with hair like grey cotton down, he whispered, "I don't want no trouble mister, you say quiet I is quiet."

"Then move nice and easy," said Jake.

He then took the guard back to the bush and the rebels sat him down against a tree, and tied him loosely, Jake then took a roll of Guineas from his hip pocket, and counted out 50 while the old man watched, he then put 50 Guineas into the old guard's shirt front pocket.

"Now," said Jake, "You sit nice and easy, and then when I go I will give you the other 50 Guineas." 100 Guineas was more than he could earn in a year at 8 Guineas a month which is all this type of security guard could earn. "But if you make a sound I will take back the 50 Guineas and gag you."

"Yes masser I be quiet, like a fly I be." Jake then took 4 men with bolt cutters, they went to the warehouse cut off the padlock and opened the double doors wide and went inside, they could see reasonably well it was a bright moon light night, they started to unload the warehouse. Mike started to make and prepare the dynamite bombs, he got them all in the correct size bundles, Jake having emptied the warehouse of all the dynamite, which took them 3 hours, placed the bundles as planned, under the respective buildings.

Mike had wired them to the detonators, 3 bundles each placed at 30 feet intervals under the lab, and one under each warehouse, and one in amongst the earth moving vehicles.

He then with the aid of two rebels pushed the 3 ton truck up near the portakabins, in the back of it, he put two gerry cans full of petrol each containing 20 gallons. He then went back to Mike.

"OK now I go and get the old man out of bed."

Jake then went and tried the door of the lab, as he expected it was locked, so he started to scrape the door with the toe of his boot, he knew that sooner or later it would bring the big guy to investigate. Sure enough within 6 or 7 minutes Jake heard a mumbling noise, he was now making quite a racket with the toe of his boot, the muttering got louder and the door catch went and the door opened. Jake shoved the spout of the A.K. auto under the guy's chin which hooked his bottom jaw, and pulled gently, with the forefinger of his right hand against pursed lips indicating silence he said, "Keep it very quiet and nobody gets hurt."

The man obeyed and was taken into the bush with the rebels, Jake sat down and tied him, the man had a very apprehensive look on his face, it isn't a pleasant experience to have a rifle spout stuck in your throat."

"What are you going to do to me?" the man asked, in a very uneasy tone of voice.

"Well you will not be harmed, so you needn't worry on that count," said Jake.

"Then do you mind if I ask, what it is all about, seeing that there is nothing I can do about it."

"Well like I say, no one will be harmed," said Jake.

"We just want to set back ECC's operation for a spell."

"But why?" asked the big guy.

"Well in the first place, these mountains do not belong to Ligeria, they belong to Cameroon."

"Then it is the government of Cam..."

"Quiet!" snapped Jake, "It is most impolite to interrupt." The man nodded. "And you would never have got permission to mine from Ligeria, if ECC had not paid for Elido's assassination.

"Never!" said the big guy in astonishment.

"Oh you didn't know, well now." Jake was putting on an act of mock surprise, "Anyway I have no time to discuss the matter, just sit still and stay quiet."

He left the man watching him, and went back to Mike. "OK now get in the chopper and get airborne, when I see you safely out of way and clear I'll blast, then Mike fly back over as though you were surveying your handiwork, then head East over the border of Cameroon, fly North for a couple of miles, then turn and I will see you back at base tomorrow noon."

"OK good luck," said Mike. He then ran across to the chopper, got in and started the rotors and lifted off, once airborne he moved well out of range, Jake then made a last minute check, everyone was clear and ready, he plunged the detonator.

The entire complex went with one hell of a bang and flash, it seemed ages before the debris stopped falling, where the lab and warehouses had been was now just a firing inferno, Jake figured that was due to the chemicals kept there.

Portakabins' doors were now being flung open, and men were coming out, Jake's men were instructed to move out, all the spoils were in the 1 and a half ton truck, Jake released the old guard slipping him the other 50 Guineas, as he did so he winked and the old man smiled. Jake then went to release the big guy, saying.

"You have a 3 ton truck with 40 gallons extra petrol, so you are not stranded, you also have your radio, do not try to follow us, that would be futile and dangerous for you." The sound of the chopper then came over, it was deafening, it hovered for a few minutes, then flew East over the border with Cameroon.

Jake smiled, Mike was playing his part to perfection, Jake then jumped into his Range Rover and moved off at good speed, he soon caught up to and passed his men who had been stalling giving him time to catch up, then as a small convoy they moved at a good speed heading back to the base.

Wednesday 17th Jake arrived back at base, and was greeted by Pike. "Did you enjoy yourself?" asked Pike.

"Yes Sir I had myself a ball, and Major Horn got himself a helicopter, which has pleased him some, as you can imagine, I figure I've just cost the ECC in excess of nine million pounds Sterling, because I know for a fact that no insurance company will give goods cover, once they have reached Bakra docks, not even unloading is covered. Yes Colonel I am very pleased."

"Jake I've been giving your suggestion of hitting the National Guard headquarters a lot of thought they moved over to the chart table, Pike then started to explain the way he saw it. "With 6 mortars from these roof tops, maintaining a constant bombardment, we could devastate the N.G. headquarters." Pike pointed out the sections of the Cafrint warehouse roof. The warehouse was a complex consisting of a huge square 30 yards by 30 yards, with a two storey warehouse on either side, and a two storey warehouse at the back.

"Now," said Pike, "We know the heights of the buildings and the distances, therefore with this knowledge we can go out into the bush, and carry out exercises to train our gunners with accuracy, the last thing anyone would expect would be a rebel attack on the N.G. headquarters."

Their reaction would be the same as Adams was, utter disbelief.

"I admit, Captain, I also thought you were, well for the want of a better phrase, not quite tuned in. However on reflection I believe we could do it, with, as I say, a constant bombardment, of mortars and the rockets, and of course the gunship. We are back to our full compliment of 60 men, the General has sent us replacements for the men we lost, he is getting dissenters every day from the regular army, particularly from the commissioned ranks. Yes, Captain, I am confident we can do it, but we will need to be meticulous with the planning.

*   *   *   *   *

December 20th Friday,

Board Meeting ECC

"Well gentlemen I take it you have all read the report submitted by our colleague Edward, are there any comments before I go on?"

"I would like to say something Mr Chairman."

180

"Yes go ahead Leonard."

"It is obvious, to me anyway, that the Cameroons were responsible for the destruction of our equipment, so I propose strong representations should be made to their embassy here in London."

"Agreed." came the comments from the table.

"Particularly since we were not covered by insurance, we all know the situation regarding insurance cover and Ligeria, the total material cost is nine million two hundred and forty thousand pounds, plus the cost of the setback."

"Mr Chairman Sir," it was the technical director.

"Yes Barry."

"The news media have been on to me, in view of the situation in Ligeria, they want to know our intentions, I'm stalling of course, but we will have to make a statement of our intentions, we will have to do something."

"Mr Chairman."

"Yes Leonard."

"I would like to know what we intend to do, or say, so I suggest we get on to their embassy now."

"Very well Leonard all your comments and suggestions are minuted and will be acted upon, there is however one aspect that Edward didn't put in the report, because he considered it too sensitive to put into print at this time, and I agree, therefore Edward will now enlighten you."

Edward stood, he was the company Geologist.

"Gentlemen you have all read my report, when I was taken at gun point into the bush, the mercenary told me in addition to the fact that the particular mountain range belongs to the Cameroon, he said we would never have got the mining concession from Ligeria if we had not paid for the assassination of President Elido, those were his exact words. The mercenary was an Englishman from the North country Lancashire I'd say," there was a hush that had descended on the board room. The financial director broke the silence.

"That's absurd." That was the first time the financial director had not spoken through the chair, he was begging to lose his cool.

"Well," said Edward, "I am merely repeating the mercenary's

words, exactly as he spoke them."

"I don't like it." went on Leonard the financial director, "I was never happy at allowing the NSP half a million pounds to fight their election campaign, but assassination? Never! The whole thing is ludicrous, Mr Chairman I think we should have a report from the ambassador Simon Denning."

"Yes," said the Chairman, "But he did resign in October of last year."

Leonard then said, "But he made all the financial arrangements."

"Yes I am aware of that," said the Chairman, "But he was merely representing us in a private capacity, not in any way connected with the government here in the U.K. or Ligeria."

"But he had the blessing of the energy secretary," said Leonard.

"Yes I am aware of that," said the Chairman. "But again everybody had wanted the project underwritten by the British Government, a civil servant from the Home Office would have been involved with whole project.

It was the NSP that Simon became involved with, because of his association with Unico Sandies who is the leader of the NSP now Sandies was the Ligerian Ambassador in London for a considerable number of years, he and Simon associated both professionally and socially because of their respective government positions. Sandies was the Ligerian ambassador under no less than four military dictators, his son graduated from Sandhurst military academy, and his daughter from London University, it would appear that they would be the ideal people to form a Government in their own country.

That gentlemen was why the NSP was formed, so if you like the ECC became the sponsors of the Sandies, and in return we were to get the mining rights for the Uranium."

"But that didn't give us the mining rights." Commented Leonard.

"They were to become ours if and when the NSP were elected to government, and at the time there were no elections imminent, the rights became ours when Elido was assassinated, but then the Sandies were assassinated, good heavens! What are we involved with?"

Leonard was beginning to perspire, he was visibly upsetting himself.

"Please Leonard don't get yourself so upset, we will I'm sure get to the bottom of it." Said the Chairman. There were all kinds of comments now being banded about.

"Please gentlemen please." burst in the Chairman "We are at this time in a situation without precedence, I will of course speak to Simon on this subject, and I think in view of the loss suffered, and the possible danger to our people, we suspend operations there until stability becomes the norm.

That is my proposal gentlemen, anyone against, none, then it is carried. We will continue this meeting at some convenient date, after the festive season, early January.

* * * * *

Monday 6th January,

"Good evening Margaret it is nice to see you."

"Hello Charles how are you, and how is Betty?"

"We are both fine Margaret, I've called to see Simon actually."

"He is in the study I'll call him."

"No, don't bother Margaret I'll just go to the study, it is business, I don't want to bother you with it, we won't be long."

Charles Johnson, President of ECC, knocked on the door and walked in, "Good evening Simon." Simon was just going through some papers, he turned, "Hello Charles, this is a pleasant surprise, come in take a seat, I'm just finished."

"Simon, I have something of importance to talk to you about, I couldn't mention it before, because you know Betty, I'd been given strict instructions, no business discussions during the festive celebrations."

"Oh, I understand Charles. Margaret is just the same, but I can't blame them really, there is a limit I guess."

"Well Simon you know about the destruction of our camp, at the base of the Otlantika mountains."

183

"Yes of course nasty business that, what will you have to drink? We cannot talk without a drink."

"Thank you Simon I'll have a small whisky and water." Simon poured the drinks and handed one to Charles, who then went to explain the situation with reference to the mercenary and their Geologist Edward, Charles left nothing out, every detail of the loss, every word the mercenary said in his North country accent. Simon then lapsed into deep thought... Tully was a Lancashire man, a dark horse that! He had made the hit on Elido in an unbelievably professional way, he then killed his own would be killer, who had been specially selected for the job, Tully was the other man besides himself who knew the true situation regarding the Elido hit, yes it was Tully who destroyed the ECC camp, leading the Ligerian rebels, it had nothing to do with the Cameroon. It was Tully who killed the Sandies in their own home and their guards. One day he would return to England having restored power to the Elido factions, then no doubt he will come after me.' he thought, 'Then all would come out, everything would be revealed, for all correspondence between the Ligerian government and the British government is recorded with time and date when it is sealed in the diplomatic bag, the bags he never allowed to be delivered, it needed the Sandies in power to make him, and now to save him. But that could never be, not now not ever, he would be ruined, and Margaret, his name would be blackened for all time, and he could possibly be charged with Treason, if not that some other serious charge, and he could not allow that to happen.

"Simon, Simon are you all right?" There was concern in Charles's voice.

"Yes, yes I'm sorry I've not been well of late, I don't really know what is wrong with me."

"What do you say to my query Simon, can you throw any light on it?" Charles asked.

"No, no I really don't know anything, I acted in good faith, if that confounded man Tu...." at that he checked himself, and stopped abruptly.

"Go on Simon, confounded man who?"

"Oh nothing, look Charles I'm very tired perhaps we could

continue this some other time it is very late, I must retire, good night Charles." he then left the room.

Charles thought he shouldn't push it, so he went down to the living room.

His sister Margaret was in the living room, watching television, she looked up.

"Hello Charles where's Simon?" she said, as she got up and switched off the set, "And whatever is wrong? You have such a pensive look on your face."

"Oh nothing Margaret."

"Where is Simon?" she asked again,

"He has retired he is not feeling well."

"You know Charles, Simon has never been the same since he retired, I know he worries a lot, but he doesn't admit it, and he becomes moody, which is so unlike him, there is something terribly wrong Charles, but what?"

"I will talk with him again Margaret, we will get to the bottom of it, rest assured love, we will sort it out."

"Thank you Charles, I know you will, Simon thinks a lot of you Charles."

"Whatever it is, we'll resolve it, I'll be off now, good night."

"Good night Charles."

On his drive back he was deep in thought, the situation was a mess, an unbelievable mess, last year's audit showed half a million pounds cost for Uranium exploration, which in a manner of speaking it was, and it could not be written off as a loss, because of the team and equipment that was subsequently sent out there.

What puzzled Charles was, President Elido had refused to give ECC the mining concession, a British company, yet it was never mentioned in government circles, meaning the government had never been informed of the refusal, or the reason for it, most irregular, and Simon had the blessing of the energy secretary, this having been stressed during negotiations between Simon, the President and himself, during his own visit to Ligeria for negotiations.

What, if anything is Simon holding back? All correspondence at government level between the two countries comes through the respective ambassadors by hand in the diplomatic bag. For whatever reason, thought Charles, Simon is holding something back. And his retirement came as a surprise to everyone, including Margaret.

Charles arrived home at 12-15am, put his car away and let himself in the house, his wife Betty was watching a late night movie on television.

"Hello Charles, how did your meeting with Simon go?"

He went to his cocktail cabinet and poured himself a small whisky, then he sat down, "Not very well I'm afraid."

"Why ever not?" asked Betty.

"It's a long story and to be honest it is extremely difficult to figure."

"Oh, you will figure it out I'm sure. Well dear I'm off to bed now, good night."

"Good night dear." Charles replied.

He went over events over and over again, but to no avail, so he retired.

* * * * *

Denning's Suicide

That night after Charles had gone, Margaret had gone to bed, she asked Simon what was bothering him, he passed it off saying he was tired.

At 2-0am whilst Margaret was sleeping, Simon got up and got his keyring from his trouser pocket, then left the room quietly, and went to his study. He then sat at his desk, took the keyring and selected a key, he opened the left hand corner drawer, and took out his old service revolver, he then started to write a letter.

My beloved Margaret,
I trust you will forgive me this terrible act I am about to commit, my whole life I have dedicated to you and my country, mistakes I have made, and all mistakes have to be paid for. I must at all cost protect you and our good name, I love you my dear cherish my memory as you knew me.

He then signed the letter, put it in an envelope sealed it addressed it 'Margaret'.

He then put the revolver to his head, and squeezed the trigger.

* * * * *

Charles's Awakening

Charles was awakened by the telephone ringing, he reached over and pressed the mute button on his alarm clock, but the ringing continued, realisation finally dawned, he picked up the phone. "Who can that be at this time?" said Betty in a muffled voice. The alarm clock showed 3-0am, it was Margaret in hysterics, trying to tell her brother what she had found after being awoke by the gun shot. She finally managed to blurt out that Simon had shot himself. Charles was fully awake now, trying to calm her down a little. "Have you phoned an ambulance?" he was saying, but he couldn't get any sense from her.

"Margaret, for heaven's sake stop it!" She quietened, "Now Margaret," said Charles in a soothing voice, "put the phone down but don't hang up, go get yourself a brandy, will you do that for me Margaret? Do it now then come back to me." Margaret did exactly as she was told, she was acting like a robot. She got the brandy came back and mumbled "Charles" into the phone. "Now Margaret take a big drink on the brandy." She shuddered when she swallowed, but it seemed to bring her back to reality.

"Now do you think you could phone for an ambulance?" asked Charles.

"Yes, yes will you come please."

"I'm on my way dear see you shortly." Charles was out of bed, putting on his trousers, "Betty, phone the ambulance service ask them to check their Richmond depot, to see if they received an emergency call from Stretford Road, if not send an ambulance a possible suicide."

"Right Charles," she said, then Charles ran out.

He broke all speed limits, he arrived at 4-15am, the door was opened by a police woman, "My name is Charles Johnson," he said as he pushed his way in, "I'm Margaret's brother, she called me, what is it all about?"

"In the room at the head of the stairs Sir," she said. Charles took the stairs two at a time, and went right into the study,

"Who the hell are you?" asked one of the policemen, there were three plain clothed police, and a doctor, and one man taking photographs, Charles pointed to Simon, who lay across his desk in a pool of blood, "I'm Simon's brother, well that is too say, his brother-in-law, Margaret is my sister."

Then Charles seemed to gather himself, "Where is Margaret?"

"My name is Kelly, I've sedated Mrs Denning and sent her to hospital, she is in a very distressed state," said the doctor.

"Yes she was hysterical on the phone, what happened?"

"Well, it was suicide, he left a letter for his wife."

"Could I see it do you think?" The senior officer then took an envelope from his pocket, and handed it to Charles.

"Mrs Denning was in no state to read this, in fact it was just where Mr Denning had placed it, unopened, when we arrived with the ambulance, it can't do any harm please read it."

Charles took it, saying "Thank you."

Charles read the letter, "It would appear he was worried about his good name, whatever these mistakes were he claims to have made must have unbalanced him." said the senior policeman.

"Would you care to comment Sir?"

"I can't for the life of me think what could have unbalanced him." Charles still had his pyjama coat on under his jacket, and he was still wearing his carpet slippers. He sat down, this was one of the very rare occasions that Charles Johnson felt a little lost.

"Do you think I could have a drink please?" asked Charles.

"Sure help yourself." Charles just sat there looking into space, his mind was racing looking for an answer, it was something to do with his early retirement, something to do with Ligeria, it had to be. The senior policeman crossed over to him, and in a quiet voice said, "If you tell me where it is I will get you one, a drink that is."

Charles recovered himself, "Yes of course." he said, "In the cabinet," and pointed to the cabinet on the opposite wall. The policeman nodded to his colleague, who went over to the cabinet and poured Charles a large brandy, then brought it over to him.

"Thank you," he said, "Please help yourself this is a distressing situation for everyone."

"Thank you Sir, but we won't bother, do you know of any reasons that could have contributed to the situation, that could have caused your brother-in-law to become unbalanced."

"No, but I will go through Simon's affairs with Margaret when she is able."

* * * * *

6-1-1976.

Pike called Adam, Jake and their gunners to a briefing at 1-30pm, "Well gentlemen I've called this briefing to go over the plan for the N.G. attack, which will be on 25th January, the festivities that will be taking place at the headquarters, at that time will be on our side, as you put it to me Captain, half the N.G. will be drunk. However be that as it may, what is required is absolute accuracy, without which we fall and perish."

Pike got up and walked over to the blackboard, the charts of the N.G. headquarters were now vertical being over the blackboard, to make them easy for all to see.

Pike carried on. "These gentlemen are the warehouses of the Cafprint Textile Mill, now on each roof we will have 3 mortars and 1 rocket launcher, these buildings here and these two machine gun posts are the targets for the mortars." Pike indicating two 4 storey buildings. "These are the main barrack blocks that house most of the men, two mortars to each building will send a continuous bombardment, and I mean continuous, now out here as you know all buildings are built from breeze block and mortar, which means they will crumble easily, if they were brick and cement we couldn't do what we will, with our particular weapons.

189

The first salvo and subsequent salvos will be accurate, and as I say continuous, the other two mortars will go for these two machine gun posts, now they cannot be seen from the warehouse roof top positions, that is the idea of the manoeuvres you have been doing, you have the distances and the heights.

Major you set up your mortars accordingly, the same goes for you Captain, you will carry on with the manoeuvres over the next 10 days, then I will assess your accuracy.

Now the rocket launcher, one will take out the front main gate, and guard house, the second the front perimeter wall, gentlemen, after the mortars have had 3 salvos at the machine gun posts, they move their attack on to the buildings, the rocket launcher having taken out the front entrance and wall, will fire at, and through the gable ends of these particular buildings, Major is this clear?"

"Yes Sir."

"Because," went on Pike, "As soon as the main entrance and wall have gone, you lead your eight 3 toners with 122 men, the tarpaulin covers will be removed to allow the men to fire in transit. The attack will commence at precisely 12 midnight, you lead the attack Major in your jeep, you will have a driver and a gunner with rocket launcher and 8 rockets, his first target will be the machine gun posts, on the off chance they survived the mortar attack. Then he will concentrate his attack on the barrack block main entrance, because some of the guards will manage to regroup, and they will make for the main exits." Pike then flung the chart over the blackboard, revealing the second chart. "This gentlemen is the rear of the headquarters, you Captain lead the attack here, your 6 mortars concentrate your salvos on these targets." Pike pointed out the 2 storey buildings, "these are officers' living quarters, this is the recreation building and mess hall, and this is the radio room. This is the admin block, and here we have the armoury and fuel store, the recreation room, which we must assume, is where the celebrations will be held, this single storey building is the officers' briefing room, I don't expect anybody to be in there, it would be unlikely anyway.

Your rocket launchers will take out the rear entrance and guard room, and of course the wall, then you follow exactly as the Major leading your three 3 toners with 40 men. You have no roof tops to fire from, just floor level, between derelict buildings and bushlands, 10 men will guard the warehouse and 10 men will guard our rear gunners, that is just a precaution, we will leave nothing to chance.

Now gentlemen there could well be contingents of some kind that we are not aware of, so our foot soldiers will have to cope with whatever there may be. Each man will have an AK 47 automatic with 10 magazines, each 3 toner will have cases of ammunition, should they be required, but if our gunners do an accurate job they shouldn't be necessary."

Now gentlemen, and this is most important, the first salvo from both front and rear will be at precisely 12 midnight. I shall be in the gunship just out of hearing range of the N.G. as the first salvo goes I move in I can be there within 7 seconds, I shall have 12 rockets along with the machine guns I will have a co-pilot and two gunners, we will have medical facilities in the Cafprint warehouse; Gloria, Doc and our medic will set up an emergency treatment clinic."

"Why bring them into it?" interrupted Jake.

"I agree," said Adam.

"As I was saying," carried on Pike. "The bombardment will be continuous, until you Major are satisfied that the battle is over and won, then you will fire a red flare to end it."

"Permission to speak Sir," said Jake.

"Yes Captain, what is it?"

"Why bring Gloria, Doc and Gerald into it?"

"Because Captain as you once put it, this is our go for broke exercise, if we fail we are finished, dead, it follows therefore that we won't fail, and we will need our medical staff on hand."

"But Sir," broke in Jake, Adam grabbed Jake's arm, and shook his head, "Leave it Jake, decisions have all been made."

"I understand gentlemen that there is a compliment of 2,700 guardsmen, so that is odds of 15 to 1, under the circumstances I think they are pretty fair!" said Pike smiling. "For the next ten days I want you out in the bush, setting up your ranges and fire for accuracy, ten days from now I shall expect a perfect demonstration.

Thank you gentlemen the briefing is over, unless there are any questions, no? Thank you."

Pike then went over to Adam and Jake, "Will you join me for a drink gentlemen?" They all went over to Pike's tent. Gloria, Gerald and Doc were waiting.

"Gloria my dear would you be so kind and pour us all a drink please?" Pike was always the perfect gentlemen, cool, calm, never got ruffled, he was a typical British army officer, a professional killer, the most sophisticated type, the calm calculating kind, by comparison Adam and Jake were just bar room brawlers.

Gloria went to the cocktail cabinet, got 5 glasses, and poured three fingers of whisky into one of them. Doc went over to her.

"I'll pour Gloria dear," he said, as he took the bottle, and filled the other three to the brim. "Of course!" Gloria replied.

"What will you have Gerald?" Doc asked.

"A gin and tonic would be nice." he replied.

"Of course, courtesy of the ordinance depot and various other such places!" said Doc grinning. Pike then raised his glass, "I would like to propose a toast." at that Gloria poured herself a tonic, Pike then said, "To success." they all repeated.

"Success."

"You know something," Jake said, "You people are all crazy, you Gloria and Gerald, you could go down into Bakra get good jobs and live in peace, or better still go home, you Adam and you Colonel I understand you fight for a living."

"That's not all together the case," said Pike, "I have lived in Ligeria now for the best part of 25 years, I've seen a lot of changes and quite a few governments, the country had a chance under President Elido to achieve social reform, that would have given the country a chance to develop, but I'm afraid under this lot, no chance."

Gloria then spoke, "I want to see order restored as it was before Elido's demise, otherwise there will be endless slavery and killing, what is left of the Elido government are the people to bring that about, that is what this struggle is all about. General Adejumo is the only one who can do this, he is Mausa but like Elido he knows that in a modern world, tribes must unite and live in harmony, with no tribe subservient to another, Elido's government was a combination of all tribes, Mausa, Urobar, Benine, Ibo, all were represented, under this power crazed NSP backed by the National Guard, all of whom are Mausa the chaos will continue, we have all lost people dear to us, because of the NSP"

There followed an uneasy silence, after Gloria's little speech. Jake realised he had done it again, opened his big mouth, why couldn't he keep his bloody mouth shut.

Adam broke the spell, "I do it for the money myself, what is your reason Jake?"

Jake couldn't think of what to say, but all eyes were on him, "Well," he said, "I, err, that is to say, maybe I have personal reasons for agreeing with all that you have said, and like Adam I do it for the money."

"I don't think so," said Gloria, "it goes much deeper than that, maybe you fight for the same reasons you drink."

"I'll retire if I may Sir?" said Jake, this kind of talk didn't sit too well with him.

"As you like," said Pike, Jake got up immediately and made for the tent flap.

"Jake!" called Gloria, "You are a troubled man, you are amongst friends, we can help you." Jake paused at the tent flap, he didn't turn, after a few seconds he raised the tent flap and walked out. Gloria said, "You have a sick man there Colonel, a very sick man."

"He's alright," said Adam, "he's got problems but who hasn't."

"When we get order," said Pike, "Then we will be able to do something for him."

"If he lives to see it," said Adam, "which I doubt, and which he doesn't care." Jake went back to his tent, the afternoon was just ebbing, he threw off his clothes, wrapped a towel round his waist, he would take a shower, he was mad with himself for opening his big mouth, would he never learn, he had done it before, always giving himself problems, that was the one thing that he was obviously good at, he walked to the shower, he stood under it and let the water pelt him, he felt a little better now, he came out of the shower wrapped in the towel, and walked round the back of the shower block.

The block was situated on the North end of the base camp, there was nothing at the rear but a mountain range and open bushlands, then a little further on a dense forest. Jake had stood there many times before to reminisce, in the solitude of it, he was gazing up at the sun, which was just setting in the Western sky. It inflamed the Heavens in a crimson glow that changed the smooth black mountain rock to a magnificent pale marble, a beautiful sight, thought Jake, one no artist's brush could capture. But to Jake there was no beauty to equal that which he saw in Jane and their children, yet he had done them a terrible wrong, what right had he to deprive his Jane of her husband, or their children of their father, and this he had done, when he signed that blasted one year contract.

"You look so sad," said Gloria, as she had silently approached she now stood about 3 yards or so to his left, he said nothing he stood as he was, gazing up at the sky, after sometime he turned and looked at her, held her gaze paused, then walked away. Jake went back to his tent.

* * * * *

Chairman's last meeting at ECC

Friday 10th January,

"Well gentlemen I will try to clarify the situation as I see it, but I'm afraid there is actually very little I can tell you of any significance. You are all aware of the tragic death of Simon Denning, it has been a very severe blow to Margaret and myself, Simon was always very close, since we were children. It is difficult to come to terms with, but Oh! Forgive me gentlemen I'm going off at a tangent."

The Chairman was a very tough astute character, his manner of speaking was cold positive and matter of fact, yet he was under tremendous strain.

"I did speak to Simon about events we discussed at our last meeting, I learned nothing, and within a few hours or so of our meeting he was dead, there will be an inquest naturally, and the subject matter of the discussion will come out. That is inevitable with all the ramifications it will have on our company, however the inquest will be postponed until Margaret is well enough to attend."

The board room was in total silence, all eyes on the chairman, all faces grim.

"At this time she is in hospital having suffered a total breakdown, the Doctors say it could be months before she is well enough to attend an inquest. However, I accept full responsibility for what has turned out to be a fiasco in Ligeria, I therefore tender my resignation as managing director and chairman of the board of Evens Chemical Company."

Comments were being raised and objections, when the chairman's hand went up, palm forward to quieten everybody, "I have every intention of looking into the allegations of this mercenary character, I will do this privately of course, I've written to Unico Sandies requesting a meeting with him, on his agreement I shall fly out to Ligeria, it would appear that he is the only living person who can throw any light on the situation, thank you gentlemen."

GO FOR BROKE

It was 18 January, all arrangements had been finished, Pike was satisfied with the gunners accuracy, the demonstration had gone well. The trucks had all been painted to give them a civilian appearance, the convoy set off on there 6 day journey through the bush to their rendezvous. Jake sat escort in the Land Rover, Adam was driving his jeep, the journey was uneventful, when they arrived they set up camp, a reconnaissance party had been there since the 14th January, they had collected the General's men from the bush bars, so a compliment of 180 men were at the ready.

At 7-0pm Adam in civilian clothes walked into the Cafprint warehouse, he spoke to the man behind the counter,

"Good evening friend, are you the only one on duty?"

"No Sir," the man replied, "My clerk and the second storeman are in the office."

Adam nodded to his men, who raised the flap of the counter, pushed open the gate and walked in.

"Hey, you can't do that." said the storeman, Adam then produced his revolver and said, "Now be a good boy and nobody gets hurt." the man froze, they then rounded up the other employees, put them all in the office, and said, "Now if you all be quiet you get a bonus." Adam then produced a wad of Guinea notes, he gave each man 50, then said, "We don't want to steal anything, we just want to borrow your warehouse for a couple of hours." Each man looked at the 50 Guineas, they couldn't believe their luck, they only got 12 Guineas a month salary, Adam then said, "Right, I am going to lock you in, I will release you later, now be quiet."

Jake with his boiler suit over his jungle greens, drove up to the back roll shutter door, and reversed inside, his men with their arms and equipment then got out to unload their gear. Adam then took his 16 gunners on the roof, Jake having done exactly the same on the other block, which was opposite the one with Adam, separated by the drive through and turn round area.

They got their gunners set up and ready, they had synchronised their watches, they were to fire their first salvo at 12 midnight. Pike was hovering just out of ear shot of the N.G. then he would be into the affray immediately.

Adam threw off his civilian clothes, and put on his jungle greens, he then went and unlocked the office door, gave the three men another 50 Guineas, he told them to leave the back way, not to run and not to look back. Jake then got into one of his 3 ton trucks and drove round the back, followed by the others, they arrived at the rear of the N.G. headquarters, among the derelict buildings and sparse areas, there were no shanties and no squatters, not this close to the N.G. He got his men all set up.

They removed the tarpaulin from the truck and got in, all was now ready, all men had anxious faces. Adam was just moving slowly up the truck drive through, a feeling of excitement or fear or whatever, he could never really define the feeling, but on these exercises it was always there, it was all part of Adam's life.

It was now midnight the first volley struck, the front the guard room and wall just disintegrated, Adam's driver then stood on the accelerator, and was through before the debris had finished falling, Jake enjoyed the same success, the rear entrance the guard room and wall disintegrated and Jake was through. He had waited a long time for this, now the bastards were about to pay, for the death of Elido and the destruction of Joe Tully.

Jake was going to enjoy this, his rocket launcher had destroyed the radio room at first shot, Jake and his 7 men who would follow him to hell and back if needs be, were out of their truck and literally mowed down the guardsmen, as they came running out of various buildings. Men were pouring out of the main barrack block, when Adam's gunner fired a rocket and hit the front just above the door, the lot went, and the entire front wall collapsed taking the guardsmen with it.

What men got through were mercilessly gunned down they had no chance, Jake then with his 7 men crashed into the recreation room where the celebrations were being held, the men were literally spraying the place with bullets. "Stop this slaughter" cried one of the officers, before Jake blew his head off.

He was searching for the Sandies and Co., but he couldn't find them, then the roof started to cave in, as the people were all crowding to the back of the hall, for safety, all were to be buried alive. "Out" cried Jake to his men, guardsmen trying to escape over the roof were gunned down by Pike, his rockets were having a devastating effect, and his machine guns were finishing off. The entire N.G. headquarters was virtually demolished, and still the mortars were falling as were rockets. Jake was throwing hand grenades through windows of buildings, that were not completely demolished, anywhere he thought he saw movement, he was a man possessed. A small group of guardsmen came running out of what was left of the mess hall, they were all carrying A.K. 47 automatics, Jake ran at them screaming and firing, at the same time the last remaining machine gun was firing at him.

Adam then arrived on the scene, firing at the machine gun post pushing them off their aim, Adam saw a guard appear from behind a pile of rubble he threw a grenade at Jake, Adam shot him the grenade went wide, it exploded against a wall blowing out what was left of the window, this hit Jake square on lifting him off his feet along with two of his men.

Adam ran over to him and helped him up, "Hell you look like you just came off a butcher's block." he said, "I'd better get you over to Doc."

"The Sandies Adam, I can't find the Sandies,"

"Jake you need to see the Doc, to hell with the Sandies."

"The briefing room Adam, it must be!" said Jake, the briefing room was terraced onto the 4 storey barrack block which had protected it, "I must check it out Adam."

"No, wait Jake, it is protected with that last machine gun post, I'll get the rocket launcher that will shift it."

"I will do it," said Jake, he put down one of his A.K. autos, that he had been using, renewed the magazine in the other, then he took out a grenade pulled the pin and holding the detonator clip in place in his hand, he set off running in a zig zag fashion for the machine gun post, he was screaming and firing on repetition.

Bullets were kicking up the ground around him, and one took

a piece of his right tricep muscle away. Adam watched in amazement. 'Crazy bloody nut case' he said to himself. Jake ran on screaming and firing, his firing was going into the machine gun port, putting the gunners off their aim and putting one out of action.

Jake got to within 8 yards or so of the machine gun post, then he stopped, and threw the grenade as he would throw a ball, then he fell flat on the ground. The grenade went in the gun port and exploded, blowing out bits of body and gun, Jake then got up changed the magazine on his gun, then he just stood upright head held back and started to scream, "Tully is back you bastards now you pay."

Pike landed the gun ship on the end of the square and ran over to Adam, "We did it Major, fire the flare!" Adam took the flare gun from his pouch, and fired the red flare. The mortar shells were now landing on buildings already demolished, they stopped.

There was now relative quiet, Jake in the meantime had turned through 90 degrees ran to the ramp that led up to the briefing room jumped up onto it, and started to run towards the briefing room door, firing as he ran on repetition, the door was splintering and falling apart.

As he approached the door, he leaped at it turning his right shoulder towards it to take the impact, he hit the door the lot, including part of the door jamb, crashed to the floor, Jake as he hit the deck was changing the magazine then firing, he got to his feet and moved into the room, at no time since he hit the door had he stopped shooting, with the exception of no more than one second, it took him to change a magazine, Adam looked at Pike. "If I live to be a hundred Sir, I will never see the like of him again."

They both looked towards the briefing room door, it was maybe 30 yards away, from where they were standing, they could hear the screaming swearing cursing, and firing coming from the room, it was bedlam, there was also the odd shot or two coming from various areas of the compound, from rebels who were seeing movement.

There was now an uncanny silence, then Jake appeared at the briefing room doorway, he slumped leaning on what was left of the door jamb, his A.K. rifle held loosely by his side, he was covered in blood mostly his own, from his forehead down to his thighs. He

drooped to his knees, Adam and Pike ran across to him, Adam dropping on one knee by his side, he put his arm around him to support
him, Jake turned his head towards Adam, he looked to be in a trance.

The blood ran into his eyes, flowed around his eyeballs, he
didn't even blink, his jaw moved, his lips were trembling, Adam
leaned his head in close to catch the words, "Adam," he said, the
words were barely audible just a faint croaking whisper, "It's over,
please let..., me... go." then he collapsed. Adam made him as comfortable as possible on the ground, tore off his own shirt, rolled it up
and put it under Jake's head as a pillow.

He then felt his neck for a pulse, after a few seconds Pike said,
"Is he dead?" Adam replied screaming, "Dead, you could never kill
this crazy fucker." He then looked round at what was left of Jake's
men, "You! You gormless pricks get me fucking truck, now, move
move move." Adam was now screaming to the point of hysteria.
"Steady Major," said Pike, "Steady."

"Steady?" cried Adam, "I am stood up to my arse in dead
bodies and you say steady, can't you for once get ruffled, or angry,
or loose your fucking temper." Adam was beginning to quieten a
little, "Must you be always so calm?" with that Adam's voice trailed
off, he just sighed and shook his head in despair.

"Loosing one's temper, Adam," said Pike, "Merely consumes
energy and muddles the thinking. Come Adam lad, let us see what it
was that drove Jake the way it did." Pike then moved off to enter the
briefing room, Adam looked round, called over some of the rebels
that were looking on, "Come here you lot," the rebels came at the
double, Adam then stood, "Now you guard the Captain," pointing to
Jake's prostrate figure at his feet. "If a fly as much as settles on him,
I'll tear out your bellies and feed em to the buzzards, understand."

"Yes Sir," they replied, "We guard the Captain, yes Sir."

Adam then walked into the briefing room, the emergency battery lighting had come on automatically, when the transformers were
destroyed. Over by the chart tables at the far wall lay 7 mutilated
bodies. Old man Sandies' head was all but severed from his body.
Lentoy was similar, and his left arm was completely severed at the
shoulder, Buhari's chest had been blown away, both their wives Pursa

and Gertrude had their faces obliterated. Mires, the acting President, lay with his eyes open, and his lower jaw missing, his Colt revolver still clutched in his hand, and next to him lay two mutilated subalterns. Adam looked at the grizzly sight and said, "I guess we will never really know, what it was these people did to Jake, but by hell they paid." Pike replied, "He did say, Adam, that they would never see the light this coming morning, and when he said it, he made a statement of fact, with us or without us, I believe this would still have been the case."

"You and me Colonel," said Adam. "We have killed many times in battle, but this!" he said as he kicked a pile of empty magazines at his feet, "I guess Gloria was right when she said Jake was sick, well Colonel he is sick in the head." Just then they heard the truck arrive outside, Adam turned and ran for the doorway, followed by Pike, the rebel turned the truck round and reversed it to the ramp where Jake lay, "Right now," said Adam, as he eased Jake's shoulders off the ground, "Put your arms under the Captain and clutch each other's hands, got that?"

"Yes Sir," they replied.

"Ease up," said Adam, they lifted Jake on a stretcher made out of their arms, the driver dropped the tailboard, they got Jake settled in, with his head on Adam's shirt as a pillow.

"I'll see to Jake, Adam, tell my co pilot to bring the gun ship to the warehouse, I'll see you later, there is no need to rush, but at the same time don't hang about."

"Right Sir," replied Adam, the driver secured the tail board of the truck, Adam then grabbed him with both hands, by the shirt front, and yanked him up to him so that their faces were almost touching, "Now you take the Captain to Doc in the warehouse, fast and smooth, if you as much as make a ripple in the back here, I'll put you in a fucking wheel chair for the rest of your life, savvy?"

"Yes Sir very fast very smooth, oh yes Sir, no problem."

They drove to the warehouse, Pike got Jake across the men's arms as before, and they carried him in, Doc had two desks placed together end to end, for a treatment table. "I've brought you some business Doc," said Pike as they took Jake in, and placed him on the desk tops. "Heavens," said Doc, "He looks as if he just came off a bacon slicer, Gloria gasped, Doc lost no time cutting Jake's clothes away, and shouting instructions to Gloria and the medic.

Pike moved out, "I'll leave you with it Doc." he said, Doc didn't reply. Pike went outside just as Gerald drove up in a Range Rover, he was covered in grime and blood, as he dropped from his cab, shouting to the men who had brought Jake in to give him a lift, they started to unload more wounded, then he went back to the passenger door opened it and lifted out an unconscious man, and carried him into the warehouse as he would carry a child.

Pike got back into the truck they had come in, "Back to the N.G." he said to the driver, Doc and Gloria were working at great speed on Jake, the medic and Gerald were working on the other wounded. Jake had severe lacerations across his shoulders chest and stomach, his forehead and right cheek and a part of his right tricep was missing, and he had a bullet in his left hip. Doc had the blood transfusion linked up to Jake, then he started to open his hip to remove the bullet.

Pike arrived back at N.G. headquarters he found Adam.

"Well Major what is the position."

"Come Sir," said Adam and took the Colonel round to the vehicle compounds, "What's this?" said Pike.

"Prisoners Sir, but I had no choice, they came from what is left of the far barrack block, some of them bollock naked, with their hands up over their heads, what could I do?" Adam looked a little dismayed, "I couldn't just shoot them could I Sir?"

There followed an uneasy moment's silence, that seemed like an age to Adam, for always Pike's final specific instructions were the same: "Remember, gentlemen, we take no prisoners." and here was Adam with 72, then Pike spoke. "No of course not." Adam sighed with relief.

"There are 72 Sir, all squaddies with one corporal."

"No officers?" said Pike.

"No Sir," replied Adam.

"Are you sure?"

"Yes Sir they are only lads and terrified."

"Very well Major strip them down to their underpants, and turn them loose."

"You mean free Sir."

"Yes what harm can they do us, the N.G. is of now I'd say finished." Adam then started to shout orders to his men,

"Sir." He called, "We will be ready to move out shortly, there is nothing worth salvaging, except for a couple of trucks everything else was destroyed."

"Right Major I'll be in the warehouse, I'll take the wounded back to base in the gunship."

"How's Jake Sir?"

"Doc is working on him, we will just have to wait and see."

Two hours passed Adam went back to the warehouse the gunship was parked outside in the drive through, Doc and Gloria were just finishing taping Jake's wounds. Pike and Adam approached, "How is he Doc?" Doc looked shattered. "He is bad Colonel, he is in shock, deep shock, he could pull out of it or he could die, I just don't know, I've put 480 stitches into his wounds, then I stopped counting, I also removed a bullet from his hip, we have three seriously wounded men here Colonel, one with a collapsed lung, one with the jugular vein severed, if it hadn't been for Gerald's quick thinking out there he would have bled to death. They all need intensive care in a modern hospital, with that they would have a good chance, as it is, at best 60-40 against." Doc then sat down on a box, with his head in his hands.

"Right Adam," said Pike, "Get the men to make up three beds in the gun ship I'll have all the wounded back at base in 14 hours."

"Right Sir," said Adam, the men then got busy under Adam's supervision, making beds up out of cotton waste wrapped in linen sheets, they found in the warehouse, they then got Jake and the other two wounded men bedded down and comfortable, also 24 wounded men sat down and comfortable, Doc, Gloria and the medic were also settled in the ship.

Pike then said to Adam,

"I will see you back in 6 days' time, you will have no trouble going back." Adam then stepped back and the rotors caught, then

Pike lifted off.

All the men were ready in convoy, it then moved off, Adam leading in his jeep.

Jake was unconscious for two days, Gloria never left his side, she worked wonders with all three serious cases, she had taken no rest, Jake finally opened his eyes, Gloria called Doc over, "I think he is coming to Doc." he leaned over and took his pulse. "Well he is definitely getting stronger."

"This is becoming a habit Jake," said Doc, Jake's lips moved, but no sound came. "Bear with me Jake I will get you a little pick me up." Doc then went and got a phial and syringe, and gave Jake an injection, in his hip. Jake moved his head and looked at Gloria. "Welcome back Jake." she said with a smile, Doc pulled up a chair and sat down.

"Well Jake you had a very successful exercise, I saved the newspapers for you, that I sent the orderly sergeant into Kasunu for, the Cat gets all the publicity these days." Jake then said something, Doc moved closer, "Come again Jake." he said,

"I could sure use a drink." Jake whispered, at that Doc laughed out loud and slapped his thigh, "Jake is back alright."

Gloria, Jake could use a drink what do you make of that."

Gloria smiled, "Yes, he's back."

"Well Jake I will get you a small brandy, OK just a wee drink, you see Jake at this time you are full of antibiotics, because infection is too easy to get in this part of the world, and antibiotics and alcohol don't mix." Jake then whispered. "Then do away with the biotics or whatever."

Doc then went smiling into his office and poured Jake a small brandy, and mixed it with a little cool boiled water, he then took it to him, lifted his head and held him steady, and put the glass to his lips, Jake drank slowly. Then Doc lowered his back onto his pillow. "Why don't you get some sleep Gloria, you have spent the last two days looking after the wounded, it is 11-0pm now I will give you a call at day break, Jake will be able to talk by then, and he will be much brighter," Gloria nodded, "You're right Doc." She got up and moved out of the ward, stopping at the exit to look back, before she went through the door.

Wednesday morning 6-0am Doc went over to Jake who was lay wide awake, "How do you feel Jake?" asked Doc.

"I ache all over." he replied.

"Any pain?"

"Yes Doc my left hip, and my right upper arm are giving me some gip. What is wrong with them Doc?"

"Well Jake, I removed a bullet from your hip, and you lost a piece of your right tricep muscle, I will give some pain killers for them, are you saying Jake, you don't remember taking those particular injuries."

"I guess not Doc, everything was happening so fast, do you think you could get me out of bed, if I could just move around a little, it might help."

"Not for a couple of days yet, I will raise you to a sitting position, OK then I will get you some breakfast."

Doc then called a medic for some extra pillows, they got Jake to a sitting position, "That's better," he said, "What other injuries did I take Doc, I appear to be covered in bandages like a bloody mummy."

"Let me put it this way, I put 480 stitches in you, your face shoulders chest and stomach, it appeared you had been put through a shredder, only joking Jake, it must have been flying glass, Gloria and I removed a lot of fragments before stitching you up. How you lost part of your tricep, I just don't know, but you will heal O.K. and recover, you will limp a little for a while, but you can live with that, and your scars."

"This is the second time you have brought me back, from wherever it is, I seemed destined to go Doc. I guess I owe you a second time."

"Gloria must take a lot of the credit Jake, she has nursed you constantly since we got back. I made her take some sleep last night, once you had regained consciousness, it will be her first time in bed for six days."

"Then that makes two people I owe."

"Nonsense, what do you fancy for breakfast?" said Doc."

"A bacon butty would go down well, with coffee."

Doc then got a pot of coffee to take to Gloria, and gave the medic instructions regarding Jake's breakfast. He then took the coffee to Gloria's tent, he walked in and put the coffee down on her bed side locker, she was asleep lay on her back, covered only by a sheet, Doc could see that she was naked, under the almost transparent sheet, that is to say it appeared transparent, he shook her gently, she awoke with a start, so that her breast became uncovered. She was, thought Doc a delightful woman.

"Steady, steady." He said in a soothing manner, "I've brought your coffee," she looked at her watch, then pulled the sheet up to cover herself. "How is Jake?" she asked.

"He is coherent, and right now he is sat up eating a bacon sandwich, I will send you one across if you like."

"Not just now Doc thank you, the coffee will be fine."

Doc then left and went back to the ward, Pike was there talking with Jake. "You have done a good job here again Doc," said Pike, Doc just nodded, Pike went on, "I'm just telling Jake, the General has been in radio contact, he is very pleased and somewhat surprised at the damage we inflicted on the National Guard, which is now virtually extinct. What is left of the government, under pressure from the army chiefs of staff, have asked for a cease fire of all gorilla activities, there are to be no elections at this time. So now we just wait and see what transpires. Jake then said to Pike. "Do you think you could persuade Doc to let me get up Sir, it's not on pissing in a bottle in bed, it's just not done."

"It is here," said Gloria, Doc and Pike turned to her approaching the bed, she looked at Jake, and said, "We don't tell you how to conduct a battle, you don't tell us how to care for the sick, and you Captain are still a sick man."

She then leaned over and gave a quick kiss on the nose end, which was the only part of his face visible under the bandages. "There's no answer to that I guess," said Jake and they all laughed, "Except to say I'm not sick, I'm injured, and there is a difference."

Seven days after their return, Jake was helped out of bed, by Doc and Gloria, he had a crutch under his left arm, "Now," said

Doc, "Your hip will take some time to heal internally, externally you're fine. So try and keep as much weight off your left leg as possible, it will be a little painful for a time but that is only to be expected."

"OK Doc." Jake was dressed in only his shorts, the bandage's and stitches had all been removed from his wounds, all had healed cleanly, but he was badly scarred. One scar which started at the centre of his forehead, ran across over his right eye, then down his cheek to the corner of his mouth. He was also scared right across his body from shoulder to shoulder, and it was the same down across his chest, down to his stomach.

Jake then started to move quite well. "Great!" he said, and started off for the back door and the toilet, followed by the medic.

The medic waited outside the toilet, when he came out he said.

"And now the shower." Jake was moving quite well on his crutch, he stood under the shower and let the water pelt him, it felt great. The medic left and returned with a towel, and a clean dry pair of shorts.

Adam had just arrived back at base, he went direct to headquarters, the Colonel is in clinic Sir, said the orderly sergeant, Adam then made his way over, the Colonel Gloria and Doc, were talking to the other two men who were seriously injured, they were both now up and making a good recovery. Adam approached saluted Pike then shook hands, "I expected you back earlier Major," said Pike.

"Well Sir, the men were exhausted, and so was I so we had a couple of days relaxation at Gwamba Edge, the fishing was good, and me and the men were able to unwind, we are now ready for whatever you have planned Sir."

"You earned your rest Major," said Pike.

"How's Jake?" asked Adam.

"He is fine," said Doc, "He's out just now."

"Out?" said Adam in disbelief. Just then the back door opened and in hobbled Jake, followed by the medic. Adam looked at Jake in amazement, and said, "Would you believe it, look at the man, don't that beat all." Adam then went to meet him, and took him in a gentle hug, "Its good to see you on your feet Sunshine, it is indeed." He said holding Jake by the shoulders at arms length, there was a genuine look of brotherly affection in Adam's eyes, "You nut case, you bloody nut case, it is good to see you."

"Well in that case, if you are so pleased to see me, why not buy me a drink."

At that Adam roared with laughter, "Jake, buy you a drink, I will buy you a brewery."

"No time like the present." Jake replied.

"Hold it," said Doc, "At 7-30am, and you full of antibiotics Jake I'd say leave it just for today, your off medication as of this morning, so lets leave it until tomorrow afternoon, all being well we will all have a drink to celebrate."

"O.K," said Adam, "He is the boss Jake, let us not upset the good work he has done, eh pal?" he said putting his arm around Jake's shoulders. "Tomorrow we will make up for lost time." He whispered, Jake smiled "O.K. by me." he said.

* * * * *

March 3rd.

It was now 6 weeks since the successful attack on the N.G. headquarters, Jake was sat in his tent, it was just after dinner, at 9-30pm, Adam had just gone to one of the villages, when Gloria, outside Jake's tent, said, "May I come in?" And knocked on the tent pole.

"Yes please do." he replied, she went in, he offered her a chair, one of two he had in his tent, "Would you like a drink?"

"No thank you." she replied. "It is very quiet now in the camp everybody is well, so there isn't a lot to do."

"No," said Jake, "And all our activity has ceased, one has all the time in the world, to think and reflect."

"What are your thoughts Jake, or are they too private?"

"No, I try not to think, one could drive oneself up the wall doing that," he got up, and was about to start pacing, when he checked himself, Gloria stood up and went over to him, they stood looking at each other, then they were in each other's arms, Gloria kissed him full on the lips, Jake responded, then he broke, and held her at arms length, he said "No, I can't, I mustn't."

They stood looking at each other, then she said, "You must love her very much," at that Jake's eyes looked up at the tent roof, he turned quickly, dropped his head so that his chin rested on his chest, and put both fists on the table in front of him, and leaned forward. After several seconds, she said, "I'm sorry Jake, I didn't mean to cause you pain, I'll leave." Jake turned, "No please, don't go, I'm sorry, I..." he paused, "I can't explain."

"Your Jane is a very lucky woman, to have a man such as you."

Jake looked in surprise, "How could you know?" he said.

"In your delirium Jake, you called for her, I take it she is your wife."

"Yes." he said.

"Will you go back to her?"

"If only I could," he said, "If only I could."

"But why not?" came the reply.

"No, not now," said Jake, "My hands, no," Jake now seemed somewhat bewildered, "My hands have shed too much blood, I am no longer the man she married, it is all such," he was searching for words, "A mess, a goddamn bloody unholy mess, excuse my language."

"I have often wondered how you got mixed up with this situation, you are not a mercenary like Adam are you?"

"Me? Good heavens no, I'm an engineer I came out here to do a particular job," he then sighed, raised and let his arms fall to his side, "its a long story, I don't really know myself how it happened," he stopped, looked at her, he spoke quietly and slowly, "Whatever was, what is, I don't know, I am a dead man, the person that I was, was reported dead, and the fact is the man I was is dead."

"No you mustn't talk like that, you are very much alive, you have had a very bad time, the scar's you bear are not only on your body, but they will fade," she went up to him, "You are a good man Jake, you must fight this feeling of guilt, your heart is still as it was, it still belongs to Jane, if it didn't you would have taken me then, and we both know it."

He looked at her, "Oh if that were only so." he said.

"It is Jake, believe me it is."

The following day, Pike sent for Adam and Jake, "Well gentlemen I have some good news. General Adejumo has been on to me by radio, and the conflict is over. Yes gentlemen we were successful in brining down the National Guard and the NSP dominance of Ligeria, the General's meetings in Bakra, Kano and Kasunu, with the military chiefs of staff, and what is left of the government, after lengthy negotiations General Adejumo who was President Elido's Chief Minister, is to head a coalition government of various chiefs and staff and civilian representatives of all tribes. Therefore disbanding depots are to be set up, in Lago, Kasunu, Kano and Benine, where we register each man, who will be given a free pardon and 1000 Guineas, an air ticket, or cash fare to anywhere in Ligeria he wishes to settle. Gloria and Gerald will be asked to organise and head a major relief programme, for all refugees, we gentlemen get a blank cheque to kit ourselves out, and make our necessary arrangements, he wants to meet with us in Bakra the 28th of March. So our next task is to strike camp, and transport all arms and equipment to, in our case, Kasunu."

"Right then," said Adam, "I guess we are all out of a job."

"Hardly," said Pike, "But we will leave that with the General."

"Buy you a drink Jake?" said Adam.

"Would you leave that until later please gentlemen, then I will join you, I've had the men assembled in their mess tent, I would like to speak to them all, and I would like you both to be with me."

"Sure," said Adam.

They all walked over to the rebels mess tent, all the men were there sat waiting, there were now 39 out of the original 62, Pike standing in front of them all, with Adam and Jake, said,

"Gentlemen, I've called you all together, to let you know that the conflict is over and we won." They all started to cheer and shout, Pike then spread his arms, "Gentlemen please," they all quietened,

"Tomorrow we will strike camp and proceed with arms and equipment to the disbanding depot in Kasunu, where each one of you will receive a free pardon, the Major, Captain and myself will be with you, and the same applies to us of course, you will each receive 1000 Guineas, and an air ticket or cash fair, to wherever you wish to settle. Your leader General Adejumo will form the new Ligerian government," another burst of cheering went up, Pike then spread his arms for silence.

"Now one very important piece of business we must attend to here and now, is to bury the myth of the Cat, Captain Cross, whom you all insist on calling Captain Cat, is in fact just an ordinary mortal like the rest of us, he is not and never has been a devil, so we bury him and the myth, here in base camp, now when you go out into the country again, amongst your own people, any questions you are asked about this devil the Cat, you will answer, that he is dead and buried up here in an unmarked grave.

The myth ends here and now, and I want that understood. What Captain Cross is, what he always has been, is a well trained British army officer. Is that understood gentlemen?" One rebel then at the front, remarked, "O.K. if you say he is dead Sir, then he is dead, you're the chief."

Jake then stepped forward and shook the man by the hand, all the men then rose and went over to shake hands with Jake, it became like a rugby scrum.

Adam then said to Pike, "How about that drink Colonel, Jake knows where to find us." They went over to Adam's tent, leaving Jake with the men, some 25 minutes later Jake walked in. "I now have 39 blood brothers," he said smiling, Adam then poured him a drink, "You know Sir." Jake said, "If I had fraternised with the men a little, socialised on the odd occasion, I don't think this devil myth would have taken hold, but we live and learn I guess."

"Well tomorrow gentlemen we strike camp, how long will it take Adam?"

"We can do it in a day Sir I reckon, I say we could move out by midnight."

"Excellent," said Pike.

As Adam had said, by midnight of the following day, the convoy moved off, on their 3 day journey to Kasunu.

The convoy consisted of eight 3 ton trucks, five Range Rovers, four Land Cruisers, two jeeps a diesel tanker a petrol tanker, to fuel up on the way and a refrigerated truck.

One jeep carried Gloria, Gerald with Jake driving, Adam was driving his own jeep, with a spare driver and two gunners, followed by two Range Rovers with 6 gunners.

Bringing up the rear, were three Range Rovers four Land Cruisers, all with gunners, Pike never took any chances, each man carried a A.K. 47 with 4 spare magazines.

Shans free pardon, would mean that he was not wanted, for any previous civilian crime, so he was a very happy man.

On arrival they were met by Pike, who had gone ahead in the gun ship, his pilot had taken the chopper. All arms and equipment were checked in and accounted for, at the depot.

Then the rebels moved over to the hall, where they were registered, they had all been booked into small hotels, and were to return to the hall the following morning.

The following day they were all assembled in the hall, where they received 1000 Guineas, and a free pardon, plus the air ticket, some rebels preferred the cash fair. This exercise was supervised by Pike, Pike and Co were booked in the Queens hotel, they were all fixed up with civilian clothes, all made to measure, at the best Kasunu tailors, with specific instructions to have them ready in two days.

Now Jake was enjoying the luxury of civilised accommodation, with piping hot water to bath in every morning, decided to treat himself to a shave, having bought from reception a safety razor and shaving brush. On the 27th of March they all flew down to Bakra, to meet the General. Jake was wearing a single breasted light weight suit, in mid blue, Adam wore a single breasted blazer in dark blue with grey slacks, Pike a tan safari suit, likewise Gerald in grey, Gloria wore a floral dress, with white open toed sandals, white elbow length gloves, and a neat matching handbag.

They were met at the airport by two chauffeur driven limousines, and taken to the Hilton Hotel, where they had been booked in.

"The General will see you all tomorrow, at 9-0am we will collect you," stated the senior chauffeur.

It was now 4-30pm, they all went to their separate rooms, and had arranged to meet in the bar at 7-0pm, Adam and Jake were in the bar at 6-0pm.

At 6-50pm Pike arrived, "Good evening gentlemen," he said.

"Good evening," came the reply from his two officers.

"What will you have to drink Sir?" asked Jake.

"A whisky please with water," Jake called over the waiter, he got Pike his drink, and replenished Adam's and his own, then Jake seemed to freeze, "Would you look at that!" he said.

Gloria came in with Gerald, she was wearing a black off the shoulder fitting evening dress, with a black diamanti wrap, the gown was split just off centre, right up to the thigh, she had a gold chain and pendant around her neck, that just came to rest on the cleavage of her ample bosom.

"Good evening," said Pike as he took her hand,

"Good evening," said Jake. "You look beautiful Gloria."

"A picture," said Adam,

"Such compliments," she said, "but they are appreciated."

"One so beautiful, and yet so talented is rare," said Jake,

"You are indeed a remarkable woman Gloria," said Pike.

They all then went into the restaurant, Pike ordered the wine, Gloria ordered chicken Maryland, Pike and Gerald ordered beef curry, Adam and Jake ordered 'T' bone steak and salad. During the small talk, during and after the meal, Jake was explaining the situation of the young girl, he had met on the flight out from U.K., some 2 years or so ago.

How he had come across her some 6 months later, and how she had changed, how she had been beaten and cowed down, he explained the circumstances of how he came across her, at the stand pipe washing clothes, "She is probably dead now," he said.

"Not necessarily Jake, a woman can be very tough and resilient where her children are concerned, she wouldn't die easy Jake, and leave her children to fend for themselves, in the kind of environment that you mention."

"I hope you're right Gloria, because I have every intention of rescuing her, if she is still alive, regardless of cost, I was actually afraid to interfere before, but now I'll free her, and the devil take anyone who tries to stop me."

Pike had been listening to the story, looked at Adam, who also heard, Pike then with a look of concern on his face, he didn't want any more blood baths, not now, said, "An interesting story that, Jake. If you put it to the General, I feel sure he will be sympathetic."

"I will handle it Colonel."

"Jake don't misunderstand, but please consider - we are no longer at war, and we don't want to spoil the situation we have now. Now like I say, don't misunderstand. *If* she wants out, and you are prepared to help her, and arrange things for her, I am sure the General will afford you every legal assistance."

Gloria then put her hand over Jake's, "The Colonel is right Jake, I will help in every way I can, and Gerald here is a legal council by profession, so the girl will get free of her situation if we can find her."

Jake then looked round the table at all the faces, Adam was thinking, "Jake is about to start the whole bloody war over again, and there is not a thing anybody can do to stop him, it is kill, or be killed, and any excuse will do."

Adam then said, "Jake you and I have never tried the diplomatic approach, to anything, but I know we can do it, what do you say we give it a try?"

All eyes were now on Jake, and he knew what they were thinking.

"Very well," he said, "I know what you say is correct."

Adam then looked across at Pike, who he knew would be relieved, but Adam knew that if the diplomatic approach failed, there would be the inevitable bloodbath.

The following morning they all met at breakfast, they ate and were all drinking coffee, when the chauffeur arrived, it was

8-50am. They all left for government house, they sat waiting outside the cabinet office, after five minutes or so, the General came out with two more uniformed colonels, and three men in civilian clothes. The General was very pleased to see everyone, he shook hands and hugged Pike, when he came to Gloria. "My dear, you are as beautiful as you are brave, I have a full report on all you have done, and you Sir he said shaking Gerald's hand warmly." The General then introduced everyone, the two colonels and three civilians, new who Jake was, for they had been briefed, by the General, but they were not to mention it, the Cat was buried and was to stay buried. It was Colonel Shagari who spoke. "It is a pleasure to meet you gentlemen, and to know, that we are now on the same side, you were a formidable adversary Colonel Pike, but now as a team, I feel we can build a strong United Ligeria," Colonel Okelo then said, "Those are my sentiments exactly."

"Come then Ladies and Gentlemen, we have a lot to cover." commented the General. They all went over to the Generals office, and sat down, the General then outlined what he intended, and how he was to leave all rehabilitation of refugees going back to the civil war with Ibo tribe to Gloria and Gerald. "I trust you are prepared to take on the job, which will be difficult, you will have every possible assistance, and no interference."

"Of course I am honoured to be asked," said Gloria, Gerald also. "You, Colonel Pike, I would like you to head my civil service, and tackle the unenviable task of stamping out corruption, which will be difficult, but I know you are the man for the job."

"I would be glad to take on the Job General."

"Excellent," said the General, "You will get no interference from my office or the military, but you will be able to call on their assistance as you require. You Major Campbell I would like you to set up a major overhaul of our military training programme, no expense spared, you will liaise with Colonel Shagari and Colonel Okelo.

Now the National Guard, or what is left of it, will be regrouped, under totally different parameters, to those employed in the past, all tribes will be enlisted unlike before when it was exclusively Mausa only. Never again will any one tribe be allowed to get to such a place of eminence as they did, both myself and President Elido were powerless their hold was so firm. I think this last conflict taught us a lot gentlemen, that is why I want you for this task Major Campbell."

"I am honoured Sir," said Adam. At this point the two colonels asked to be excused and left.

"You, Captain Cross, will assist the Major, I understand you are a strategist."

"Thank you General, but I think if you will allow, I am seriously thinking of returning to England, I haven't as yet decided what I am going to do, I just don't want to commit myself, not at this time anyway."

"Very well Captain, whatever you decide you will get every assistance, I only ask that you inform me immediately your decision is made."

"Yes Sir, thank you."

"I thank you Captain, Ligeria is in your debt, all you people in this room we owe you all."

"But you see General I have no passport, no papers of any kind, I have only what I stand up in."

At that point Mr Links came in, he handed the General a telex, who read it then passed it to Jake, "Read this Captain, then pass it round if you please." Jake read the telex, it was a bank statement showing a bank transfer for 30,000 Dollars to his wife Jane's account to their bank back in Manchester, where 1200 Dollars a month was transferred to, it was similar for Adam and Pike, he looked at the General as he passed Adam the telex.

"But why?" asked Jake of the General,

"Because," said the General, "A great deal of money was set aside, in case there was a conflict such as there was, oh yes Captain I can assure you, this last conflict was imminent, it had been on the cards for a couple of years or more, so money was put aside just in case, so you see Captain, the NSP with the support of the National Guard, wasn't just something that could be brushed aside, we know for a fact that they got money from somewhere, our intelligence tells us from this British company, who wanted to mine Uranium in the Olantika mountains, which are on the border with the Cameroon. Now the border has international recognition, but still the Cameroon dispute it, and this is the reason President Elido would not allow mining to take place. Can you imagine what would happen if Uranium started to be mined there, in addition to the upheaval caused by the mining, and all that is involved. You would have Guerrilla raids by the

Cameroon, that would ultimately lead to a full scale war, Chief Elido could see this, I can see it, therefore we shall leave well alone. Any agreement reached between this British company and the Sandies government will not be honoured. Not by the New Ligerian government. Try and imagine the size of the possible conflict, Ligeria and the Cameroon at war, Ligeria seeks aid from Britain, Cameroon seeks aid from Germany, can you see the ramifications of that situation? All this was explained to the British Government, via their ambassador Simon Denning, I might add we never did receive a favourable reply, in fact we never received a reply of any kind for that matter. So unlike the British, that." he said as an afterthought.

"No," thought Jake, "You can bet Denning never sent those letters."

"I did hear that this man Denning committed suicide, for whatever reason," said the General. At that Jake's ears picked up, "Denning committed suicide, did you say?" asked Jake.

"Yes, buy why, nobody knows. He was involved with the Sandies and this British company, and on their behalf entered the negotiations with Chief Elido. However, this is now all in the past, this last conflict has resolved all that. Neither myself or my good friend Chief Elido knew when it would happen, but the NSP and the National Guard were pushing for civilian elections, but you see there are no political parties to speak of, other than the NSP and to have given in would have put the Mausa in power for all time, it was only money that was holding them back. However be that as it may, one million Dollars was deposited in the National Bank of Ghana. Well we didn't spend one half of that, so you all get a bonus, it will be the same for Major Horn, who is due in a couple of days. Mr Links, Captain Cross requires a passport, see to the details will you please."

"Yes Sir."

"There is just one difficulty Sir," said Jake, all eyes then looked at Jake, "My name is not Cross, that is my alias, my name is Tully, Joseph Tully."

217

"Well I'll be damned," said Adam, "Didn't I read about you just before I left U.K. it said you were abducted by the President's assassins and were presumed dead, at least that is what the papers said at the time."

The general then spoke, "Were you not the young man who was building the new Presidential office suite, Chief Elido spoke very highly of you."

"Yes Sir, that was me."

The general then went on, "You know the Sandies interrogated Akeja Construction for weeks, they were convinced there was some hidden passage way or entrance, to the suite that allowed the assassin to get in and out. They were under the impression that Elido had this so called hidden arrangement installed for whatever his reason, which is nonsense of course. However they got nowhere naturally, so Steven Sandies had the entire block taken down brick by brick, so the suite no longer exists, what a terrible waste. However, be that as it may."

"No," thought Jake, "Steven Sandies would think I would get him the same way, he wouldn't take any chances that one. It also proves they didn't figure out how I did it."

"Well Sir, they did try to kill me." Jake then showed him the scar round his neck by the garrote, "But they didn't succeed."

"I bet whoever it was tried that came worse off," said Adam. "Am I right Jake?"

He just looked at Adam and nodded, at that Adam laughed.

"That doesn't surprise me Adam, in fact I would expect it," said Pike.

Jake then went on, "So I disappeared and changed my name, I took out the Sandies as you know, because I knew they would never rest until they got me, they were the people responsible for the whole bloody nightmare, and then I joined up with your rebels General, and as I didn't, at the time, feel that I could trust anybody, I kept my alias."

There was total silence everybody looking at Jake, the General broke it, "Well Captain that is no problem, you did register with the British embassy when you took up residence in Ligeria."

"Yes Sir," replied Jake.

"Then there is all the information necessary on record, at the embassy to get you a new passport."

"I would appreciate it Sir, if there was no publicity, that would make things difficult for me, life is going to be difficult enough, without reporters pestering me, particularly when I return to the U.K."

"Anything you say Captain I can appreciate what you say, Mr Links you will attend to this, not a word to the papers, any undue enquiries from the embassy, you refer them directly to me."

"Right Sir," said Mr Links.

"Thank you General I appreciate that, there is just one other thing, a little domestic difficulty, I would like to put to you."

"Shoot Captain," said the General.

Jake then told him the story relating to the young girl he met coming out here. "Well Captain this is Ligeria, not Britain, you know it took Britain 700 years to develop your system of democratic equality, and social reform, you cannot expect Ligeria to do it over night, but like I say Captain anything we can do for you we will, if the girl wants to go home, and you want her too, then we will send her." Pike was very relieved at the generosity of the General, who then picked up the phone and spoke into it, "Send Lieutenant Babangida in please."

A few minutes passed then in came a very good looking immaculately dressed young military police officer, who came to attention and saluted the General, "Lieutenant, Captain Cross here has a little domestic difficulty, I want you to help him in any way he requires."

"Very well General," he said.

"I'll assist the Captain, General."

"No Major, I have other things to discuss with you." Adam thought to himself, "General, that could be one hell of a mistake."

"The Lieutenant can handle this little affair."

"I hope so." thought Adam, who then looked across at Pike.

"Its O.K. Adam," said Jake, "Believe me I won't do anything you and Colonel Pike wouldn't approve of. Thank you General, I really appreciate what you are doing for me."

"You are welcome son, welcome." Mr Links then said, "Before you go Captain, will you please come and sign the relevant documentation for your passport, and I'll take your photograph also.

"Yes of course we won't be long Lieutenant."

"I will accompany Captain Cross Sir if I may," said Adam. The General looked at Adam and smiled, "I know you are worried Major, but believe me all will be well."

A military police sergeant was waiting just outside the office, as Jake and the Lieutenant came out he came to attention, "Is the vehicle outside Sergeant."

"Yes Sir."

"Very good, wait with the vehicle we will only be a few minutes."

"Very good Sir," he then turned and went out. He also was immaculate, "they are a smart bunch," thought Jake.

FREEDOM

Jake and the Lieutenant came out of government house, after attending to the passport details, went straight to the Range Rover, the Sergeant was sat at the ready in the drivers seat.

"Where am I to head for Sir?" asked the Sergeant. Jake explained the area on the outskirts of Lepapa, that he was looking for a particular white girl, a friend of his, and that the General was going to send her home, back to England.

"That will be no problem Sir," said the Lieutenant, "It will be easy, we will call in more men if need be."

Jake was relieved at the Lieutenants confidence, "I'm sure you're right," said Jake, they drove to the area where Jake had met the girl at the standpipe, he directed the driver round the high rise block of flats, the mud hut type of dwellings, made from corrugated iron, packing cases and mud, all the usual rubbish that these people use.

There was an open sewer that ran between the dwellings, the stench was indescribable. "She is in one of these," said Jake. He went in the first, no luck, they tried many but to no avail, Jake was thinking out his next move, when he saw what could have been one of the twins, Jake looked at him and there was a look of recognition on the child's face, the boy ran into one of the dwellings, Jake walked over and entered the place. The boy ran to his mother who was just putting food on a rickety old table, there was no windows, just two holes, with no glass, about 12 inches square.

To Jake's left there was a toothless old man, sat on a cushion on the floor, chewing on an old clay pipe and blowing foul smelling smoke into the already polluted atmosphere. To Jake's right, sat an old settee cushion, were the girls husband and brother, at least that's who Jake assumed they were. They were both drinking, this would be their breakfast thought Jake.

"Hello Lucy," said Jake, he had remembered her name, he was stood just inside the doorway, when her husband, Alex she had called him, jumped up and ran at Jake, cursing. Jake promptly hit him with a straight short right hand blow to the solar plexus, and he put all his weight behind it.

The man went down as though he had been pole axed, his brother was then on his feet when the Lieutenant, who had just entered the dwelling, stepped past Jake and smashed both fists left and right into the mans jaw. He went down, the old man just sat in the corner, and didn't take a blind bit of notice, just kept on chewing his pipe.

Lucy had grabbed the child, and was pressed back against the black mud wall, she looked terrified. "Don't be afraid Lucy," said Jake, "Remember me? I am the guy you met on the flight out here." The girls eyes filled with tears as Jake said, "I have come to take you home." There was total silence, the Lieutenant stood over the cowering brothers. "Yes Lucy." Jake said, "You are going back to Middleton where you belong, you and your boys, you have nothing to fear. You and your sons will come with me now, I will get everything arranged for you, then you fly home." Jake realised that this was indeed a delicate situation, the girl had been beaten and ill treated for so long, she was now totally confused, frightened and unable to trust anyone or believe anything.

What he needed now was Gloria, she would know what to do, but he couldn't leave now and go back for her, he somehow had to cope, he stepped forward very steadily, and held out both hands, one to the boy and one to the girl, "Don't be afraid, I am your friend." The boy, who had been rejected by his father Alex, and the other members of Alex's family, reached out and took Jake's hand, Jake smiled, "Good boy, now how about Mum?" at that she reached out and took his hand, "Fine," he said.

"Shall we start on our trip back home to England?"

He then very gently stepped backwards, the girl and her son also moved with Jake, the Lieutenant just stood looking down at the brothers, who were now very much afraid, because under successive military dictators, the military police always held ultimate power. Jake stepped backwards slowly until they were out of the door. He then squatted down and asked the boy, "Where is your brother?" He pointed across the sewer to a dwelling, "Go bring him." Joe said.

The boy looked up at his Mum who nodded, he then flew, and leaped over the sewer and ran over to the hut. After several seconds the two boys came out, jumped over the sewer and both came running, grabbing at their mothers skirt.

The Lieutenant came out of the house, and the Sergeant turned the vehicle and reversed down to Jake, who then helped the girl into the vehicle, then passed up the boys.

"Do you still have your passport Lucy?" he asked.

She was now beginning to realise that all was well, she recognised Jake, she was beginning to loose the terror she first had, because her husband and brother had been beaten down by these men, something she never believed was possible.

She pointed back towards the dwelling, and whispered, "My husband has it, if he hasn't already sold it." The Lieutenant then walked back into the place and there came some muffled shouting, and the sounds of more blows being struck, the Sergeant then quickly dropped down from the vehicle, and ran into the hut, there was now some screaming and more blows being handed out, then silence.

The Lieutenant and the Sergeant then came out, both just as immaculate as before. The Lieutenant then came up to Jake. "One passport Sir." He said as he handed it up to him.

"Thank you Lieutenant," he said, turning to Lucy, "Are there any possessions you have, that you would like to take with you?" She shook her head, she had, as Jake guessed, only what she stood up in.

"Take us to the Hilton hotel please," said Jake.

"Very well Sir." answered the Lieutenant.

"You got that Sergeant?"

"Yes Sir, the Hilton." They didn't lose any time, the Sergeant obviously had no regard for speed limits.

They arrived, and Jake walked right up to reception, "I want a family room please on the first floor."

The clerk at the reception desk looked down his nose at Lucy and her boys, Jake leaned over the desk and snapped, "Now!"

The clerk jumped with a start, "Yes Sir, a family room on floor one, we have this one Sir room 101. It has a double bed and a single bed."

"That will be fine," said Jake, taking the key, "Come on," he said to Lucy. He then turned to the clerk and said, "I see that Miss Vora is in her room, will you phone her and ask her to meet us in room 101, the name is Cross."

"Yes Sir right away." Jake then took Lucy and her boys to the lift and pressed the button for floor one.

They walked out of the lift, and down the corridor to room 101, Jake opened the door stepped back, and gestured Lucy to enter, she did, and looked round with eyes open in amazement, she had forgotten what decent things looked like, she just gazed in wonderment.

The two boys ran over and jumped on the double bed, as you entered the room, directly in front of you was a large double window, with long golden drapes, to the left of the window was the double bed, then a side cabinet, then the double wardrobe, in the left hand wall was the door to the bathroom, on the right hand wall was a settee with a glass topped occasional table, on the right of the door was a writing desk and a straight back chair, and opposite was the single bed, and a large set of drawers.

Jake went on in a very gentle voice, "Now Lucy, you and the boys stay here for a few days, while I make all the arrangements, then you fly home, anything you want, anything at all, phone and ask reception, they will provide it."

She looked at Jake with tears welling in her eyes, "Is this for real?" she asked, "Am I really going home, or is this a dream?" "No dream Lucy you are going home, with your sons, where you belong." Just then was a knock on the door, and Gloria walked in, "Hello Jake, what is it?"

"I want you to meet a friend of mine, Lucy this is Gloria, Gloria this is Lucy, and her two sons, I wonder would you take her shopping and get her some decent clothes, they will be flying back to U.K. in a few days." Gloria then reached and took Lucy's hands in hers saying, "It will be my pleasure Jake, now Lucy I think first we will take a shower, then after we will visit the hairdresser, I know this excellent beauty parlour in Bakra," Gloria was carrying on.

Just like a woman, Jake thought but she would soon have Lucy thinking straight again.

They then walked over to the bathroom, the boys following on behind. Jake then thought, and went into his hip pocket, he pulled out a wad of notes, he counted 500 Guineas, he then knocked on the bathroom door, it was opened by Gloria, Jake gave her the money. "Take this for starters, I'll get more, so don't skimp, if there isn't enough put to, I'll square up with you on your return, I do have a blank cheque."

As Jake walked out, he was thinking, whatever happened to that simple, lovely girl, he had first met on the plane? Then she had been happy, full of life and gaiety, and now she was a wreck. Gloria would sort things out, she would see to it that Lucy recovered, she was the best qualified, to allay the girls fears, reassure her, and get her thinking like a normal person again.

Jake went round to room 116, knocked on the door and waited, Gerald opened the door. "Hello Jake come in, what can I do for you?"

"Well Gerald, its like this, I've got that young girl away from her husband, Lucy is her name, she is in room 101, Gloria is with her. Well I know nothing about legal matters, but before Lucy goes home in a few days time, I would like her to get a divorce, and legal custody of the children, she can do this in England of course, but it would be a long drawn out affair. So, I know I can fix a judge, or whatever, or whoever, but where do I start?"

"Well Jake, after hearing your story, and knowing the General had agreed to help, I got all the necessary papers ready, knowing that you intended to do exactly what you said. Gus Links, the guy we met with the General, is the minister for home affairs. So divorces finishes up on his desk." Gerald then went to his briefcase and he took out some papers. "These are the necessary papers, ie custody warrant and divorce papers, now for speed, if we could get the husbands signature, it would make it easy. Otherwise it is a long drawn out affair with a court hearing, then a judge signs to give custody etc."

"That is no problem Gerald, I'll get the husbands signature, and the judges too if needs be."

"Just the husbands, Jake, just the husbands!" said Gerald smiling, "Then I'm sure any time period can be fixed."

Jake took the papers, "Thanks Gerald, I appreciate this, believe me, I'll have the signature within the hour." He then went into reception, the Lieutenant and the Sergeant were sat waiting, "I'm sorry gentlemen, I didn't think it would take so long, I now need to go back and get the husbands signature."

"Right Sir." and they left.

In the meantime, Gloria came out of the bathroom and picked up the phone, reception answered and put her through to room 116. Gerald answered, "Could you come to room 101 please Gerald, I want you to do something for me."

"I'll be right there." he answered. A few seconds passed, then Gerald knocked on the door, "Come in," said Gloria, he went in, she then quickly explained the situation. "I want you to look after the boys for a couple of hours, whilst I take their Mum shopping. They have no decent clothes, you could take them swimming in the hotel pool, we can get swimming trunks from the reception shop, you can't very well take them anywhere else."

"I will think of something," said Gerald. She then phoned reception. "Could you please send up two pairs of children's swimming trunks, to fit boys aged 6 years, I know you have them in your shop book them to room 101, thank you."

She then went back to her own room and got some of her own clothes, a shirt and a skirt, a pair of open toed sandals, and underwear, she then went back to room 101. Lucy came out of the bathroom wrapped in a huge bath towel. "Gerald, this is Lucy." Gerald took the tiny hand in his. "How do you do Lucy." He said, Lucy tried to smile and nodded, there was a knock at the door, Gerald went and opened it, it was the swimming trunks, he then went over to the boys who were stood naked, he gave each a pair of trunks, "Try these fellows." he said, they put on their trunks and looked at Mum, their eyes shining, they had never had anything new, not that they could remember, "Can you swim?" asked Gerald, they both shook their heads.

"What do I call you?" he asked, they both looked at Mum. Lucy in a very small voice said, "This is Terry, this is David."

"Now then," said Gerald, "Shall we go and I will teach you?"

Gloria squatted down and spoke to the boys. "You two go and have your swimming lesson, and I will take Mum shopping and buy you both some new clothes, you would like that wouldn't you?" they both looked up at Mum, who nodded.

"Come on boys," said Gerald, offering them his hands, they both took Gerald's hands and went. After they had gone Gloria said, "Try these on Lucy, they will be a little on the large side, but they are only for shopping, Lucy let the towel fall to the floor, she then picked it up folded it and placed it over the chair back. Gloria noticed that her body was covered in fading bruises, Lucy then picked up a pair of silk panties, she put them on and just like her two sons, a look of wonderment came over her face.

Such lovely things, just the basic ordinary items, were now things of unbelievable wonder to someone who had been beaten and forced to live and endure total debauchery and torment.

Recovering from an unbelievable nightmare, was what Lucy was now beginning to cope with, it would not be easy. The situation, Gloria realised was indeed a delicate one.

When she was dressed, Gloria brushed Lucy's hair using her own brush and hair drier. The hair was natural with a lovely shine, the ends were ragged split, but the hairdresser would correct all that thought Gloria, the texture was good.

Some three hours later, Gloria and Lucy returned to the hotel, Lucy was dressed in a white print floral dress with matching short sleeved coat top, with it she wore white gloves and a small matching hand bag, with white open toed shoes with a one inch heel. Her hair was styled and trimmed, reaching down to her shoulders. Her face had the minimum of make up, just a hint of lipstick, she looked lovely.

Gloria put two suitcases on the reception desk. "Take these to room 101 please."

"Yes Ma'am." the receptionist replied, the cases held the rest of the clothes for Lucy and the boys. Gloria then took the other case from Lucy, and said, "Come, let's find the boys."

227

They both went out to the swimming pool, around the pool were the usual li-lows deck chairs etc, at the rear of the pool there was a low wall about 18 inches high, with a wide opening at the centre, with 4 steps leading down to a large lawn area. Gerald had bought the boys a junior cricket set, and he was teaching them the rudiments of cricket.

The two girls walked over to them, the boys looked up in total surprise. "Gee don't Mum look pretty," said Terry. Lucy squatted down and grabbed them both, hugging them to her, Gloria unpacked the case, then she and Lucy started to dress the boys in identical open neck shirts, short trousers, socks and sandals. When they were dressed, and looking very smart, very pleased with their new found prosperity, both stood in front of their Mum, with their eyes shining, Lucy grabbed them both to her, hugging and rocking them. The whole situation, Gloria realised, had to be handled with great care, to avoid Lucy having a complete breakdown. What has kept the girl going has been the welfare of the children, but now they are safe, she might just let go, and that would be disastrous. Gloria looked at Gerald, who understood the situation.

"How about some lunch fellows?" he said, "With ice cream!"

"Yeah!" they both chorused, and broke from Mum.

"Shall we go Lucy?" said Gloria, they all walked back to the hotel and went into the buttery, and sat down and picked up the menu, "How about roast beef and Yorkshire pudding?" said Gerald, they all agreed and ordered. The meal was served, and the two boys got stuck in with their fingers, so Gerald cut the roast beef for them, and showed them how to use their forks, to feed themselves with.

The boys had taken a shine to Gerald, he was the first person that they could remember, that had shown them any interest. Lucy ate her meal slowly, the boys then had ice cream, the others had coffee, Lucy still had a feeling of un'reality, but slowly it was sinking in, that she was free.

Jake and Adam then came in, looked round and spotted the party, they walked over to them, Jake said, "Hello Lucy," Looking at her now, he recognised the girl from the plane, she had aged, and the sparkle of the eye was missing, but time would rectify that he figured, she was still very attractive, and he would see to it that she got her chances.

"You look lovely Lucy, and your sons look very smart." tears welled up in her eyes. "How can I ever th.." Jake held up his hand palm forward to stop her, "Don't try Lucy, it isn't necessary, anyone who has come through a nightmare such as you have is entitled to a chance, and if we can be instrumental in giving you that chance, then it is our duty to do so."

Lucy was at a complete loss for words, Gloria then said, "Lucy my dear, we will all recover from our nightmare, she then looked at Jake and said, "all of us Jake, all of us."

"I would like you to meet a friend of mine, Lucy, this is Adam."

Adam walked round the table to her, took Lucy's tiny hand in his rather large one, and said, "My pleasure Lucy." Adam could be quite polished when he wanted to be, thought Jake.

They all then walked over to the lounge and Adam called the waiter over, "Would you excuse us gentlemen we have rather a lot to do," said Gloria.

"Of course," said Jake, the two women and the boys then left, and went back to room 101. Jake gave Gerald the documents he had got Lucy's husband to sign, "Thanks, I don't see any difficulty now, these will be backdated two years if need be." said Gerald. Jake then said, "That could be arranged Gerald."

"Well what I intend to do is mention your name, and that should do it, and Mr Links is the authority anyway, and we have his blessing."

"This is Lucy's passport, I want the name changed to Jones, her maiden name, the name in the passport is Musheveni, the boys are on the passport, so it will save a lot of trouble in the future." "Well that is British embassy business Jake, but I will see what can be done."

Adam then said, "You got the husbands signature alright then, what did you do break his legs?"

"No," said Jake, "But I would have." Adam laughed, "You are a rum lad Jake." The waiter had been standing there since Adam had called him over, Jake had his government pass clipped to his lapel, and Adam wore his newly tailored dress uniform, of the Ligerian infantry, with Major's crowns on the epaulette, so these were powerful men by Ligerian standards.

"Two very large malt whiskies," said Adam, "What will you have Gerald?"

"A gin and tonic to celebrate."

"Got that?" said Adam to the waiter.

"Yes Sir,"

Lucy and Gloria were trying on the boys clothes, they both had new identical suits, and Gloria was turning up the trouser legs to the right length. "Reception will get them altered by their own seamstress." Gloria was saying, the shoes fit perfectly, 3 Tee shirts, and 3 shirts with collar and ties, all fit, they were all now kitted out.

When Gloria was satisfied with the fit, she went to the phone and called the reception, "Would you send your seamstress to room 101 please."

Now reception had been briefed to give every assistance in this particular case, for Captain Cross.

"Yes Ma'am came the reply."

The seamstress arrived, checked the work that was required, the boys still had the trousers on, "I will have them ready by 6 O'clock Ma'am, will that be alright?"

"Yes thank you, that will be fine," said Gloria.

Gerald finished his drink, "Well I'll get these papers over to Mr Links now, I'll see you both later."

"I'll come with you Gerald, I need some money."

Jake collected another 2,000 Guineas from the ministry, to square up with Gloria.

Jake and Adam were having a drink in the bar at the hotel, when 'Captain Cross' was paged. Jake went to reception, where there was a government courier, "A package for you Sir."

Jake accepted the package from the courier, it was in fact a large envelope, "Sign here please." Jake signed, then went back to the bar and opened the envelope. There was Lucy's new passport, her decree nisi, and the official papers giving her custody of the twins, the name in her new passport, was Lucille Jones, plus the children

Terence and David Jones.

There was also his own passport, made out to Joseph Tully, with an entry visa, and resident visa, dated 1st September and 15th September respectively, Jake smiled at this, and passed them to Adam, who read the visas and smiled, "When you have friends in high places Jake, anything is possible."

"Yes," he said, looking through Lucy's papers, all were backdated. Jake looked again at his photo, gone was the bushy unruly hair, what he saw was a scarred face, with crew cut hair which looked like a clothes brush.

"Well Adam I've a little business to attend to, I'll see you for dinner, say 7-0pm in the bar."

"O.K. I'll be waiting."

Jake drove over to government house, he went to Gus Links office, and knocked on the door, "Enter." came a voice from inside, Jake went in. "Good morning Captain, I take it you got the package I sent you."

"Yes thank you Gus, I really appreciate everything you have done."

"My pleasure Captain." he replied.

"Well Gus, I need something else, and then I shall make my reservation to fly back to U.K., with the Generals approval."

"Of course Captain, what is it?"

"I want £500 pounds Sterling in Travellers cheques with £50 cash, and 2,500 Guineas, to book Lucy Jones and her children's air fare."

"The cash is no problem, I can give that now, the travellers cheques you will have to collect from Barclay's in the city of Bakra, I will give you the necessary authorisation to enable you to collect them if that is agreeable."

"Yes, thank you," said Jake, "That is fine." He then made out the documentation, and he then phoned Barclay's and spoke to the manager, telling him to have everything ready.

Jake thanked him and left.

Jake got the travellers cheques from Barclay's, then went on to the Swissair travel office, he went in and asked to see the manager.

Jake was shown into the managers office, he thought to himself the government pass clipped to his lapel works wonders.

He introduced himself to the manager, a white man who spoke perfect English.

"A pleasure to meet you Sir, what can we do for you?"

"I wish to book an accompanied flight to Manchester, England."

"That we can arrange Sir, is it children?"

"Actually," said Jake, "It is a young woman with her two 6 year old twin sons, she has been quite ill for some time, so I consider it advisable that she be accompanied all the way, she must not be left at any time, she is to be thoroughly looked after, and this of course we will pay for, is that understood?"

"Yes Sir, that can be arranged."

"Then," said Jake, "I wish to meet the stewardess or whoever will be accompanying her."

"Certainly Sir, when will the party be leaving?"

"On the 11-20am flight tomorrow morning, I will book the flight now."

"Very well Sir," he then pressed the intercom and the clerk came in, the booking was made first class. Jake paid the man in guineas, "I will have the stewardess concerned here at 5-0pm Sir if you care to call back."

"I'll do that," said Jake and left.

As Jake walked into the hotel, Gloria, with Lucy and the boys, were just about to enter the lift, Gloria saw Jake, "I'll follow you up Lucy, go ahead."

She then walked over to Jake, "Gerald tells me all has been taken care of."

"Yes," said Jake, "He has done a great job." He took out the divorce and custody papers, and the passport in Lucy's maiden name. "Gerald is quite a character."

"He is," said Gloria, "He is a wonderful man and believe me I know, he is a tower of strength."

"Yes I can see that Gloria." They walked over to the lift and pressed the button, they arrived at 101 knocked and entered, Lucy was sat on the bed, looking at a comic book with the boys, she smiled when Jake approached her and in a gentle voice, said, "Lucy, you fly home tomorrow morning with your boys." She closed her eyes momentarily then opened them again, here are your tickets, and here Lucy is your decree nisi, you did tell me a couple of years ago, that was what you wanted, well it has all been taken care of, here are the custody papers, you have legal custody of your sons, nobody can ever hurt you again.

And here is your passport in your maiden name, you are now Lucy Jones, you are no longer Mrs Musheveni, and your sons are now Terry and David Jones."

She was now clutching the papers to her breast, and rocking slightly, she then held back her head, and a slow weird high pitched sound was emitted between her clenched teeth. Gloria sat down quickly besides her on the bed, and put her arms around her, and cradling her head started to talk in gentle tones, "Why don't you have a good cry Lucy, we are all your friends, we care my dear." Gloria went on, reassuring her, Lucy then dropped her head and let go, she started to sob uncontrollably.

Gloria then pursed her lips, and raised her eyebrows, she looked at Jake and her lips mouthed the words, "Thank heaven." She then nodded at the boys, who were looking at their Mum. Jake got the message, and got the boys out of the room and took them downstairs to the buttery, and got them both an ice cream, reassuring them that their Mum was alright.

He then went over to the shop and got the boys a comic each, he sat down with them, he was worried, things were gong to well, he didn't want any upset now, 20 minutes passed then Gloria came into the buttery.

"How is Mum?" the boys asked immediately.

"She is fine boys there is no need to worry." She then nodded to Jake, and they walked out of earshot of the twins, who now were looking at their comics. "Everything is fine now Jake, something had to go, and fortunately it was just a good cry, she will be fine now, up until now Jake the girl was afraid to speak, or even move, for fear it might upset the whole situation, the girl was almost out of her mind, she is asleep now with exhaustion, nervous exhaustion, 4 or 5 hours sleep and she will be able to hold a conversation with you."

"I am so pleased," said Jake "You are a remarkable woman Gloria, I could get her away from those two goon's, but I couldn't possibly have done what you have."

"Like I say Jake we are a good team. Oh and while you were out Doc got in, he was held up at the hospital, they were stuck for a surgeon and he felt obliged to help out."

"That is good news Gloria, tonight we will have a celebration dinner."

"I will look forward to that Jake, and I know Lucy will."

It was now 5-0pm, Jake went to the Swissair travel office and the clerk took him straight into the managers office, there was a very attractive young woman there, who was introduced to Jake, "This is Pamela," Jake then gave Pam detailed instructions about looking after Lucy. "I can assure you Sir, Lucy will be well looked after, you need have no worries, I've travelled world wide caring for people."

"Yes I understand thank you, I know Lucy is in good hands," said Jake.

He then went back to the hotel and to room 101, he knocked on the door, it was opened by Gloria. "Oh Jake come in Lucy is in the shower, and she is fine."

"I am so pleased," he said, and sat down, the boys were reading their comics, then they started to talk and argue with each other, they were now just two happy 6 year olds. The bathroom door opened and Lucy walked in dressed in a large towelling robe. Gloria said, "Right boys, come on, tonight you are having an early dinner, because Mum is going out, O.K. fellows what will you like for dinner?"

"Hamburger and lots of chips," they both shouted, Lucy smiled. Jake thought, a lovely smile, the girl from the plane was back.

"Right," said Gloria, "lets go!" and they left.

"How are you Lucy?" asked Jake.

"I'm fine, I haven't felt this good in such a very long time, and I owe it all to you, you have saved me from an unbelievable debauched existence, and more important you have saved my children, they shouldn't have to pay for their mothers mistakes, how can I ever repay you?"

"You repay me Lucy, my going home with your two sons, and forgetting the last two years, dismiss the whole period from your mind, you are now Miss Jones, so you take it from there, when you meet your parents be tactful, try not to cause them the pain that knowledge of your existence over the last two years would cause."

"I realise that, thank you." Lucy then looked round and gestured with her hands, "and all this, the lovely clothes, it must be costing a fortune, and I have nothing, I am penniless."

"Forget it Lucy, a small price to pay for your happiness, and your children's. "Oh yes," Jake went into his pocket and produced the travellers cheques, "Here is a little something to start you off when you get home, sign them on the top line Lucy." He handed the cheques to Lucy.

"But there is a fortune here."

"No," said Jake, "£500 won't got far these days, they are with the courtesy of the Ligerian government."

"But I couldn't accept this, forgive me, I don't know what to call you, people call you Jake or Captain, and I seem to think of you as Joe, I'm still a little confused."

"Jake will do Lucy, and the money is yours, yours and the boys, I'll go now Lucy, I expect to see you at 8-0pm sharp, looking like a princess." Jake got up, as he was going through the door, he heard he saying, "You're so kind." he stopped and looked back and said "Us Brits in a foreign country have got to stick together, or we are all lost." He then winked and closed the door behind him.

At 7-50pm he realised he hadn't made arrangements for Lucy being collected at Manchester airport. He went to room 101 and knocked on the door, it was opened by Gloria, "Jake." she said, "We are just about to come down."

"Well," he said, "I have just remembered, we haven't made arrangements for Lucy being collected, have you phoned your Dad Lucy?"

"They are not on the phone Jake."

"Well is there anyone you can phone?"

"I could phone the paper shop in our road and ask them to bring Dad to the phone, they are good friends of ours, the Richards."

"What is the number?" asked Jake.

"633-0077," she said. Jake lifted the phone and said, "This is Captain Cross." He then gave them the exchange and number, saying "This call is urgent, I want it now, O.K.?" He put the phone down, Terry and David were in bed reading their comics, "How are things fellows?" asked Jake. "Great!" they both said in unison, "we are going home tomorrow!" Jake smiled "I know, I bet you are looking forward to it." The phone rang, Jake picked it up and gave it to Lucy. "Hello," she said, "Oh Elsie this is Lucy Jones, yes! Lucy Jones! I'm ringing from Ligeria... yes the twins are fine." There was some further small talk, "Do you think you could bring me Mam and Dad to the phone please?" She then looked at Jake smiling, "She said don't go away, she is a love." A few minutes passed and her Dad came on the phone, he said, "Is that really you Lucy?" "Yes Dad, oh I'm so pleased!" and with that she burst out crying, a gentle cry tears of joy, but she couldn't speak, Jake took the phone off her, "Mr Jones, my name is Jake, I'm a friend of Lucy..... yes Fred, O.K. Fred, if you have your pencil ready I will give you Lucy's flight details, she will be on her way home tomorrow... yes she and the boys, they can't wait to get home, she will arrive in Manchester early evening.... Yes here goes, flight LAG 243 leaves Bakra 11-20am arrives Zurich 4-50pm then flight No.347 leaves Zurich 6-20pm and arrives Manchester 6-20pm your time. Thats the one hour time difference. Lucy has had her little weep now I will hand you back." He gave Lucy the phone, "Hello Dad I feel such a fool, it was so good to hear your voice......no I couldn't write Dad, it's such a long story, is me Mam there?.....Yes Dad, Jake is a very dear friend......the twins are fine, looking forward to tomorrow. Hello Mam." Lucy started to cry again, but she was fighting it, and managed to carry on talking, "Yes Mam like I say it is a long story....no I will never come back here again, when I'm home I'm staying home..... yes I am divorced, and I have legal custody of the twins. They don't ever want to see this place again either..... I'm crying because I'm happy, because I'm coming home..... great, bye Mam, see you tomorrow."

She put the phone down, had a little sniff and smiled up at Jake. "They will all be there to meet us tomorrow, Mam, Dad, Jim and Mike my two brothers, Elsie and Harold from the shop, it is just wonderful!"

"O.K. now, come on we have some celebrating to do." Jake was now behaving in his old Joe Tully manner.

He went down to the bar, Doc was there when he walked in, Doc got down off his bar stool, they shook hands warmly, both were grinning, "What kept you Doc?" said Jake. "Business." Doc replied, "I hear you have been rescuing damsels in distress!"

"Details, Doc, details." replied Jake, "Come on Doc what was all this business in Kasunu?"

"Well Jake its like this, I take all the medical equipment to the depot in Kasunu, and they ask me to take it to Kasunu Royal, well I arrive there, check everything in and when then realise I'm a doctor they start fussing around all over me, apparently they had only the one doctor and he was on the point of breaking down due to over work, so I agreed to stay on and help out until the second doctor got back off sick leave."

At that moment Doc stopped talking and was looking over Jake's shoulder. Walking towards them came Gloria and Lucy, Jake thought how beautiful they both were, Lucy wore a dress of deep brocade, with full sleeves fastened at the wrist, the skirt was full and ankle length. Gloria wore her black off the shoulder evening dress, split off centre from the ankle up the thigh, Lucy, Jake knew, once recovered from the insanity of her existence over the last couple of years, would have everything to look forward to.

For the first time in years he was feeling good and so pleased with the achievement of Lucy and her sons.

Jake held out his hand to Lucy and smiled, they held each other's gaze, then Doc spoke "Who is this delightful young lady you have obviously been keeping to yourself Jake?"

"I would like you to meet a very good friend of mine Lucy, this is Doc, and Doc this is Lucy, another very good friend of mine, so behave yourself!" he said smiling.

Doc smiled, took Lucy's hand and kissed it, "You are very

beautiful." He then to Gloria, hugged her gently and kissed her, "You two ladies," he said, "Are the most delightful sight I've seen in a very long time."

"All flannel and flattery Lucy," said Gloria smiling, "But he means well, don't you Doc." she said patting his face.

"Doc is right as always, you are both very beautiful." said Jake. Lucy was looking at Jake and smiling, they held each others gaze, then she whispered, "Thank you."

"Well ladies what will you have to drink?"

Gloria said, "White wine please Doc."

"Orange juice please," said Lucy,

"Just orange juice Lucy? O.K., but we'll have champagne with dinner." Lucy looked at Gloria, "Champagne will be fine Lucy, I drink very little myself so a glass of champagne will be fine." They were all sipping their drinks, when Adam and Pike and then Gerald appeared. Both Adam and Pike were dressed in their army dress uniforms, Jake thought to himself "Ligeria being the way it is, these are two very powerful men, dressed as they are. "Gerald was dressed in a lightweight grey safari suit. Pike walked up to Lucy, "It is nice to see you looking so radiant my dear, tell me how are you?"

"I am fine thank you Sir," she replied, "I haven't felt this good in such a long time."

"I am pleased." he said.

Pike then moved over to Gloria, Adam went over to Lucy and took her small hand in his saying, "Good evening Lucy, you look beautiful, "Thank you." she said. Then Gerald moved in, saying "I hope you feel as good as you look."

"Thank you, yes Gerald, might I take this opportunity to thank you, for all you did for me and my children, my divorce and getting me custody, it is just so wonderful."

"My pleasure Lucy, and my duty."

"Shall we take our table? and a starter with Champagne?" said Pike.

The head waiter came over to the Colonel, "This way Sir," he took them to a large round table, set for seven people, the waiters were fussing around, they had just finished setting it. They each took their chair and sat down. The waiter poured the Champagne, Pike raised his glass, "Ladies and gentlemen I would like to propose a toast, which I think is very befitting at this time, to freedom!" Everybody chorused, "Freedom!"

Lucy had never had caviar before, so Gloria explained "Take a toasted biscuit Lucy, spread it with a little pate, and then spread the caviar."

"Oh lovely," she said, then took a sip of her Champagne, "I feel like a Princess!" said Lucy smiling. "And might I add," said Pike, "You look like a Princess." Lucy smiled.

They ordered their meal, Lucy following Gloria, who understood the situation, so she made everything easy, to avoid the girl any embarrassment.

The hotel orchestra was playing lovely music and people were beginning to get up to dance, Jake said, "Lucy would you care to dance?"

"Oh," she said, "I think I've forgotten how."

"Good," said Jake, "I never knew how, so we will make a good pair!" He then got up, smiling and took her hand, they walked on to the floor, and started to dance. As the number finished, and they were walking off the floor, Lucy said, "I am really enjoying myself tonight Jake."

"So am I," he replied, "But when I'm dancing, I'm all fingers and thumbs." At that she laughed, "You mean all left feet."

"Whatever," said Jake.

"You know Jake, I thought Lucy Jones was dead, but now I realise I am very much alive, it is Mrs Musheveni who is dead.

"Of course," said Jake, "Good girl."

During the course of the evening both girls danced with all the men and all had a very enjoyable time. As the celebrations drew to a close, Adam and Pike, who had an early start the following day, said their goodbyes to Lucy, likewise Doc, who had an early meeting with the General, all then retired.

The following morning Gerald had a call from Gus Links asking him to go over to government house.

He went to Lucy's room, "Come in Gerald," she said.

"Well my dear I've come to say goodbye, I've just had a call to go over to government house immediately, the boys then came running over to Gerald from the bathroom, he bent down and grabbed them both and hugged them. "Now fellows I'll have to say goodbye and I want you to promise to look after Mum on your journey home." "Yes Mr Gerald." They both chorused.

"And don't forget, always a straight bat!"

They both then grabbed him again, they had become very fond of Gerald, he straightened up and looked at Lucy, "You have two fine boys there Lucy, you must be very proud, all will be well for you now, goodbye my dear." Lucy also held Gerald with affection, he had been a tonic for the twins, he was a very dear person.

"Thank you again for all you have done, for me and my children, they have both grown very fond of you, we will never forget you." He smiled, "My pleasure Lucy." Then he left.

Lucy then sat on the bed in silence, the twins came and stood beside her, she then grabbed them and held them tightly to her, although she knew now all was well, it was difficult for her to comprehend. The suitcases were packed she was ready.

There was a knock on the door, she let go of the children and went to answer the door, it was Gloria, "Are you ready?"

"Yes I am, is it time to go?"

"Yes, Jake is downstairs with the hostess who will accompany you and the boys, you see Lucy when Jake booked the flight, you hadn't at the time fully recovered from your ordeal, so he considered it wise to book you an accompanied flight. The hostess will look after you until you meet with your parents at Manchester."

"I see," said Lucy, "Jake is such a dear person, I will never forget his kindness, or you Gloria, you are all such wonderful people, if everybody were as you, the world would be such a wonderful place, and fools like me would have a chance.

"You are not a fool Lucy, you made a mistake, we all make mistakes from time to time, you must count your blessings, you have a lovely family and you are going home, what could be better than that?"

Lucy smiled, "Come on boys, we are going home."

Gloria then went to the phone, reception answered, "Send someone up to room 101 for the suitcases, we are checking out." She put down the phone, "Shall we go?"

Down in reception Jake had just settled the account, Lucy came over with the boys. Jake introduced Pamela, "She will accompany you on your flight home." Pamela offered her hand, "It will be my pleasure Lucy. This is Terry and David?" she said, rubbing their woolly heads, "Well I think we will have a fun time on our little trip."

The bell boy arrived with the suitcase and they all moved out to Jake's Range Rover and they all got in, Lucy, Gloria and the boys in the back, and Pamela in the front with Jake. "All set?" said Jake as he moved off. They arrived at the first class check in desk and Jake got them all checked in, and then went with them into customs, Jake went right up to the customs officer, and pointed to the suitcases, "Those." he said.

"Yes Sir," said the man, chalking the suitcase, the party then when into Passport control.

Lucy handed the new passport, to the control officer who opened it, checked it and stamped it. Then Pamela went through, followed by Gloria and Jake who nodded and touched their government pass that was clipped to their lapels.

They all sat in the departure lounge drinking coffee, the boys had a lemonade, when the flight was called they all got up and walked to the departure gate, Jake then bent down to the boys, and put his arms around them, "Now fellows it is up to you to look after Mum on your journey home, O.K.? Remember Mum is very special."

"We know that Mr Jake, we will look after her." They both hugged him, Pamela then said, "Right boys," and they left Jake and took hold of Pamela's hands, and walked towards the exit. Lucy held Gloria's right hand in both of hers, "Thank you for all you have done for me and my children, you are an angel."

"My pleasure Lucy," she said, and kissed her on both cheeks. Lucy then went to Jake, they took each other's hands, "Jake," she said, as the tear's welled up in her eyes, "How will I ever be able to thank you, what can I say?"

"Don't say anything Lucy," Jake interrupted, "There is no need to, your eyes say it all," at that she flung her arms around his neck, and hugged him, Jake's arms enclosed her tiny waist, he could feel the frail tiny body trembling, and her warm tears on his cheek, when she broke away, she kissed him on the cheek, saying "God bless you."

She then turned, and ran until she caught up to the twins. She turned and they all waved, but Jake could see the tears in her eyes glistening in the artificial light of the departure lounge.

Jake smiled and winked, they turned and walked out of the exit, on the first leg of their journey home. Jake just stood there, looking at the empty doorway, some time passed then Gloria said, "It was very important to you Jake wasn't it, to get Lucy free and away?" a couple of seconds passed, then Jake said, "Yes Gloria, very important, from the moment the Colonel called me in his office, and told me the conflict was over, I've thought of nothing else."

"You were freeing yourself Jake, but the irony of it is you are still here, you must know surely, that you must go home, it is your only chance Jake, it is either that or a life of torment, you owe it to yourself, and you owe it to Jane."

They were walking slowly through the airport. At the name Jane, Jake stopped and looked at Gloria, they looked at each other in silence, for what seemed like ages, then Jake spoke, "You're right Gloria, you're right as always, you know, last night Lucy said something, to make me think, she said she thought, and believed that Lucy Jones was dead and gone, but she realised that Lucy Jones was very much alive, it was Mrs Musheveni that was dead. Well at that time I suddenly realised, that I was thinking and acting like Joe Tully, so maybe Joe Tully is very much alive, maybe I should bury Jake Cross, and go home and take my chances."

"You must, Jake," said Gloria, they just stood there looking in each others eyes, Gloria could see the torment and the struggle going on in Jake's mind, she felt helpless, she wanted so much to convince him that he must go.

"I will, I will go home, yes I will do it, that's it, decision is made." they started to walk again, Jake's pace was beginning to quicken, "I'll throw myself into it, like I've thrown myself into every campaign I've conducted over the last couple of years. I will go and see the General tomorrow, he is tied up with the Colonel and Adam today, if he has nothing for me, and will release me, I'll book the first flight out."

"I'm so pleased Jake, it is the right thing to do, all will be well I know it."

The following morning, as Jake was stepping out of the shower, he saw his reflection in the huge mirror, over the wash hand basin, he was totally scarred from shoulder to shoulder, right across his chest and stomach, at his left hip there was a saucer shape indentation where the skin shone like silk, it was the same where the neck and shoulder meet. He remembered how he and his Janie, would lie and caress each others naked body and make love. But what girl in her right mind would want to caress this mound of scar tissue? Jane isn't any girl, she is his wife Janie, "I'm going home, decision is made, and that is final."

That morning he went to the General, who was only too pleased to release him, and wished him all the best, and hoped to meet him again some day. When Jake left the General, he booked Swissair for the following day, 11-20am to Zurich, 6-20pm to Manchester.

After dinner that evening with Gloria and Gerald, they were having a drink in the lounge bar and at 10-0pm Pike and Adam joined them. Gloria and Gerald were flying to Kano tomorrow to organise the relief campaign for the northern province so they decided to retire.

"We will say goodbye Jake," said Gloria, they both stood facing each other, "Jake," she said, "I sincerely hope we meet again under happier circumstances, such as will be now in Ligeria, you may some day decide to spend your vacation here, I would like to meet your wife Jane."

"Thank you Gloria, I shall never forget you." they then hugged each other and Gloria kissed Jake full on the mouth, she then turned and walked out of the bar.

Gerald shook Jake by the hand, "I sincerely hope you find what you seek Jake and God be with you." After they had gone,

Adam said, "She definitely has a soft spot for you Jake, she is one hell of a woman."

"She is a remarkable woman," said Jake.

The following morning, Jake went down to reception to sign his account, which would be sent to government house for payment, he noticed in his pigeon hole, a letter which the clerk got and handed to him, it was from Gloria, it read:

My dear Jake, (Joe),
There are some things a person cannot say in company. What I want to say is thank you for your part in saving my adopted country. It is you, and men like you, that enable people like me to live in a world free from prejudice and bigotry. And I owe you special thanks, for not taking advantage of me when I offered you the opportunity, I know you consider my actions to be those of a foolish woman acting out of gratitude. You are truly a man of the highest integrity, I wish you and your wife Jane, who is indeed a very lucky woman, a very happy and prosperous future and that your children may always walk as tall as their father. I will always carry you in my heart with affection, as a true and very dear friend.

With sincere affection
Gloria.

Jake then clenched his fist, enclosing the letter, and was just staring into space, the clerk leaned over, "Is everything alright Sir?"

"Yes thank you, everything is fine."

He then went upstairs to his room, sat down and read the letter over and over again, he felt like a fraud, an utter fraud, a hypocrite, he had done everything out of sheer revenge and hysteria, with nobody's interest at heart, driven on only by his own vindictive outlook.

He smoothed the letter out, folded it neatly and put it in his top pocket. "It is people like you Gloria that enable people to live in a world free from bigotry and prejudice," Jake said to himself, "Men like me are just passengers."

But all that was now in the past, he had to try and sort out his future, if it could be possible, how can one climb out of such a cess-pit, without affecting the people around him?

He just had to try, for Jane and the children, Gloria thought he could. What a mess! he thought, What an unholy confounded mess! The phone rang, he picked it up, "Captain Cross?"

"Yes?" said Jake.

"Colonel Pike is here, Sir, asking for you."

"I'll be right down," Jake went down, Pike was there with Adam.

"I have called to say goodbye Jake, I want you to know it has been a privilege to have had you on my team, and served with you in this last conflict, I hope we can keep in touch, Adam and I go back a long time, to the late forties, he was just a lad then, in what was then Palestine, but it is always nice to know where your true friends and compatriots are."

Thank you Colonel, it is much appreciated."

"I can always be reached Jake, care of government house, Bakra." They shook hands, "See Jake off at the airport Adam." Pike then turned and left.

"Well Jake, we could drive over there now, and kill the last hour in the bar," said Adam.

"Good thinking!" said Jake.

They arrived at the airport. Jake checked in at the first class desk, he had only a very small holdall.

"You travel light Jake," said Adam.

"The only way Adam, I have a clean shirt, pair of pants and socks, a toothbrush and a battery operated razor, what else does one need?" Jake then went through customs and passport control. They then went through to the bar, Adam ordered two very large whiskies, and they just sat drinking. Then they started to call Jake's flight. On the last call, they stood up and walked over towards the departure gate, then they grasped each others hands, "Well Jake, I know you will never set foot in Ligeria again, so if ever I'm passing through Manchester, and I decide to call I hope I would be welcome."

"As a friend and a fellow drunkard Adam, you are always welcome, you know that, but as a mercenary with battle plans, No way!"

"As a friend Jake, as a friend!" They then hugged each other, Jake broke away, and walked over to the exit door, he stopped and looked back, held Adam's gaze for a few seconds, then turned and walked out the door on the first leg of his journey home.

Jake was the last passenger to get on the plane, he sat down and fastened his seat belt and they took off. When the seat belt sign went off, the stewardess went up to Jake, "Champagne Sir?" "Yes thank you." he replied as she gave him a glass and poured the Champagne. Jake then took a sip of the drink, and then put it on the table in front of him, his mind now started to wonder about the last two years, it all now seemed so unreal, it was gone, irrelevant, because time just passes, it was now, and yesterday didn't matter.

He thought of the times he and Jane would sit in the lounge of his own home, and listen to music, all that seemed so real but so far away, could it ever be the same again? Would he ever know any peace? His mind was a turmoil.

His daughter would be 3 years old now, she would be a happy little girl playing, laughing, talking, and to her he would be a stranger, Jonathan would be 7 years old, working hard at school, he was a bright boy, he would be reading now, he would have his books and his toys, would he remember his Dad?

Jane, he knew, would have kept faith in him, it had never been proven to her that he was dead, then there was the money going into her account every month, she would know in her heart that it was from Joe, maybe, just maybe all would be well.

There was hope for him, how could a man create such a mess for himself, as he had done? "Is the drink not to your liking Sir?"

"Oh yes it is fine." the Champagne had been there for the last two hours untouched, they were now serving lunch, Jake wasn't interested, "Would you bring me a beer please?" he asked, Jake

then settled back and dismissed everything from his mind, he asked for a newspaper. After some time the seat belt sign came on, they were approaching Zurich. On landing, Jake left the plane and went into transit.

He got himself a beer, and sat down with his little holdall, his

246

mind started to wander back over the last two years again, Denning had committed suicide, why? Was it conscience? He doubted it, was it fear? he doubted that too, then what? If he had still been alive, would he have gone after him? He didn't know, Jake Cross in Ligeria would have, of that there is no doubt, he would have got him too, that's a fact, but Joe Tully in England, he just didn't know, all the fire the vengeance, had gone, just at this time he felt helpless and lost.

Everybody that had been involved with Elido's death was now dead, except himself.

The flight to Manchester was announced. At 7-15pm he boarded the flight, he must now think of himself as Joe Tully, Jake Cross was now buried in Ligeria, or was he?

When they arrived at Manchester it was a pleasant spring evening, April 15th, Joe got a taxi. As it drove up the drive where Joe lived, he had the driver turn into the adjacent drive way, he got out and paid him, then he walked into the garden through the back gate. Joe's stomach turned as he saw the old familiar garage and rear lawn.

Something he never expected to see again, the light in the kitchen was on, he could see from the window, he walked to the back door, put his hand on the door handle, and pressed gently. The latch went, then he pushed slightly, the door moved, there were butterflies in his stomach and his mind was racing, he took a deep breath, pushed open the door and stepped inside. He closed the door and dropped the holdall at his feet, he stood there, his left hand still on the door handle.

Jane, who felt the draught on her legs, turned, then stepped back, pressing herself against the sink unit. The sponge with the plate she had been washing fell to the floor, smashing to fragments, her eyes open wide her mouth gaping, Joe just stood there looking, there she was, his dream, his world, she had on an old pinny, with a duster hanging out of the front pocket, old trashers on her feet, her cheek and forehead grease marked, from cleaning the cooker, her hair was tied back with a scarf, he had never seen a more beautiful sight, how he loved this girl.

Every nerve in his body was stood on end screaming for her, yet he had completely lost his voice, it had deserted him, his lips mouthed the name Janie.

With that she flew across the kitchen to him, and flung herself around his neck, her feet coming up off the floor. Joe clamped his arms around her tiny waist and he held on as though the very world depended on it. There was total silence, then Jane's feet lowered to the floor, she tried to step back, but Joe's hold was too firm, so she took his face in both her hands, covering his ears cheeks and hair in soap suds, she pushed and leaned back, looking in his eyes and his face, which was scarred, and he had aged, but the look in the eye that expresses love can never age.

She then started to kiss him frantically, his scars his eyes his nose his lips, then she was back round his neck, her feet coming up off the floor. Two long years of longing, doubt anguish, and strain were about to be released. She sobbed, uncontrollably she cried, the tears flowed as water from a tap. It was similar for Joe, as the tears welled up behind his eyes, and forced their way from between closed eye lids, run freely down his face, dripping off the end of his jaw, and fell to the tiled floor of his home, at last Joe was home, to the ultimate protection, that of his Janie's love, 'The Cat' had found his home.

EPILOGUE

Joe was home and it was indeed ecstatic, his Jane was bubbling over joy gaiety and love, the children were screaming and laughing with the joy of having their Daddy home with them. To Joe it was what living was all about, he had everything. Within a week he had been on to his old firm, and they could offer him a position similar to the one he left. Joe was convinced that the nightmare was over.

He had asked Jane not to ask questions about the last two years, she had replied "If you want to tell me you will, if you don't, then I don't want to know, your home that is all that matters."

But there was one hard tough very astute business man, who wanted answers, why had his brother-in-law and close friend committed suicide, that had destroyed his sister and ruined his career, Britain being the relatively small island that it is, isn't the ideal place, for a mercenary with a North country accent to hide in.

But Charles Johnson would do well to let sleeping dogs lie, the Sandies pushed Joe Tully to their cost.